The Best Little Motel in Texas

The Best Little Motel in Texas

a novel

Lyla Lane

HARPER PERENNIAL

NEW YORK • LONDON • TORONTO • SYDNEY • NEW DELHI • AUCKLAND

HARPER PERENNIAL

 For information, address HarperCollins Publishers, 195 Broadway, New York, NY 10007. In Europe, HarperCollins Publishers, Macken House, 39/40 Mayor Street Upper, Dublin 1, D01 C9W8, Ireland.

HarperCollins books may be purchased for educational, business, or sales promotional use. For information, please email the Special Markets Department at SPsales@harpercollins.com.

hc.com

FIRST EDITION

Designed by Jamie Lynn Kerner

Library of Congress Cataloging-in-Publication Data has been applied for.

ISBN 978-0-06-346932-7 (pbk.)

Printed in the United States of America

25 26 27 28 29 LBC 5 4 3 2 1

To Dolly Parton

For the wit, sparkle, and charm you brought to the role of Miss Mona, the paths you've carved for women everywhere, and your tireless advocacy for literacy.

Chapter One

CORDELIA SAT IN THE BREAK ROOM, POLISHING AN APPLE WITH A WIPE. Her phone buzzed against the plastic card table as she set out her lunch supplies, but she just glanced at the number before she let it go to voicemail. She didn't deal with business or social matters on her break. While the area code caused a flutter of trepidation to beat against her breastbone—a dead snake could still bite, after all—she quickly shook it off. It had been twenty years since she'd last heard a peep out of Sarsaparilla Falls.

Getting on with sanitizing the remainder of her lunch, a task that took ten of her allotted thirty minutes, she put her hometown out of her mind. But when that area code came up three more times, she reluctantly set aside her apple and picked up the phone.

"Is this Miss Cordelia West, daughter of Sherilynn West?" The unfamiliar voice had a stuffy quality to it, like he'd just come out of a dust storm and didn't want to breathe through his nose. "Former resident of our great town of Sarsaparilla Falls, current resident of Dallas?"

Cordelia pulled the phone away from her ear to check the number again. Was this one of those phishing calls where they tried to get you to say yes on the phone just so they could sign you up for all sorts of services you didn't want or need? It was hard to tell these days.

Just to be safe, she opted for "How can I help you?"

"My name is Arbuckle Jenkins. I'm an estate lawyer here in Sarsaparilla Falls. I worked with your great-aunt, Penelope. She ah . . ." The man cleared his throat. "I apologize for bringing you some news that might be a bit of a shock, but it seems she's passed away."

It was indeed a shock, as Cordelia didn't know she had a great-aunt. Or any remaining relatives in Sarsaparilla Falls, for that matter. "I'm so sorry to hear that."

"Yes, well." The sound of cloth rustling came over the line, as if he were dotting his face with a handkerchief. "These things happen."

"Forgive me for asking, but how did I come by my relation to her?" Her momma didn't have any living relatives that she knew of, and surely her daddy's kin would've come forward by now, especially if they were from the same small town where she had been born.

"Are you the daughter of Travis West?"

"Only biologically." No one had seen hide nor hair of her daddy since she was eight months old.

"Well, there you go. He was her nephew."

A million questions rose in Cordelia's mind, but since she hadn't seen the man who could best answer them in near thirty years, she kept them to herself. She rooted around in her purse until her hand found the side pocket where she kept her pen and notepad. "If you give me the address for the funeral service, I'll send flowers."

"No need for that." Mr. Jenkins hacked and the soft thump of his fist hitting his chest reminded her of her momma beating their rugs with a broom when she was young. "Funeral's already done. It took us some time to track you down. Your momma left town real abrupt-like some twenty years back and no longer lives at her last forwarding address."

Cordelia's back stiffened at his admonishing tone. She'd had twenty years to distance herself from the lonely girl she'd been in Sarsaparilla Falls, and all it took was a two-minute phone conversation to undo that thread of time. "The town didn't seem like it had much interest in our comings and goings back then."

"Yes, well." The rustling of papers filtered over the line. "Be that as it may, there is certainly an interest in your whereabouts now."

This sounded like a mess, and Cordelia didn't care for messes. As a child, she kept her dolls in their boxes, careful not to crinkle the cellophane. She'd line them up in her spotless room and admire the way their hair gleamed, never tangling, and the way their clothes remained pristine, never wrinkling.

Unlike her momma—who often had lipstick stains on her teeth, ketchup stains on her shirts, and unidentifiable stains on her white sneakers—Cordelia strived to be the definition of cleanliness. According to their neighbor Pastor Reed-Smythe, it was next to godliness. Seeing as Sherilynn was the only woman in town who'd ever been turned away from church on account of her showing up four Sundays in a row drunker than a kernel in a corn whiskey barrel, Cordelia figured she could use all the godliness she could get her hands on.

It was a shame Pastor Reed-Smythe didn't extend those judgments to his own backyard. His son, Archer, had been a hellion from the get-go. He collected dead flies, lit fires on purpose, and rolled around in mud puddles. In the summer, Cordelia would practice sitting still while the grass tickled her ankles. She wanted to see how long she could go without twitching. But

Archer ruined that for her when he wandered over from next door and blew a loud raspberry on his arm, breaking her concentration and making her jump. He'd laughed, and she'd gotten a powerful urge to stick her finger into the empty slot where he'd lost his two front teeth.

It was the grossest image she'd ever conjured in her young life. That night she'd had to wash her hair three times just to scrub it from her head.

Every Sunday morning, he'd come out of his house in a nice clean suit, with his dark hair smartly combed and not a speck of dirt to be found anywhere on his face. He almost looked like the kind of boy she wouldn't mind being friends with. But then he'd call her Delia, which she hated, or stick his tongue out at her, or tell her Satan was going to eat her toes, and she'd remember why she disliked him so much. Since he was the pastor's son, folks in town would see him coming up the street dragging a cloud of dust behind him and just smile and nod and say things like "boys will be boys." But if Cordelia had so much as a speck of lint on her sweater, they'd draw closer together and sneer and say things like "blood will tell."

By the time Cordelia was ten years old, her momma had gotten so sick of being a pariah that she moved them way on up to Dallas and promised to clean up her act. A handful of false starts later, she attended her first AA meeting. But by that point Cordelia had already formed what the experts called her "core sense of self," and there was no turning back from the girl who just wanted people to see her as respectable.

No one from Sarsaparilla Falls bothered to stay in touch with them. The only person who had written her was Archer Reed-Smythe, who had sent her a letter informing her he could still smell her across Texas, along with a drawing of a stick figure she presumed to be her next to a large pile of garbage.

She didn't write him back.

As a teen, she was the only one in her class who had pressed creases in her jeans. She wore her long golden-brown hair straight and flat. No makeup, no jewelry, no loud prints or embellishments of any kind. Her big blue eyes, dark lashes, and wide mouth that tended to smile even as she frowned made some of the boys in her class think she was friendly, but she quickly disabused them of that notion. Boys were just one more thing that fell into the category of messy.

In college, once she'd cleared her gen eds and settled on a major, she figured it was time to partake in the adult tradition of dating. She tested the waters with a handful of movie nights with a few different guys, and, after taking an adequate amount of time to research why her stomach twisted into knots every time Harmony Salto's arm brushed hers in their tightly packed Postmodern Lit lecture, a few women as well. That was a shock to her momma, who sometimes still struggled to overcome some of Sarsaparilla Falls' more antiquated ways of thinking, but it didn't take long for Cordelia to decide dating didn't get any less complicated in adulthood. Soon after she scrubbed her last relationship from her dorm, her roommate requested a room change because the overpowering scent of bleach had begun to make her sick. After that, Cordelia was mostly alone again.

Once she graduated from school with a master's in library and information science, she felt as though she could finally live like she'd always wanted: a respected librarian with a tidy apartment, a neat wardrobe, and free from the shadow of being the town drunk's daughter.

All that seemed imperiled by this call.

Cordelia pulled herself from the grainy memories of her past. "And just why is anyone from Sarsaparilla Falls interested in my whereabouts after twenty years?"

"Your Great-Aunt Penelope has named you sole heir to the Chickadee Motel."

Cordelia's brows pinched together. What kind of nonsense name was the Chickadee Motel? Not any place that respectable people could take seriously, that was for sure. Besides, she didn't know the first thing about running a motel.

"I'm not sure if hospitality would suit me." Just the thought of touching sheets other people had slept in made a cold drop of sweat slide down her spine. "Can I sell it?"

"I'm afraid not," Mr. Jenkins said. "There's a developer by the name of Sean O'Leary who's sniffing around here, and he'd love to get his hands on the Chickadee, believe me, but her trust states that it may not be sold until the current residents move out or pass away."

"People live there?" She knew even less about being a landlord than she did about running a motel. "Can I ask them to leave?"

He laughed. "You can try, but the town wouldn't be too happy with you. The Chickadee is . . . something of an institution, and we, the good folks here in Sarsaparilla Falls, think it's best to just leave things the way they are."

Cordelia didn't give a single fly's carcass about the town's feelings. But if the residents were on some kind of cheap rental plan, they might not want to leave anyway. Not in this economy. "And what happens if I decide not to take it on?"

She had a good life. A job she liked well enough, a dirt-free apartment, and a weekly lunch date with a now-sober Sherilynn. There was no need to complicate it with unpleasant business in a town where she had an unpleasant history. And a residential motel with a no-sale clause sounded like the type of mess she'd spent her entire life avoiding.

"If you decide not to take on the Chickadee, ownership will pass to your momma."

She pinched the bridge of her nose. That wouldn't do. Not at all. The only reason her momma had been on the wagon these past twenty years was because she'd finally gotten away from Sarsaparilla Falls and all the ugly memories of Cordelia's daddy walking out on them. Her momma had a good life in Dallas too, but Cordelia feared she wouldn't be able to resist the opportunity to return to that town and take ownership of an alleged institution—if only to rub it in folks' faces for all the years they'd called her trash.

Cordelia released a long-suffering sigh. "How long do I have to decide?"

"You have a month to make a proper decision. If you're still not sure by the first of June, you'll forfeit your right to ownership and the Chickadee will then pass to Sherilynn."

Chapter Two

CORDELIA SAT AT HER USUAL TABLE AT THE COOP AND SCOOP, FOLDING and refolding the paper napkin she'd set neatly in her lap. The red-and-white-checkered tablecloth crinkled as she shifted it, so the edge of the squares lined up perfectly with the edge of the Formica booth. Then she rearranged the single-serve jellies, so they all faced the same way in the plastic caddy. Setting things to right had a way of soothing her nerves, like a cigarette or a double shot of whiskey did for others.

It had been two days since she'd taken that phone call from her deceased Great-Aunt Penelope's lawyer, an odd fellow who'd locked her into a situation where she couldn't yet see a means of escape . . . unless she could convince the residents of the motel to sell. She had three weeks of vacation saved up and figured she could get things sorted one way or another by then. She just wasn't sure what she'd tell her momma.

Cordelia glanced at the rooster-shaped clock hanging above the bar. Sherilynn was ten minutes late, but that was to be expected. Her internal alarms ran on snooze. And seeing as how Cordelia always ran ten minutes early, they were like two trains passing each other in a second-grade math problem. They didn't mean to be opposites. They just were.

"Sorry I'm late, sweetheart." Sherilynn West breezed into the Coop and Scoop like she did most things in life, in a whirlwind of chaos and cucumber-melon body spray. "I was on my way here when I saw this old dresser with the cutest knobs you ever did see sitting on the side of the road like trash. I couldn't just leave it there."

Cordelia's momma had traded her addiction to gin and tonics for an addiction to rehabbing furniture people left out on the street. She rented a booth at an upscale consignment shop in Highland Park and churned out a decent living. It never ceased to amaze Cordelia how much money rich people were willing to spend to look shabby just because it was chic, and her momma was the queen of capitalizing on the trend.

There was no telling what kind of trouble she'd get into if she got her hands on whatever furnishings had been left behind at the Chickadee.

"I ordered our drinks already," Cordelia said. "I hope you don't mind."

"Not at all." Her momma beamed as she took in Cordelia's appearance. "You look different. Did you trim your hair?"

Cordelia shook her head.

Her momma tilted her head. "A facial?"

"I haven't made any aesthetic changes at all." She picked at the corner of the napkin in her lap as she wiggled into the small opening she'd been given. "But I have some news. You might not like it, but hear me out."

"Okay." Her momma drew out the vowels on a long, wary note.

"I'm going to miss lunch for the next three weeks. I'll be out of town." There was obviously a bit more to it than that, but Cordelia wanted to dip a toe in and test the waters before elaborating. "I'm looking into a few job opportunities."

"What about the library?" Sherilynn wrinkled her nose as if she could sniff out the bull. "You love that job, and you worked so hard to get it."

"I'm just looking. I'm not committing to anything yet." She hadn't figured out how to bring up Sarsaparilla Falls to her momma, but she wanted to do it slowly, the way new parents let their house cats sniff around toys and blankets to keep them from smothering the baby in their sleep. "You know how rough it's been at work lately."

It pained Cordelia to admit the downtown library she loved had changed so much. With book bans heating up, her job had become more of a stress than a joy. The only silver lining was at least she didn't live in Florida. Not that Texas was much better. When she went to school, she never thought she'd be putting her actual life on the line to protect children's right to read.

But selling the motel would go a long way toward funding her education if she did decide to switch careers. Maybe she'd look into something that required less daily interaction with the public, like quality control management or taxidermy.

"When are you leaving?" Her momma blinked several times, as if she was still expecting Cordelia to announce she was pulling her leg. "If you give me a little notice, I can arrange things at work and see if I can make the trip with you."

"I appreciate it, but I want to do this on my own. I'll be heading out tomorrow. If I like what I see, I'll give my two weeks' notice." Cordelia doubted it would come to that. A quick sale would be best. The lawyer had said the town wouldn't want to see the motel sold off, but what did she care about the town? All they'd ever done was give her grief.

Sherilynn opened her mouth to argue and closed it again when the waiter came by with their drinks. Cherry Coke with extra syrup for Sherilynn and room temperature water, no ice, for Cordelia. Her momma's expression had turned stony, so Cordelia ordered their usual, chicken and waffles with a scoop of ice cream on top and a plate of beans and greens. The waiter didn't need to ask who got which.

Sherilynn sipped her Coke, licking off half her pink gloss as she smacked her lips. "Are you experimenting with drugs? You can tell me if you are."

"What?" Cordelia nearly dropped the napkin she'd been fidgeting with. "What would make you say a thing like that?"

"This isn't like you. Since when have you ever sought out change?"

"I'm thirty years old. Don't you think I ought to be doing something with my life? Finding some kind of direction?" Cordelia only said that to placate her momma, who'd always had a yearning in her soul for something she could never quite reach, but it didn't stop an ache from blooming in her own chest.

Did she want something more for herself? But what if the real reason she was so keen to check out this motel was because, deep down, she did want another life?

She dismissed the notion. Those occasional aches she got to try new things or be someone different came from her upbringing and her natural instincts to follow in her momma's footsteps. That was all. She'd been fighting those instincts her whole life, and mostly won against them, but every now and again they'd sneak up on her and make her feel like doing something dangerous.

"I'm sorry. I'll support you no matter what." Her momma reached across the table and squeezed her hand, and Cordelia felt an immediate rush of affection for the woman who'd raised her. "You know I will. What can I do to help?"

Cordelia chewed on her bottom lip, the guilt of not being fully forthcoming worming its way into her consciousness. "I could use some help packing for my trip."

"Sure. That'll be fun," Sherilynn said, in the same way one would call a root canal fun.

The waiter brought their food, and they let the comfortable silence settle between them while they ate. Cordelia still wasn't sure how to bring up Sarsaparilla Falls, or what her next steps would be if she couldn't sell. Maybe it was enough to tell her momma she was going out of town, and she'd find a way to spill the rest when she got back. She didn't really intend on staying down there. She just had to talk to the residents and see if she could negotiate a deal with them.

"I appreciate you." Cordelia poured a teaspoon of apple cider vinegar on her turnip greens. "Enough about me now. What have you been up to this week?"

Sherilynn shimmied her shoulders like a pitcher about to throw a strike down the middle. There were few things she liked more than talking about herself. "I had a meeting with my sponsor, and she's got me doing some extended step-four work, digging deeper into my past and looking more honestly at situations I might've glossed over thinking I was the victim."

"I thought you completed the twelve steps years ago?" Cordelia had sat through her momma's step-nine amends when she was thirteen, and the awkwardness of it was *not* something she wanted a repeat performance of in her thirties.

Her momma gave her a pitying, silly-goose-with-its-neck-caught-between-fence-posts look. "The steps are ongoing. It ain't a one-and-done deal."

"How was I supposed to know that?" Cordelia muttered. "I'm not in AA."

Her momma went on as if she hadn't heard her, talking about her business and gossiping about people Cordelia had never met. Sherilynn had a full life. It seemed as if she had no shortage of things to talk about and situations to laugh over. Hearing about all her momma's sober living adventures should've been encouraging. She was doing well, staying on the wagon, and enjoying the fruits of her hard-won labor. Cordelia couldn't help but stack up her own life against her momma's stories only to find it lacking. Like holding up an HD color photo next to a vintage black-and-white and expecting the images to be similar.

Maybe Sherilynn would be just fine running the Chickadee. Maybe Cordelia was the one hanging on to her momma's ghosts thinking they wouldn't haunt her.

Pushing her greens around on her plate, Cordelia decided to test the waters. "Do you ever think about Sarsaparilla Falls?"

"Only every day," Sherilynn said. "It's an important part of my recovery to stay aware of who I was while living in that town. Why are you asking?"

She'd somehow managed to make "that town" sound like a slur. Maybe she wouldn't fare so well there, after all.

"I was just thinking of it the other day. What it would be like to go back."

"And do what?" Her momma wrinkled her nose like she'd spotted a skunk at a lawn party. "Spending weekend nights at the local bar? Try to attend church again? There ain't a whole lot else going on there, and between the two, I think you know which I'd prefer."

"I know." The only church her momma ever attended now was the AA meetings in the basement of the local Presbyterian church on Tuesday nights. "I didn't mean we should take a vacation there or anything. I was just thinking about it, is all."

"That town is as poisonous to me as sitting in a bar just to hear the band play." Her momma motioned for the waiter to bring them their bill. "I've been sober long enough to know what I can and can't handle, and Sarsaparilla Falls is firmly in the can't camp."

"That's fair." All thoughts of sharing her news about the Chickadee went right out the window. There wasn't anything more important to Cordelia than her momma's sobriety. "Forget I mentioned it."

Her momma waved her hands around her head. "Already forgotten."

The waiter brought the check, and they each paid their individual bills, her momma putting hers on a credit card with Goofy on it, and Cordelia paying in exact change, plus tip, from her beaded coin purse. Cordelia didn't bring up Sarsaparilla Falls again. With any luck, her momma would plumb forget to ask her where she intended on staying while she was gone.

This would be fine. It's not like the people who lived at the Chickadee could stay on forever. One way or another, she'd find a way to sell so she could keep her anonymous life in an anonymous city and forget all about the small town where she'd been born.

Chapter Three

CORDELIA STOOD ON THE PAVEMENT OUTSIDE THE CHICKADEE, LILAC roller suitcase propped up beside her. Flat land and flecks of pale green from dry scrub brush spread out as far as the eye could see, with only a single winding dirt road to break up the deserted landscape. A hot wind blew a tiny twister of dust around her ankles and she cringed as it clung to the fabric of her most responsible pair of pantyhose. The ones she wore for job interviews and trips to the DMV.

The motel didn't look like any she'd ever seen before. With a cotton-candy-pink exterior, white scalloped trim, and the front walk of each room sectioned off with spindly iron fencing, it looked more like a dollhouse than a flophouse. Flowers in sunset hues bloomed from giant terra-cotta pots, and at the center of the L-shaped parking lot a sparkling and well-cared-for pool stood out like a jewel in a concrete wasteland. Even Cordelia couldn't find fault in the aquamarine oasis, and she abhorred public swimming facilities. They ranked right up there with nail salons, playgrounds, and bus stations.

She'd been informed before arriving that there were six rooms for rent, but only three were occupied. When she'd inquired about renting out the other three rooms, Mr. Jenkins made a noncommittal sound and said she'd have to take that up with the current residents. The more questions she asked, the more he deferred to the residents. As if she were the owner in name only. What kind of lease did her Great-Aunt Penelope sign with these people?

As Cordelia rolled her lilac suitcase toward the short end of the L, where the front office and her adjacent apartment were located, she took in her surroundings. She had to admit the Chickadee was much nicer than she'd been expecting for a motel ten miles outside of town, but she still didn't understand what made it such a treasured institution. As a business, it didn't make much sense. They weren't close to any kind of tourism or facilities that would require an overnight stay. The only scenery to be found in this part of Texas was tumbleweed, gravel, and scrub grass. People could get that kind of view anywhere.

The sign for the Chickadee was painted a powder blue, and underneath the motel's name, in scrawling cursive, it read ROOMS BY THE HOUR, BUT WE GUARANTEE YOU'LL NEED A WHOLE LOT MORE THAN THAT.

Cordelia certainly hoped people would need a room for more than an hour, especially as it would take them nearly fifteen minutes just to get out here from town.

She walked past the third room when a gentleman of about sixty-five, wearing a wrinkled white linen suit, a wide-brimmed Stetson, and a satisfied smile stepped into the sun from the fourth room. He tipped his hat to her, looking her up and down as if she were a fattened calf at the county fair and he was handing out blue ribbons.

She turned her nose up and kept walking. She was not about to accept judgment about her appearance from a man in a wrinkled suit.

The blinds behind the fifth room rustled, but she kept her focus straight ahead. Before she could steel herself to meet the residents and see exactly what kind of mess she'd gotten herself into, she needed to get her bearings. Unpacking and putting things in their proper place would calm her nerves. As would a spot check with her trusty lint roller. If the apartment was in a state of disarray, she'd probably spend a full two days cleaning before she could be expected to attend to anything else. It was a good thing she'd packed trail mix and carrot sticks. She didn't know if a grocery delivery service would come this far.

She'd just rolled her suitcase over a sidewalk crack in front of the sixth room when the door burst open to reveal a busty blond who couldn't have been younger than her late fifties, wearing a practically transparent black lace bodysuit with dangling garters that swayed as she squealed in delight. With soft brown eyes, sky-high Texas hair, ruby-red lips, and a beauty mark on her left cheek, she looked like a pinup model getting ready to collect her first Social Security check. She wrapped Cordelia in an enormous hug that threw her off balance.

"You must be the new madam." The older woman smelled like Love's Baby Soft, as if she had aesthetically stopped aging in 1985 even as her face and body kept on going. She squished her sizable chest against Cordelia. "My name is Daisy. Belinda Sue and Arline told me to let you get settled in first, but I was so excited to meet you. I just couldn't help myself. Miss Penelope, rest her soul, was the only madam I'd ever known. Though we were all sad to see her pass, it will be exciting to see what someone new will bring to the table. I hope it will be parties. We've missed having parties around here."

"I haven't decided to stay in an official capacity yet," Cordelia said. "I'm only here for a few weeks right now, to take stock of what's being asked of me."

Daisy bounced on her toes. "But you just have to stay. Sarsaparilla Falls is the sweetest little town. Safer than a bank vault. Except for that nasty break-in over at Porter Sheldon's place last week, but he was visiting his niece, wasn't even home. And the only thing that got stolen was a dusty old book anyway, so really no harm done. Let me show you around."

She talked a mile a minute, and Cordelia only picked up on every other word. She nodded as Daisy pointed out the pool, Belinda Sue's and Arline's rooms, and kept using the word "madam." Was that what they called the motel manager? Strange title, but it wasn't the oddest thing about the Chickadee, so Cordelia could hardly let herself dwell on it for too long.

The more Daisy talked about the other ladies, the more Cordelia had begun to understand that aside from being a motel, the Chickadee served as a retirement home for single women of a certain age. That must've been what Mr. Jenkins had been talking about when he called it an institution. He could've just told her as much. Cordelia wasn't heartless. She wouldn't throw senior women in their golden age out on the street. She'd be willing to use some of the proceeds to make sure they got set up some place just as nice, but she also had no problem leaving the Chickadee be until it was time for the residents to move on in a more permanent way.

"Please take a breath." Cordelia put a hand on Daisy's thin upper arm to still her fidgeting, nearly shuddering when she came away with what appeared to be rolled-on glitter. "I have no intention of changing things. I have a job at a library in Dallas, and I assume the motel can run itself, as it seems to have been doing since Great-Aunt Penelope's . . . departure."

"See. The thing is." Daisy nibbled on her bottom lip as she tilted her head, studying Cordelia like she'd just fallen off the turnip truck. "The Chickadee don't really run itself."

"Nonsense." Cordelia removed a wet wipe from her purse and meticulously scrubbed between her fingers to remove all traces of glitter. "I saw a gentleman leaving on my way in, and the pool is immaculate. I'd say things have been running just fine around here."

"Belinda Sue gives Antonio Reyes a monthly discount for changing the filter and general maintenance. He's a real whiz with mechanics. The pool was Miss Penelope's pride and joy." Daisy's eyes filled, but before a tear could fall, she returned her gaze to Cordelia with a bright smile. "I'm sure you're itching to get unpacked and settled in. We're having happy hour by the pool at five if you're feeling up to it. It's Belinda Sue's thing, she likes us to have time together to wind down."

With that, Daisy flounced back to her room and shut the door with a soft click. Cordelia tipped her sunglasses down and continued to roll her suitcase toward the front office. Her great-aunt's lawyer had given her a key on a flashy keychain that resembled lips. She'd be replacing that first thing with something more understated and utilitarian. Like a Swiss Army knife or a spoon from one of the fifty states.

After Cordelia unlocked the door and stepped inside the small office, she took in her surroundings. For a front office, it didn't appear to be all that functional. The air reeked of dollar-store potpourri. Several old steamer trunks stood against the wall, with feather boas and sequined garments spilling out of the open lids. A mannequin wearing a floral wreath and an electric-blue wig had been propped in the corner. The back wall that should've held the room keys was papered over with a gaudy palm tree design. The counter where guests should've been able to check in held dusty boxes filled with an odd assortment of party supplies. Balloons, plastic champagne glasses, cheap replica tiaras, and a ten-foot-long rubber snake.

It looked like the backstage of a cabaret. Where was the computer system? The keys for the empty rooms? The little bell customers could push if there wasn't anyone at the front desk? Daisy had said the Chickadee didn't run itself, but it looked as though it didn't run at all.

How had that older gentleman in the wrinkled suit paid for his room? Or had the residents just let people come and go as they pleased in the absence of an owner?

But Great-Aunt Penelope's lawyer said she'd passed just six months ago and had been running the Chickadee all on her own, right up until the day she was T-boned outside the H-E-B. How could the front office have become so disorganized in such a short time?

Feeling her skin prickle from the layer of dust she'd stirred up by opening the door, dust that was surely settling on her as she stood there in horror, Cordelia made her way to the side door, which had a slightly crooked EMPLOYEES ONLY sign hanging over it. She passed through a short hallway that held the boiler room and a bathroom she couldn't bring herself to inspect just yet. The door to her new apartment was painted bubble-gum pink with white trim and she couldn't help but be charmed despite herself.

Holding her breath, hoping Great-Aunt Penelope kept plenty of Lysol on hand, Cordelia turned the key, pushed open the door, and exhaled.

Much to Cordelia's relief, it appeared she'd shared a tidy gene with her deceased great-aunt. The air was staler than discount deli bread, and it held the old notes of a fruit basket turned sour, but nothing a little airing out wouldn't fix. A mauve couch sat against a wide window adorned with goldenrod curtains that had little tassels at the hem. A lamp with a stained-glass hummingbird shade hung on a chain over a moss-colored velvet chair. Next to the chair, a copy of *Woman's World* and a pair of paisley print readers sat on a mid-century modern end table.

The little kitchenette featured cherry-red appliances and

a dining nook that held a table for two. At the back of the small apartment, a narrow space with a double bed covered in a hot pink bedspread and a sewing machine served as the only bedroom. It had a connected bathroom with just a corner shower stall, no tub. That didn't bother Cordelia much. She hated the idea of cooking herself in what amounted to a large bowl of water.

The style wasn't exactly to her taste, but it was furnished and clean. It could've been a lot worse.

She unpacked her suitcase, then pulled a book off a skinny shelf decorated with spider plants and crystal hippos. All of Great-Aunt Penelope's books featured women in shoulder-baring nightgowns clutching shirtless, windswept men. They made her sensible A-line skirt and eggshell blouse feel too tight. Cordelia considered herself well read—it was part of her job, after all—but she didn't often indulge in romance. She didn't like to feel things.

A few chapters in, she found herself wondering how one managed to make love on a horse without falling off. She jotted down a note to research later.

As she stood up to stretch her limbs, the sound of high-pitched laughter drew her attention. She'd opened the window to let in some air, and the scent of sun-warmed tar and chlorine wafted in on a gentle prairie breeze. She peeled back the curtain to get a peek at the pool party.

Three older women sat on striped beach recliners, sipping cheap margaritas from comically large glasses with pineapple wedges and bright-blue paper umbrellas. She recognized Daisy, who wore a pink polka-dot bikini. She had her curly blond bouffant tied up with a black checkered handkerchief. Despite her wrinkled skin and sagging jowls, she had a youthful glow about her. As if she approached the world like it was still fresh and new.

Daisy chatted with a red-haired woman who looked to be in

her sixties. She wore a no-frills black one-piece and styled her hair like Lucille Ball, but she had the face of an accountant. Cordelia liked her immediately. She reminded Cordelia of the cranky old women who yelled at the library staff for shelving a gardening book in the true-crime section even though they hadn't come in seeking a gardening or true-crime book. Her favorite patrons. Cordelia had nothing but respect for those who appreciated order and lacked social shame.

The third woman, somewhere in her late sixties, kept her dark-gray hair cut short and wore a floral bikini with a matching swim skirt. She sat slightly off to the side, keeping her own company. And though the other women included her in conversation, she didn't do anything other than nod or shake her head in response. If she hadn't opened her mouth to take a drink from her margarita, Cordelia might've wondered if she had a jaw condition.

She hadn't intended to join the pool party, but when Daisy caught sight of her in the window, Cordelia had no choice but to wave back. It was her first day here. The last thing she wanted to do was come off as unfriendly to the residents she was hoping to negotiate with. Closing the curtain, Cordelia released a long-winded sigh, then went into the bedroom to change into her bathing suit and sun hat.

Chapter Four

CORDELIA'S SANDALS SLAPPED AGAINST THE BLACKTOP AND SHE SHIFTED her gait to stop the offending noise from drawing any more attention. Her bathing suit was plain blue, with a bow that tied across her chest. It looked nice against her pale skin, but suddenly felt too loud next to the red-haired woman's even plainer black.

"Yoohoo! Over here!" Daisy waved her hand wildly as she spotted Cordelia opening the gate to the pool area. "We're so glad you could make it. Belinda Sue thought you'd need more time to get your bearings, but I told her you had a real friendly way about you and that you'd be down here in no time. I mean, who can resist a pool party? Am I right?"

"Lord, Daisy, let the poor girl catch her breath before you hit her with all of you." The red-haired woman in the black suit stood and offered her hand. She had a firm, dry grip. More proof that this was Cordelia's kind of person. "I'm Belinda Sue, and this here is Arline." She nodded to the woman in the floral suit, who just nodded back without speaking.

"Nice to meet y'all." Cordelia bent her knees and tipped her chin as she greeted them. A semicurtsey to show her respect to her elders. "I hope y'all will have a little patience with me as I figure out how things work around here."

"Of course, dear." Belinda Sue patted the plastic chair beside her, directing Cordelia to take a seat. "Feel free to ask us anything you'd like to know."

"Thank you for your hospitality." Cordelia drummed her fingers on the armrest of the plastic beach chair as the three women stared at her expectantly. She didn't like having that many eyes on her at once. It felt like being watched by a spider. "Have y'all lived here long?"

Belinda Sue frowned, as if she'd been expecting another question. "I suppose we have. Daisy and I arrived in eighty-six and Arline joined us in eighty-eight."

"Eighty-nine," Arline said. Her voice creaked like it didn't get a whole lot of use.

"Eighty-nine," Belinda Sue repeated.

Cordelia was as confused as a goat on Astroturf. Surely these women hadn't been living in a motel for this many decades? Why hadn't they gotten apartments? She'd assumed they'd formed a little retirement community here, but this was something else altogether. They must've come here when they were fresh out of high school.

"I'm sorry." Unused to so much fresh air, Cordelia coughed and patted her chest, which Daisy took as a sign that she needed a drink. And though she'd never been much of a drinker on account of her personal history, Cordelia thought a little liquid courage might not hurt in this situation. She took the dressed-up glass of liquor and punch Daisy passed to her and drank deeply. "Are you saying y'all have been renting rooms since you were teenagers?"

Daisy shook her head enthusiastically. "We weren't quite teenagers, though it's sweet of you to think we look that young, but me and Belinda Sue weren't allowed to start until we were twenty-one. Arline might've been a bit older, maybe thirty. We don't know for sure. And don't bother asking, she'll never tell you."

"What do you mean by allowed to start?"

"That was Penelope's rule. We had to be old enough to have figured out some of life before we could be one of her girls. She had a funny way about her, but it all made sense in the end."

Cordelia wasn't sure how much of life they'd had figured out if they'd chosen to live in a motel for the bulk of their lives, but she'd grown up with enough judgments from strangers to know when to hold her tongue on other people's personal business. Still. The odd way Daisy phrased it, that she started here, made it sound more like a job than a living arrangement.

"You . . . work here?" Maybe they were part of the staff. House cleaners and bookkeepers and whatever else a motel required to run. But that only left three vacant rooms and a staff of three for three rooms seemed a little excessive. But then again, by Cordelia's standards, everything was a little excessive.

"Of course, dear." Belinda Sue gave her a look similar to the one Daisy had given her when she first arrived. Like Cordelia's brain was made of ink and she couldn't dot an *i*. "All of us are working girls. Didn't Arbuckle explain it to you?"

"I bet he didn't." Daisy giggled and bounced a little on her beach chair.

Cordelia's shoulders stiffened. She'd been the butt of plenty of jokes growing up and didn't care one bit to be set outside the loop. "I was told the Chickadee was a local institution and that's about it. If I'm missing something, I hope y'all can fill me in."

"Dang it, Arbuckle. No-good, useless son of a gun," Belinda Sue muttered under her breath. "Here's the thing." She gave Cordelia a tight smile that didn't fit the natural contours of her pinched, agitated face and folded her hands in her lap. "The three of us are the last of the chicks, working girls, here at the Chickadee. Everyone else has either passed on or moved away to other towns, other jobs."

"The younger generation all got themselves webcams now," Daisy said.

Belinda Sue snorted and shook her head. "The ones who got snap in their garters, anyhow. And that's the only sort Penelope would ever let cross this hallowed threshold. She didn't do business with common folks."

"She had a reputation to uphold," Daisy said. "You understand that, don't you?"

Cordelia could understand a reputation better than just about anyone else. She knew all the ways it could build you up and even more ways it could break you. She valued a good reputation above all else, because once you had a good one, it could carry you places you could never get to on your own.

"I certainly understand the need to be respectable." Cordelia tapped a finger to her lips. "But what did the running of this place have to do with y'all?"

"She was our madam." Daisy lifted her chin as pride radiated through her voice. "We're the best in the business."

There was that word again. "Madam." But this time, instead of finding it strange and mildly amusing, a pit opened in Cordelia's stomach. Deep and endless. It was just beginning to dawn on her that "madam" probably wasn't just a South Texas way of saying "female landlord."

She cleared away the lump of panic that had seen fit to settle in her throat. "What kind of business do you do?"

Belinda Sue took on a more serious expression. "Well now, the proper term these days is 'sex worker.' But what we do is provide a community service—"

"For pay," Daisy interjected.

Belinda Sue nodded. "For pay. But a community service at heart. We service the husbands in all the nearby counties so their wives can get on with other doings."

"Other. Doings," Cordelia said, not quite sure how her jaw was still working when it had dropped clear on down to her feet. Mr. Arbuckle Jenkins had some serious explaining to do.

"Quilting bees, book clubs, canning jams, you know." Daisy twirled her wrist. "All those hobbies many of the respectable ladies in town like doing in peace without having their randy husbands pawing after them at all hours of the day. Of course, we don't mess with the husbands whose wives don't wholeheartedly approve. We have some single clients too, but most our visitors are married."

"So the husbands come and see y'all?" Cordelia's voice squeaked on the last syllable. This was fine. She was not a cartoon dog casually drinking coffee while the room burned around her. This was. Just. Fine.

"Not all at once," Daisy said. "Unless they pay extra, but we haven't had any requests like that in oh"—a dreamy smile overtook her face as she sifted through her memories—"maybe twenty years. Not since Earl Cruiser died. Isn't that right, Belinda Sue?"

"God rest his soul." Belinda Sue closed her eyes and pointed to the sky before directing her gaze back to Cordelia. "For the most part, we have our regulars and routines. We each offer a specialty. Daisy is our sweetheart. She handles the men who like to be cooed and coddled and treated like the center of the universe."

Daisy threw Belinda Sue a mischievous grin. "I've always been real good at spoiling babies, and what are men, if not just a bunch of overgrown babies?"

"Indeed." Belinda Sue grinned back. "And I tend to the men who like it when a woman has what I refer to as a firmer hand, if you know what I mean."

"Or a whip," Daisy said brightly. "They like that too."

Cordelia pressed her fingers into her temples. This couldn't be happening. She couldn't be having a civilized conversation about whips with a group of senior ladies. They should be wrapping their furniture in plastic and having dinner at four o'clock, not satisfying the sexual appetites of old married men who didn't want to bother their wives.

"I'm sure they do," Cordelia said absently. She leaned forward, cradling her forehead against her knees.

Belinda Sue rubbed her hand up and down Cordelia's spine. "It's not as bad as all that now. You'll get fifteen percent of whatever we make, and you'll only have to get out the shotgun once or twice a month."

"Even less than that now that Jimmy Dodge Buck got himself into the AA," Daisy said. "He used to have a real mean temper when he drank, nothing Miss Penelope couldn't handle, but that's all behind him now."

"My momma's in the AA too." Cordelia couldn't think of what else to say as she tried to wrap her mind around the situation.

They expected her to know how to hold a shotgun, for crying out loud. She was Texas down to her bones, but she wasn't *that* kind of Texas. She lifted her head and shifted her gaze between Daisy and Belinda Sue. They wore matching nervous expressions.

As she glanced away from them, her lungs tying themselves in knots, her gaze settled on Arline, whose head tipped forward as she lightly snored, though her watery eyes remained open and fixed on the surrounding open plains. Cordelia couldn't tell if Arline was asleep or just completely uninterested in the discussion at hand.

"She's awake." Belinda Sue nodded toward Arline. "She just breathes like that."

"Oh. Of course." Cordelia's cheeks pinkened at having been caught staring. She tried to recover by changing the subject. "And what is it you do, Arline?"

Arline didn't so much as blink.

"It's not personal," Belinda Sue said. "Arline doesn't talk much."

"Only when she's got something important to say," Daisy said.

"But it's not important for her to make conversation. Her particular skill set doesn't require all that many words." Belinda Sue snapped her fingers at Arline, drawing her attention from wherever it had wandered. "Arline. Show the new madam what you do for your regulars."

Arline took out her teeth and set them on the clear-topped table beside her.

"Okay. I think I've seen enough here." Cordelia got to her feet and began pacing. "Y'all seem very nice, and I'm happy you have your system worked out, but this really isn't what I was expecting to find here, so if you'll excuse me."

"I told you she needed time," Belinda Sue said to Daisy.

"I'm just going to . . ." Cordelia pointed behind her and turned around to leave, only to run smack-dab into a hard wall of muscle. "Oof."

Cordelia tipped her head back. And back. And back. Until her gaze landed on a face she might've called ruggedly handsome, if he hadn't been raising his eyebrows at her like she was half a bubble off plumb. There was a familiarity to him she couldn't quite place her finger on. Though she was certain she'd never met a man with this much . . . virility.

He had dark hair that curled at the tips, a strong square jaw, and a mustache that suited him, despite Cordelia having a serious aversion to all manner of facial hair. It made most faces look unkempt, but it made the gentleman standing before her seem stronger for it. Sturdy. Cordelia's stomach fluttered unpleasantly, and she pressed a hand to it to steady herself.

She took in his wide chest and tapered waist. He wore a white button-down with the sleeves rolled up and black suspenders. Her ex-girlfriend had worn suspenders, an article of clothing that implied a level of fastidiousness Cordelia found hard to resist. Much to her disappointment, she soon discovered her ex wasn't neat or orderly, but on those rare times when she looked back on their relationship, she'd remember those suspenders fondly.

"You okay there, darlin'?" The man's grin turned to a smirk as he eyed her floppy sun hat. She suddenly found herself wishing she'd risked the burn.

"I'm fine." Fine. Fine. Fine. "I was just . . ." Leaving? Running away? Immediately seeking a pillow to scream into? "Going back to my great-aunt's apartment."

His tawny brown eyes lit up. "You must be the new madam everyone is talking about."

"People are talking about me? Why? What are they saying?" A montage of scenarios flashed through her mind, each more horrifying than the next. The old whispers of "Blood will tell" rang in her ears on repeat.

"Whoa." He held his hands up. "Relax. People are just sayin' the Chickadee got itself a new madam. Don't know much more than that, not even your name. Arbuckle Jenkins has been real tight-lipped about things. Possibly for the first time in his life."

"This here is Penelope's great-niece. Cordelia West," Belinda Sue said.

"From Dallas," Daisy added in a lilting tone that could've just as easily have said "From Paris," or "From Rome."

"Well, well, well. This day is certainly full of surprises." The man rubbed his jaw, the gesture much too casual for the shock evident in his wide eyes. Clearly, he wasn't used to being caught off guard and didn't much care for it. "I know it's been twenty years, but let me be the first to welcome you back to Sarsaparilla Falls, Delia."

The nickname she hadn't heard in years, on account of her specifically hating the shortening of proper names, the familiarity of his grin, and the trouble brewing behind those whiskey-colored eyes all hit her like a two-ton truck going eighty down a dirt road. She knew this man. He had once been as recognizable to her as the back of her own hand.

Archer Reed-Smythe.

All grown up.

Chapter Five

CORDELIA WALKED BACK TO THE APARTMENT SO FAST THAT SHE DIDN'T have the wherewithal to adjust her stance. The incessant flap, flap, flap of her sandals followed her all the way across the blacktop like the chatter of magpies.

Once inside, she shut the door and pressed her back to it, her heart hammering hard enough to make her teeth rattle. She fanned her overheated cheeks. Archer Reed-Smythe, the pastor's devilish son, had grown into a man too handsome for his own good. Cordelia didn't trust men of that caliber. They had a way of looking at women like they knew the exact shade and style of their underwear.

That was all to say, Cordelia had only ever dated people who made her feel comfortable and actively avoided those she found overtly attractive. Not that she'd been thinking of dating Archer Reed-Smythe. Not when he was paying a visit to the Chickadee for what she feared could only be one reason. She just hoped he wasn't after Arline's specialty.

Cordelia changed out of her bathing suit and back into her professional attire, which seemed a little silly given the circumstance, but she was still, above all else, a lady. Snatching her phone off the charger where she'd left it, she dialed Mr. Arbuckle Jenkins. He picked up on the first ring, and his jovial greeting made her jaw clench.

Cordelia couldn't keep the snapdragon from blooming in her voice. "Why didn't you tell me the Chickadee was a cathouse?"

"Not just any cathouse, but the best little one in Texas." The jolly good cheer of his tone only served to make her more upset.

"That's not funny. We're not putting on musical theater here, Mr. Jenkins. This is my life. You knowingly withheld information from me. I think that frees me from any responsibility."

"Miss West. You've always been free from the responsibility. If you'd like to back out, I'll just call up your momma and let her know—"

"No." Cordelia squeezed her eyes shut. "No, please. That won't be necessary."

She couldn't imagine what her momma would do if she found out she'd inherited a brothel for seniors. Would it be enough to bring her back to Sarsaparilla Falls and all the ugly memories that had knocked her off the wagon time and time again? That wasn't a risk worth taking. She had to keep this from Sherilynn for as long as possible.

"Okay, then." The clunk of Mr. Jenkins's cowboy boots hitting his desk reverberated through the phone. "I happen to know Belinda Sue personally, and I'd be more than happy to ring her up and ask her to go over the basics with you."

Cordelia grimaced at the thought of just how personal a relationship he had with Belinda Sue. Did he prefer the hand or the whip? The vision of him squealing like a pig under Belinda Sue's ministrations nearly made her retch.

"I understand the basics," Cordelia said. "Though you should know, I'll be writing you a strongly worded one-star review on Yelp for this."

She hung up and flung her phone on the bedside table, then face-planted into the mattress. She had no way out of this. She couldn't sell. Who would buy a cathouse full of golden-aged sex workers? What about the law? Sex work wasn't legal in Texas. Would she be on the hook if there was some kind of trouble? Perhaps Archer had been right all those years ago, and Satan had it out for her. She'd never been a religious sort, but if all those churches turned out to be right, this was surely the most direct path to hell.

Cordelia allowed herself fifteen minutes to eat sorrow by the spoonful before she stood and organized her thoughts while she organized her sock drawer. Her Great-Aunt Penelope must've lost her mind when she wrote her trust. Why didn't she leave the Chickadee to Belinda Sue? She looked like she wouldn't mind showing unruly patrons the business end of a .45.

If only Cordelia had gotten the chance to know her great-aunt. If she'd spent a single day in Cordelia's company, she'd have known Cordelia fit in about as well as a porcupine at a nudist colony. Just one more reason for Cordelia to curse her spineless father for walking away, abandoning any chance of connecting his only child with her only family. His shadow had a long reach.

After Cordelia finished organizing her sock drawer, her mind still wasn't as clear as she'd hoped, so she rearranged the towels in the bathroom closet by size and color, polished the knobs on the kitchen cabinets, and vacuumed a perfect diamond pattern into the living room rug. At the end of her mini cleaning spree, she still felt unsettled, but her spirits had lifted significantly. Perhaps her situation wasn't as bleak as she'd feared. She had a roof over her head and a job that offered her respectability, if not comfort, in Dallas.

Just because she owned the Chickadee didn't mean she had to be its madam. That wasn't a condition of the trust. Mr. Arbuckle Jenkins said she couldn't sell out from under the chicks, but he never said she had to stay. And having her name on the deed didn't make her a madam any more than renting her first apartment from a hoarder made her a trash collector.

Maybe she could turn the day-to-day operations over to one of the remaining chicks. They'd all get to stay, and Cordelia would be free from any legal obligation. Belinda Sue certainly appeared to have a head for this business. It would be like a promotion.

With that settled, Cordelia took out her notepad and began jotting down a list of things she needed to pick up from the grocery store. A quick trip into town would also allow her to check out the library and pick up a few more serious books that didn't make her think about men like Archer Reed-Smythe. She'd just folded her list and tucked it into her purse when there was a light tapping on her door.

"Miss Cordelia? It's Daisy. Is it okay if I come in?"

Cordelia's brows pinched at the interruption, but now that she'd decided to turn operations over to Belinda Sue, she only needed to stay for a few more days, a week tops, and she didn't want to give the impression she was a she-bear in satin. She opened the door, careful to keep her expression neutral. "I was just about to head into town, but I've got a few minutes. Would you like something to drink?"

"No, thank you." Daisy walked in and made herself at home, touching the knickknacks on the shelves and rubbing the rubber plant leaves between her fingers. "I just wanted to make sure you were okay. You sure left in a hurry after Archer arrived."

Cordelia internally groaned. "I didn't want to disrupt your business."

Daisy paused her fidgeting to spin around and face Cordelia. Her ruby-red lips popped open before she released a full-bellied laugh, bright as the sun. "Oh, honey, no. I wish." Her lashes fluttered. "Archer Reed-Smythe is way too young and much too handsome to take up with the likes of us."

A tension Cordelia didn't know she was carrying in her shoulders loosened. "What was he doing here then, if he wasn't here for business?"

"He was looking for his daddy, who *is* one of my clients and closer in age to our regulars." Daisy gave her a sly little smile. "Archer would suit you, though."

"I don't think so." Cordelia sniffed. "He used to steal Barbies from the girls in class and hide them in a dirt hole in his backyard he called a booby trap."

Daisy laughed. "Boys will be boys."

"So they say."

While Cordelia had no doubt Archer had likely matured in the last twenty years, there was still a roughness that wafted off him like cologne. Wild boys grew up to be dangerous men. The kind who couldn't be tied down with barbed wire.

"And how long has the good Pastor Reed-Smythe been a card-carrying member of the Chickadee?" Cordelia asked.

Daisy's chest puffed up proudly. "For the past thirty years."

"Isn't that something?" Cordelia couldn't help but be amused by this information. She didn't remember much about him, since her momma had been banned from attending church, but he sure did like to complain about how often they mowed their grass.

"I remember when you were little." Daisy picked up one of the crystal hippos and nervously rubbed her thumb over its enlarged backside. "I asked Miss Penelope why she didn't offer you and your momma a room when her no-good nephew left you two high and dry. She said you still had your house and the Chickadee was no place to raise a child."

"Did my momma know Penelope?" Cordelia found it hard to believe that Sherilynn would keep a relative from her, considering how short they were on them. Even one tied to her deserting daddy.

"No. From what I understand, Travis wasn't real fond of Penelope's profession and didn't acknowledge her as kin. His parents were from another county, so not many people knew anyway, and she wanted to respect his wishes by keeping her distance. Once he was gone, she didn't know if it would be a good idea to approach Sherilynn. Back then, your momma . . ."

Cordelia held up a hand. "No need to say more."

Her momma used to make a spectacle of herself. She could turn a cloudy day into a tornado, and she would steal anything that wasn't nailed down. The sheriff had once fished her out of the wishing fountain in town, where she'd jumped in buck naked and tried to grab enough quarters for her next six-pack. It was that more than anything that made her such an outcast. Sarsaparilla Falls could deal with the drinking, they could even deal with her lack of responsibility, but they drew the line at her outlandish exhibitions.

"Right. Still, I wish we'd done a little more to look after y'all back then, but then y'all moved away and that was that."

"We ended up okay." It touched Cordelia that Daisy considered her at all when everyone else in town had treated her like she'd steal the flowers off their grandmas' graves.

"I hope we can do better by you now." Daisy took both her hands and guided her toward the couch. The stiff, paisley-print fabric creased under their weight. "I'm sorry Mr. Jenkins wasn't more forthcoming. Belinda Sue told me to give you some time, that you'd come around to all of us eventually, but I can't stand letting things hang without clearing the air. I feel downright awful for assuming you knew what was what this afternoon."

"It's not your fault," Cordelia said. The earnest expression on Daisy's soft, doe-like face could've melted an ice block in a blizzard. Cordelia would've expected Daisy to be tough as nickel steak after nearly forty years in her line of work, but there was an innocence to her that Cordelia couldn't help but find endlessly endearing. "I grew up in this town and never once felt welcome in it until I met you."

As soon as the words passed her lips, she tasted the honey-sweet truth of them. Daisy had greeted her with warmth and openness and hadn't asked a thing of Cordelia before accepting her into her cotton-candy-pink corner of the world. Some people were born good, and some were made good, and then there were people like Daisy, who were just good for no reason.

"If that ain't the kindest thing anyone has said to me in a long while." Daisy beamed. "You just made my week, honey."

Cordelia tilted her head as she studied Daisy, who looked as fresh as the flower she was named after. The eager sparkle in her eyes and the flush to her cheeks clued in Cordelia on just how badly Daisy wanted her approval. It wasn't often someone looked up to Cordelia. She found the pedestal most disagreeable on account of her fear of heights. Not to mention, the idea of a woman thirty years her senior thinking of her as a mother figure was ludicrous. But the parts of her that had grown hard and unyielding in the cracked concrete where she'd been raised softened. Maybe being needed, no matter the capacity, wasn't so bad.

"How did you end up at the Chickadee? If you don't mind me asking," Cordelia said.

"I was always the pleasing sort, and I liked attention." Daisy settled against the couch and crossed her ankles. "My momma thought I'd grow up to deliver singing telegrams."

"That's sweet. Did she approve of your profession?"

"Oh, Lord, no." Daisy chuckled. "The cheese would've fallen off her cracker, but she passed on a month before I started at the Chickadee. I was raised by a single momma too. Having no place else to go and no plans for my future, I asked Miss Penelope to take a chance on me, and it turned out I liked the work. It kept me on the straight and narrow."

"Really?" Cordelia raised an eyebrow.

"Absolutely." Daisy nodded vigorously. "Miss Penelope had no tolerance for bad-mouthing or substance abuse or petty fights. She hired good girls and kept us off the streets. Taught us about charity and community and gave us a purpose. When the tornado of ninety-three tore through town, Miss Penelope not only donated the money to rebuild the businesses lost to the storm, but she swung a hammer with the best of them and expected her girls to help out too. She donated to the public library when their funds got cut. She donated school supplies so the teachers wouldn't have to take out of their own pockets to stock their classrooms. The entire town owed her a debt of gratitude."

"I wish I'd had a chance to meet her." A twinge of regret hit Cordelia on two fronts, for never getting the chance to meet the only extended family she'd ever heard of, and for being so quick to judge the Chickadee without understanding what kind of place it had in town.

"She liked you. Kept an eye on you from a distance. Said you were like Yellowstone. All hard and unassuming on the outside, but a spitfire under the surface."

"I'm not sure about spitfire." Cordelia found her thrills in color-coded binders and a well-organized spreadsheet. She liked her food beige and avoided anything that sparkled.

"You've got more of Miss Penelope in you than you realize." Daisy gave her a knowing smile. "She left the Chickadee in your care for a reason."

"We'll see," Cordelia said. Though Cordelia had no intention of being a madam, it wouldn't hurt to finish out the week with an open mind. What a funny twist of fate that she had landed right back in the town she'd spent near her whole life trying to outrun.

Her grocery list and trip to the library forgotten, Cordelia put on some tea and sat out front on the porch rocker with Daisy, listening to the wild stories from her younger days. By the time Daisy had made it to her thirties, Cordelia's ears had turned the shade of a cherry bomb pop, but she couldn't think of the last time she'd been so entertained. Turned out, wild girls grew up to be cheeky, delightful women.

As the sun set over the flat expanse of land that surrounded them, Daisy stood and stretched her limbs, the crack and pop of her bones the only thing that betrayed her age. "I appreciate the talk and tea, but the pastor should be along any minute now, so it's probably best if I get back to my room."

They said their goodbyes, and Cordelia went back inside and turned off the part of her mind prone to overanalyzing.

Great-Aunt Penelope had left a stack of Salisbury steak TV dinners in the freezer, and since it was too late to go into town, Cordelia decided to make do. She set up her dinner in the living room and watched the evening news, giving up on the rubbery meat after two bites. It went cold before she finally threw the rest in the trash. Her upbringing instilled a real fear of waste in her, but even she had her limits.

She'd just put away the gold-trimmed TV tray decorated with watercolor bluebirds when there was once again a light tapping on her door that she'd already come to associate with Daisy. But Daisy was supposed to be with Pastor Reed-Smythe. According to the sign out front, she should've been occupying him for longer than an hour.

But when Cordelia answered the door, there stood Daisy, eyes wide as she twisted her fingers so tight her knuckles glowed white under the silvery moon. All the muscles in Cordelia's body hugged her bones, but she wouldn't allow herself to panic. Not yet, anyway.

"Please don't tell me you need me to drag out the shotgun on my first day here." Cordelia had meant to keep her tone light, but her thin, papery voice betrayed her concern. While she didn't put much stock in the idea of God, she wasn't looking to test that theory by pulling a gun on one of his own.

"No, I don't think that'll be necessary." Daisy's lips were free from their ruby-red coloring, and for the first time, Cordelia could see just how small and lined she was beneath her thick layer of makeup. "This is beyond the usual sort of help."

Cordelia motioned for her to come inside, then moved toward the kitchen to put the kettle on the stove. Near anything could be fixed with a strong-enough cup of tea. "What's going on? You look as full of pains as an old window."

Unable to hold it together any longer, Daisy burst into tears. "I think I killed the pastor."

Chapter Six

CORDELIA ROUSED THE OTHER LADIES FIRST THING. THIS WAS NOT THE type of situation she was up for handling alone, and considering the median age of the Chickadee patrons, this couldn't have been the first time a man's heart gave out in one of these rooms.

Thankfully, Arline wasn't occupying any business that evening, and Belinda Sue sent hers away with a discount for the next night. On his way out, she took off his cowboy hat and plunked it on her head, which seemed to satisfy him enough. That left just the four of them.

And the pastor, of course.

Daisy flicked on the lights to her room, and Cordelia took in the scene. The walls were painted a soft pink with a cabbage-rose border. Matching pink shag carpeting covered the floor. Cordelia felt like a genie trapped inside a Pepto Bismol bottle. The marble-topped vanity housed a charming perfume bottle collection, a bouquet of roses waiting to be clipped and placed in the heart-shaped vase next to them, and a bottle of wine and one glass.

Daisy had a mini fridge, a small icebox freezer, a hot plate, and a microwave. A three-panel wooden partition painted with peacocks separated a small sitting area from the king-size bed. Lingerie in silks and lace, jewel-bright tones and muted blacks, were thrown over the top of the partition, and the satin sheets on the bed were a deep mauve.

And in the middle of the massive bed lay Pastor Reed-Smythe, a sheet pulled up to his neck, dead as a doornail.

Belinda Sue stood over the pastor, wearing a black rubber catsuit and six-inch stilettos with spikes on the heels. She poked at his knee, his arm, and his neck with the tip of a wire hanger. He didn't move. She swatted his thigh. Nothing.

She tossed the hanger to the side. "Welp. He's dead, all right."

"Oh, God. Oh, God." Daisy tucked her mouselike hands under her chin, her mascara creating sooty tracks down her cheeks. "What are we gonna do, Miss Cordelia?"

Cordelia crossed her arms as she thought over the options in front of them. She didn't know how she'd been put in charge of this operation. Her degree didn't have anything to do with bioremediation. "We ought to close his eyes."

Daisy nodded, her blond beehive bobbing with the motion. "Good idea."

The four of them looked at one another, silent and nervous as flies in a glue pot. No one wanted to make the first move. Unable to stand the mounting tension a moment longer, Cordelia marched over to the pastor's body. "This is well above my pay grade, y'all."

The pastor appeared gentle in death. Gone were the traces of the stern man who had been her neighbor for the first ten years of her life, who told his son to stay away from "that West girl" as if he hadn't been raising Satan's spawn under his own roof. As a child banned from church and ultimately deciding religion wasn't a necessity, Cordelia hadn't thought much about him over the years, but now she couldn't help noticing just how much he resembled his son. No wonder Sunday services had been so popular with the ladies in town.

She pushed the pastor's eyelids closed with the pads of her fingers. The room released a collective wheeze.

"That's already much better." Belinda Sue clapped her hands, a loud crack that made the hair on Cordelia's arms rise. "Who wants to grab his feet?"

Cordelia choked. "Pardon me? Why on earth would we be grabbing his feet? We need to call the police."

"And tell them what, exactly?" Belinda Sue fixed her gimlet eyes on Cordelia. If Belinda Sue had been holding a ruler, Cordelia was certain the back of her hand would've gotten a thwap. "Do you think the pastor wants it known that his heart gave out in Daisy's room?"

Daisy began to cry harder. "If I'd known he was having heart troubles, I would've been gentler with him. He was always so kind to me. We can't let it get out that he was here. He deserves to be buried with his dignity intact."

Cordelia moved closer to Daisy and awkwardly patted her shoulder. It was the first time Cordelia had felt this protective toward another living being since she had stolen a chicken set to be butchered from the county fair when she was five. She'd hidden him in her closet and got a serious tongue-lashing when her momma discovered the puddles of poop and peck marks on the walls. Her momma shooed the chicken out of the house, where it ran into the street and promptly got run over by the mailman. After that, Cordelia did her best not to get attached.

Daisy had a way about her though. Cordelia had never met someone who had so few reservations about how much she craved affection. Although Cordelia wasn't in the habit of handing it out, Daisy made her want to try.

"Well?" Belinda Sue tapped the toe of her stiletto against the plush shag carpeting. "Are we moving him or not?"

Cordelia released a resigned sigh. The Chickadee might've been an institution that did a lot of good for the locals, but the nature of the pastor's death would be far too salacious for the town to just let pass. He'd be made a mockery of for years to come, and seeing as how he was dead, it wouldn't touch him none. It would all blow back on his family and Daisy.

"Let's start by sitting him up to see what we're dealing with here." Cordelia had heard dead bodies could weigh a ton, but since this was her first time handling one, she didn't know if this would require all hands on deck. Surely, it would be easier to move the pastor through town without everyone in tow.

"If you sit him up, his eyes are gonna pop back open," Arline said.

"For heaven's sake." Belinda Sue threw her hands in the air. "He's not a babydoll."

Arline shrugged and pressed her lips together. With Daisy too distraught and Arline too uninterested to participate, it fell to Cordelia and Belinda Sue to lift the pastor into a sitting position. They each took a side, grabbed an arm, and heaved him forward. Daisy released an earsplitting scream, and Cordelia and Belinda Sue immediately let go. His body hit the mattress with a dull thud, the springs creaking from his weight.

"Told ya." Arline cackled.

"Fine." Cordelia pressed a hand to her chest to catch her breath. "It's probably better if his eyes stay open anyway if we're going to move him elsewhere and act like he was alone."

Daisy nibbled on the fist she had pressed to her mouth. "I can't touch him if he's staring at me like that. It's not right."

"Here." Belinda Sue yanked one of the satin cases off a pillow. "We'll put this over his head. Then we can pretend we're just hauling a sack of grain."

"I didn't grow up on a ranch like you did." Daisy rocked back on her heels. "I don't know what it feels like to haul grain."

"Well, here's your chance to learn." Belinda Sue covered the pastor's head, then motioned for Cordelia to take her place on his opposite side, while Daisy and Arline had to be coaxed into grabbing his ankles.

The chicks didn't possess a whole lot of upper-body strength. It took them nearly an hour just to drag him the fifteen feet to the door. Whoever said dead weight was a lot heavier than living weight wasn't kidding.

Cordelia's phone jingled, startling her into dropping the pastor's arm. Belinda Sue immediately lost her hold, and his head hit the thick carpet with a soft thud. Thankfully, nothing cracked.

Distracted and flustered, Cordelia answered her phone without thinking of just sending it to voicemail. "Hello?"

"Sweetheart." Her momma's shrill voice pierced her eardrum. "It's been an age."

"It's been a day," Cordelia said.

Arline dropped the pastor's ankle and glared at Cordelia like she was holding up the show, but it wasn't like they were in a hurry. The pastor was already dead. He wasn't going anywhere they didn't take him.

"I was about to drift off to sleep when I bolted upright out of the blue with the feeling something terrible had happened," her momma said. "Is everything okay there?"

She glanced at the pastor's unhinged jaw poking out from under the pillowcase. "It's as fine as it can be. Just settling in."

"Then why do you sound so out of breath at half past ten?" Her momma didn't miss a trick. One of the unfortunate side effects of her sobriety.

"I'm . . . um . . ." She glanced around. What was she supposed to say? "Moving a stack of Bibles." She winced. It wasn't the worst thing she could've said. Probably.

"What are you moving Bibles for?" Cordelia could've sworn

she heard her momma narrowing her eyes. "Did you end up finding religion down there?"

"It's more like it found me." She pressed a hand into her back, already feeling the muscles knotting together. "Listen, I've got to go. It's real late and I'm finishing some important work here. I'll call you tomorrow."

"Wait, I just—"

Cordelia hung up before her momma could finish her sentence. Her phone jingled again, but this time she sent it to voicemail. There would be hell to pay for that later, but she was already up to her neck in it, so what was a little more fire and brimstone?

"Finally," Belinda Sue said. "Can we get on with moving this body now?"

Cordelia brought her car around. It took considerably more effort to lift the pastor's body into the trunk. They ended up doing it in sections. Left side, then right. The upper half of his body, followed by the lower half.

Belinda Sue tilted her head. "We can't drive into town with his feet sticking out like that. We're gonna have to fold him up some."

"Ew." Daisy flapped her hands. "I can't do this. I can't."

Arline spit and cracked her knuckles. Shoving Belinda Sue out of her way, she bent the pastor's knees and shoved them up against his chest. "There. Done."

Belinda Sue patted Arline's back. "I do believe this is the most I've heard you speak in a single night in near thirty years."

Arline grunted in response.

Cordelia opened her driver's-side door. "Where should we take him?"

"We can't drop him off at home," Daisy said. "Stella won't need that kind of trouble. She's about to have enough on her plate."

"We'll take him to the church," Belinda Sue said, her lips pressed into a firm line.

A sick feeling churned Cordelia's gut. She didn't know what the afterlife held, but planting the pastor in the church probably wasn't scoring her any points in the game of eternity. "Is it appropriate to bring a dead body there?"

"Of course it is," Belinda Sue said. "Where do you think they hold funerals?"

Cordelia found she couldn't argue with that logic.

Belinda Sue used to skin jackrabbits, so she wasn't as squeamish as the rest of them. She fished the pastor's keys out of his pocket and started up his car without issue. The old Cadillac roared to life, and a small smile touched Belinda Sue's stern face as she ran her hand over the buttery leather seat. Arline jumped into the pastor's car with her and the two of them donned sunglasses like they'd just landed starring roles in a Miami crime drama.

Daisy opted to ride with Cordelia and remained mostly quiet, a worrying change for her, as they drove into town. They had a good ten-mile stretch of dirt road, and the only light came from the vast field of stars overhead. Halfway to the gas station that marked the outskirts of Sarsaparilla Falls, Cordelia could've sworn she saw the pinprick of headlights in the distance, but it was just a blink, then it was gone. Must've been a trick of the open sky.

It was right after midnight when dirt turned to tar, but it might as well have been three in the morning. Shadows stretched across the sidewalks and the ding of a tin can rolling down the street sounded loud as bullets against the otherwise quiet night. They passed a bar with five cars and a motorcycle out front. The neon sign for the Harbor Bar still had the same letters burned out as when she was a kid. The locals probably still called it the Orb.

They didn't pass another car on their way to the church. If anyone peeked out their window, the pastor's Cadillac would be recognizable to those who attended church. Which was to say, everyone. But Cordelia had specifically asked for the most nondescript car on the lot. With any luck, no one would glance twice at her vehicle.

Right before the entrance to the church, Cordelia shut off her headlights and pulled around to the back to park. She popped the trunk and stared down at the pastor, right where they'd left him. Moving his body still didn't feel right, but they were in deep now.

Belinda Sue stepped up beside her, flipping through the keys on a keychain engraved with the Lord's Prayer. "Which one of these do you suppose opens the church?"

Arline took Cordelia's emergency blanket out of the back, wrapped it around her hand, and punched through a glass window in the back door.

"Gosh darn it, Arline." Belinda Sue scowled. "We had the keys right here."

"Why did you feel the need to break the window?" Cordelia steepled her fingers and pressed them against her lips to keep from screaming. "Now it looks like a crime scene when he was supposed to have died here alone."

"It's my fault for letting her come along. Arline gets a thrill out of breaking the law. It's why we can't take her anywhere." Belinda Sue once again took charge and motioned for Cordelia and Daisy to follow her. "Let's go find us a cart or one of them rolling chairs."

The church didn't turn on their air until June, but May in South Texas could get hotter than a billy goat in a pepper patch. Not exactly an ideal condition for storing a body. Though Cordelia figured better a hot church than the cool satin sheets at the Chickadee. The broken window would be a problem, but nothing they could do about it now.

As they crept through the church, every creak and groan made them jump. Pipes. Just the pipes. Not God coming down from on high to personally smite them.

Seeing as the four of them weren't regulars at church, it took them a while to locate the pastor's office. The desk was solid oak with various chips and nicks that spoke to its age. Shelves stuffed with books on theology lined the walls. A picture of the pastor proudly shaking hands with Kirk Cameron was the focal point of the room.

The pastor did indeed have one of those rolling chairs, high-backed black leather with a plush seat. On top of his desk, papers with next week's sermon, fully written, were spread about. Belinda Sue clicked on the desk lamp. Arline swiped a stapler and a paperweight and tucked them into the pocket of her floral caftan.

"This is a real nice office." Daisy trailed the tip of her finger over a divot in the desk. "I think he would've liked knowing we brought him here."

Belinda Sue wiped her forehead with the back of her arm. "Let's just hope he puts in a good word for us with the man upstairs."

She grabbed the chair and rolled it down the hall. A single squeaky wheel created a seesaw rhythm Cordelia found oddly comforting. Her gaze darted around the walls, picking out faces she recognized from her childhood in the potluck and fundraiser photos. She couldn't quite remember their names. They sifted like sand through her faraway memories.

Hauling the body out of the trunk ended up being easier than lifting it in. Cordelia and Belinda Sue ended up doing most of the work. Daisy couldn't look at the pastor's crumpled form without tearing up again, and Arline didn't make any move to contribute.

They had just wheeled the pastor into his office when a distant shrieking caught Cordelia's attention. "Does anyone else hear that?"

"Honey, I can't hear my TV when it's at top volume and I'm sitting right in front of it," Belinda Sue said. "Can you be a little more specific?"

"It sounds like . . ." Cordelia strained her ears and all the color drained from her face. "It sounds like police sirens."

"Arline probably triggered an alarm." Belinda Sue practically shoved them out the door. "That's our cue to hit the road."

Belinda Sue, Daisy, and, much to Cordelia's surprise, Arline blazed down the hall toward the back door. Cordelia tried to keep up, but her lungs burned. All that cardio the ladies did entertaining the patrons of the Chickadee paid off in spades.

"Oh, Lord." Belinda Sue clutched at her side. "My hip just popped."

Cordelia shoved her forward. "Put some ice on it later, we've got to move."

They burst through the back door just as tires squealed against the pavement a block away. As the sirens grew closer, the blaring screech of them rang in Cordelia's ears like a gong. If they got caught, this whole night would be for nothing. Everyone would know the pastor had been with Daisy, and to top it off, they might face charges for tampering with a body.

That thought alone gave Cordelia a final shot of adrenaline to get her legs working in time with her brain. She jumped into her car and had the engine revving as the chicks hopped in. Choosing to leave the lights off, she ran her car over the concrete parking stops at the back of the lot and peeled through the grass.

Belinda Sue pumped her fist and let out a Texas holler loud enough to get the neighborhood dogs barking as Cordelia aimed for an opening in the fenced yards that took them down a deserted alley. Her heart hammered in her throat as she weaved her car along various back streets, and even though she'd long left the sirens behind her, she didn't turn on her headlights again until they hit the dirt road that would take them back to the Chickadee.

Chapter Seven

YOU COULDN'T MOVE A BODY WITH SOMEONE AND NOT DEVELOP AN INstant lifelong bond, which helped, considering Cordelia couldn't leave Sarsaparilla Falls anytime soon. In light of recent events, the chicks weren't fit to discuss taking over the motel just yet. Not to mention, it would be suspicious as all get-out if she blew out of town right when the pastor turned up dead, considering his well-known ties to Daisy. Cordelia didn't think there was anything to connect them to the body, but she couldn't be sure, so she decided to hold off on discussing official Chickadee business until after the funeral.

And though she didn't intend to run the Chickadee, her personal plight took a significant back seat. Her plan was to lie low for the next week, then see what was what in town. If everything appeared fine, and the chicks were back on even ground, she'd turn the running of the operations over to Belinda Sue so she could get back to Dallas.

Easy peasy.

Over the past few days, Cordelia had discovered Belinda Sue had been a rancher's daughter, tough as nails on a fifty-year-old fence. She'd grown up hog-tying calves in the local rodeo, which was how she'd developed a particular skill she put to use on her regulars. After her daddy's ranch had been scammed out from under him by the same development company that wanted to buy up the Chickadee, he died of a broken heart. Miss Penelope offered Belinda Sue a job straightaway and told her she could do whatever she wanted, so long as she was up-front about the rates and rules.

Arline ended up at the Chickadee with a pack of twenties splattered in red dye and a jar of petroleum jelly after a bank robbery gone wrong, and that's all she would say on the subject.

Daisy painted Cordelia's toes a bright coral pink, which made Cordelia squirm every time she looked at her feet. It felt like too much fuss. But fussing was what Daisy did best. Cordelia found it easier if she just went along with it.

After painting her own toes, Daisy put the cap back on the polish. "I think Miss Cordelia and I should go into town today."

Belinda Sue set her sunglasses atop her victory rolls and pierced Daisy with a hard stare. "We said we would wait a week. It's been four days."

Daisy fidgeted in her beach chair, restless enough to worry the spots off a ladybug. "I know what we said, but I'm getting antsy out here, and it'll look strange if Miss Cordelia doesn't go into town at least once. We don't want people thinking she's unfriendly or that these aren't normal conditions."

"Fair point." Belinda Sue put her sunglasses back on and relaxed against her beach recliner. "Grab me some strawberries while you're out. I've got a hankering."

Daisy clapped her hands together. "Sure thing." Not wanting to give Belinda Sue a free second to change her mind, Daisy grabbed Cordelia's hand and dragged her to her apartment. "Go on and get changed. I'll meet you by your car."

"Shouldn't we take your car since the police might be looking for mine?" Cordelia asked.

"I don't drive. Haven't in years." Daisy waved a hand in front of her face, swishing away invisible gnats. "And don't worry too much about your car; the church doesn't have cameras."

"How do you know?"

Daisy grinned.

Cordelia's lips pinched like she was sucking on a lemon a week past its prime. "Forget I asked."

Wanting to make a good impression on the town that'd thrown her away before she cut her first tooth, Cordelia wore her most professional gray pantsuit and clipped her hair back with a no-nonsense barrette. Of course, all that professionalism was undone by Daisy's flamingo-print halter dress and matching flamingo earrings that skimmed her bony shoulders.

She gave Cordelia a wide grin, her ruby-red lips shimmering in the sunlight. "Let's light a shuck, daylight's wasting."

As they took the dirt road, kicking up dust on their way, Cordelia pointed to a small collection of pickup trucks about halfway to the gas station—in the general area where she thought she'd seen headlights the night they moved the pastor's body.

"What's going on over there?" she asked.

Daisy glared at the group of trucks. "Those are the developers trying to run us off our land, same as they did to Belinda Sue's daddy. Dick Abernathy retired and moved to Houston, but he left the business to his son, Corbin, who says he's more honest in his dealings than Dick, but I can see them horns holding up his halo."

"If he can just take land like that, what's stopping him from doing to us what he did to Belinda Sue's daddy?" Cordelia asked.

Daisy lifted a shoulder. "Miss Penelope's trust was ironclad. Everyone knows it. And I'd never say this to Belinda Sue, but her daddy couldn't ride and chew at the same time, if you know what I mean. Still. He didn't deserve what happened to him."

"What happened?"

"It was ugly business." Daisy glowered, and the expression looked about as natural on her as a nun's habit. "Everyone in town thought he lost his land on account of being behind on his taxes, and Dick snapped it up for a song."

"I'm guessing he wasn't behind on taxes?"

"He might've been. He swore up and down he wasn't, but he wasn't the best bookkeeper. Though it was also common knowledge that Dick Abernathy had some kind of blackmail over the county tax collector, so, like I said, ugly business."

"Why is he just hanging around out there?" A sense of unease prickled the back of Cordelia's neck. Truth be told, that feeling had been following her ever since they moved the pastor's body into the church. "Is he trying to intimidate y'all?"

"Could be." Daisy held her arm out the window and her paper-thin skin flapped on the wind. "He done bought up a bunch of empty land around the Chickadee, but Miss Penelope owned fifty acres smack-dab in the middle of the fancy golf course he planned on building. He can't get his hands on the one piece of land he needs, and he's fit to be tied."

The terms of Great-Aunt Penelope's trust finally made sense to Cordelia, and a satisfied smile touched her lips. "I'll bet she loved dangling that over him."

Daisy laughed. "She sure did. And the thing was, she could've bought up ten motels for what Corbin offered and moved the Chickadee anywhere else. She never said so out loud, but we all knew she did it for Belinda Sue, for her daddy, and what they lost because of the Abernathys."

The more Cordelia learned about her Great-Aunt Penelope, the more she liked and respected who she'd been. Even though she said a cathouse was no place to raise a child, Cordelia wondered just how different her life might've been if she'd been raised around a woman who was as generous as a spring harvest in peat moss. But every day she spent with Daisy, Belinda Sue, and Arline, she felt like she was getting pieces of her all the same.

They pulled into town and parked across from the drugstore. Main Street still looked the same. Bank, drugstore, diner. The old men who used to sit in front of the H-E-B market had been replaced by newer versions of old men, but they wore the same loose slacks, button-down plaid shirts, and aviator sunglasses. They got to their feet and tipped their hats when they saw Daisy coming up the walk, swinging her hips in her halter dress like she'd been born to draw men like flowers attracted bees.

"Miss Daisy, you're looking mighty fine today." A man with a silver comb-over and a sly grin clutched his hat in his hands. "Might have to pay a visit to the Chickadee this week."

"Please do. I've missed seeing your face, Hank." Daisy lavished him with an adoring look. If Cordelia didn't know better, she'd think this gentleman was Daisy's one and only. "And tell Maureen I loved the cookies she sent last time and would love the recipe."

"Will do." Hank rotated his hat in his hands. "Her sister's coming up from Corpus Christi next week. They'll be gabbing into all hours of the night, so she might just send me over to get me out of their hair."

"That'll be fine, just let me know when I can pencil you in." Daisy stood on her tiptoes and planted a kiss on his cheek, leaving behind a lipstick print so perfect it could've been drawn on. "It was good to see you. Take care now."

They walked about five steps before Hank stuttered out, "And welcome back, Miss Cordelia. Everyone's real pleased you're taking Miss Penelope's place."

"Oh." Cordelia stumbled over being addressed with warmth from one of the market men. "Thank you." She gave him an awkward wave. "I hope you enjoy your next visit."

Daisy giggled and pushed her in the back to get her moving again. "You're so silly, Miss Cordelia. I told you people in town would be welcoming; you don't need to act like a nervous Nellie. You're the madam of the Chickadee, and that's not nothing."

"Mm-hmm." Cordelia didn't comment further. She hadn't gotten around to explaining to the chicks that she had no intention of staying, and wasn't sure how to break that news to them yet. Cordelia had never been good at engaging in conflict.

They entered the store and proceeded to get on with their shopping, Daisy stopping every aisle to say hello to a patron or the wife of a patron. Everyone greeted Daisy with genuine smiles and offered Cordelia the kind of respect she'd only ever dreamed of while growing up. It seemed as though Mr. Arbuckle Jenkins wasn't lying when he said the Chickadee was an institution, and everyone in town appreciated the service it provided.

There were a few people Cordelia recognized. The Newman brothers, who still smelled like a couple of wet dogs. Ashby Clover, who rode in the mayor's convertible as the Pumpkin Patch Festival Queen the year Cordelia started kindergarten. Bert Baker, who chipped his front tooth trying to jump a rail in the park on a dare, now walked around the store with a baby strapped to his chest. And Rayla Towne, who moved to Houston to work for NASA, but still came back every other week to volunteer at the local animal shelter. A collage of faces from her childhood that had shifted and changed, even as the town around them remained the same.

"Miss Daisy." A man in his late fifties with a bristly beard and small eyes took off his John Deere hat and clutched it in his hand. He handed Daisy a flyer. "Would you be so kind as to put this up in your room? The sheriff is more interested in helping that real estate fellow from Catterwood, Sean O'Leary, scout out land than he is in solving crime these days."

Cordelia looked over Daisy's shoulder at the poster offering a cash reward of twenty dollars for anyone who had information on a recent break-in, or forty dollars if anyone had heard of an old miner's journal reported to be sold to a nearby pawn shop. If so, people were instructed to contact Porter Sheldon.

"Oh, Porter, honey, I'd love to. Really." Daisy handed back the flyer. "But I'm not sure it fits in with my decor. Next thing you know, everybody will be wanting to pin things to my wall, and that's not good for ambiance, you know?"

"Yeah. I know." Porter put his hat back on. "Thought it would be worth a try."

"I'll be sure to pass the word along though." She gave his cheek a pat.

"Thanks, ma'am. Appreciate it."

They walked up a few more aisles, grabbing a package of gummy worms for Daisy and cooking spray for Arline to do Lord knew what with since she didn't have a stove.

"There's Stella." Daisy pointed to a woman who stood alone in the baking aisle holding a bag of flour and staring off into space like she wasn't quite sure how she got to the store.

She looked nearly the same as she had in Cordelia's youth, with sleek raven-black hair twisted into a tight bun, wide tawny eyes, and understated makeup. Even her style screamed elegance, though she wore only a plain black shift dress. She had a softness about her that made her the perfect pastor's wife. The picture of a nurturing soul.

"Should we say hi?" Cordelia whispered. While it seemed like the polite thing to do, as Stella had been her neighbor for the first ten years of her life, she didn't want to bombard her with the woman her husband had been spending time with for the last thirty years.

"Probably not." Daisy maneuvered their cart toward the produce section. "Stella didn't have a problem with my arrangement with the pastor, but it'll stir up gossip, and that's not a nice thing to do to a woman in mourning."

Daisy put Belinda Sue's strawberries in their cart, then

grabbed Cordelia's upper arm. "Ooh, don't look now, but here comes Honey Stevens. She don't like me on account of her obsession with the pastor. I'm surprised she's not wearing a black veil."

Cordelia turned her head to take in a woman of about sixty wearing a skintight leopard-print leotard with neon-pink leg warmers and a matching headband that pushed back a pile of blond curls sprayed stiff enough to be a storm shelter.

An old memory prickled the back of Cordelia's mind. Twenty years ago, Honey Stevens had been too busy gossiping to pay attention to where she was going and bumped into Cordelia as she was coming out of Parson's Drugstore. Instead of apologizing, like any good Texas woman would, she yelled at Cordelia right in the middle of Main Street while she doused her hands in sanitizer like Cordelia was a germ who was trying to invade her ecosystem.

Honey's blue eyeshadow cracked as she raised her brows at the sight of Daisy. Her gaze passed over Cordelia as if she weren't worth noticing, and Cordelia couldn't decide whether to feel offended or blessed at the obvious brush-off. Bracelets jangling as she waved, Honey made a beeline toward Daisy with her reusable shopping bag dangling off her overly tan, speckled arm.

"Now you've done it," Daisy said. "I told you not to look."

"Well, if it isn't Daisy Dawson. I haven't seen you in a dog's age." Honey fluffed her immobile curls. "I'm sure you heard the news."

"It's a tragedy." Daisy's voice couldn't have been flatter if it had been pressed between a stack of Bibles. "He was a good man."

"The best." Honey's thousand-watt smile dimmed by several degrees as her eyes filled with tears. A practiced move, if Cordelia had to bet the farm on it. "I'm not sure how this town is supposed to move on when he was the center of it."

"I'm sure people will find a way. They can be real resilient like that." Daisy began to guide Cordelia away. "If you'll excuse us."

Honey's eyes narrowed. "Truth be told, I thought you'd be

more broken up, but here you are, out strutting through town without a care in the world."

"It's not my place any more than it's yours, as you'd do best to remember." Daisy leaned in closer to Honey and lowered her voice. "I hope you're respecting his wife's time of grieving. She doesn't need to hear how devastated *you* are right now."

Honey turned up her nose. "I'd never."

Daisy gave her a short nod and walked away, her heels clicking on the concrete flooring, leaving Cordelia to hurry to catch up to her. As they turned into the next aisle, Daisy clenched her fists and released a low growl. "If I hear one word about Honey bothering Stella right now, I might be tempted to slap some sense into her. That fool woman would fire a missile if she thought she could take credit for a war."

Cordelia didn't say anything, just hummed and placed a jar of pickles in the cart. She didn't bring up her brief history with Honey Stevens. Memories only had as much power as a person was willing to give, and Cordelia wasn't willing to give Honey a lick. And perhaps Honey had her own problems now. Back in the day, she'd been a nurse at the local hospital and married to a town councilman. She wore a diamond the size of a small boulder. There had been rumors that her ring was a fake and her husband was a conman. Cordelia never set much store in rumors, but she had noticed the absence of the ring and the husband today.

Daisy and Cordelia continued to shop, but it wasn't until they made it to the baking aisle that Cordelia realized why Daisy wanted to come into town so bad. It wasn't just because she was itching to socialize, though that was probably part of it; she was also fishing for information. Aside from a few mentions of Porter's reward and the Abernathys hurting local builders by going into business with an out-of-town real estate developer, almost every conversation revolved around the pastor.

Had Daisy heard about his tragic passing? Did anyone know he was having heart troubles? Or did the intruder scare him so bad his heart stopped? Wasn't it a shame the church didn't have cameras? Why did the intruder only take a stapler and a paperweight? How were Stella and Archer holding up? Whose turn was it to bring Stella a casserole? What would happen to her house seeing as it was church-owned?

Not one whisper about the pastor and Daisy or the Chickadee. As far as everyone was concerned, he'd passed away in his office from heart failure during a break-in, where he'd been working late on the coming week's sermon. Cordelia could hardly dare to believe they got away with moving a body.

Though that feeling of elation appeared to be short-lived. As they were loading groceries into Cordelia's trunk, the loud clang of metal on metal jarred their attention as a woman ran her cart straight into theirs.

"Pardon me." The woman with the cart had a short bob of black hair and a mole the size of a nickel on her right temple. She smiled at them with what could only be described as clear malice. "Well now, if it isn't the local whore and her pimp."

Cordelia's blood burned hotter than the hinges of hell. Who was this terrible woman and where did she get the gall? Everyone else managed to be polite. Even outright friendly. She'd almost forgotten where she was and where she'd come from, but she could feel it rising in her now. That shadow of her momma's poor reputation, daring her to fight fire with fire.

Cordelia gave her the kind of hard-edged stare she generally reserved for book banners and people who left carts in parking spots. "You look lost, honey. Did the circus leave town without you? That's all right, I'm sure there are a few children's parties around here that could use a spare clown, bless your heart."

Now she'd gone and done it. Cordelia hated confrontation

with every fiber of her soul, but it was too late. She'd have to accept the consequences of her irrational outburst. It wasn't every day her momma's influence took hold, but it could be ugly when it happened.

Daisy cackled with delight. "Like I said, Miss Penelope didn't make mistakes."

The woman before them looked ready to do a murder without reasonable cause, and suddenly Cordelia didn't feel so bad. "I doubt y'all will be laughing when it comes out that my husband happened to see the pastor's Cadillac and a car that looks an awful lot like this one leaving the motel last Friday night, right before the church was broken into."

Cordelia stiffened, but Daisy appeared unfazed. "Why, Edna Abernathy, are you telling me Corbin was at the Chickadee last Friday? What a scandal." Daisy placed a hand over her chest. "Oh, I do hope for your sake that doesn't get out."

"That's not what I'm saying, and you know it," Edna hissed. "I think you had something to do with the pastor's death, and when we prove it, that nasty little establishment of yours will go up on the auction block. So enjoy those laughs while you've got them."

"Okay." Daisy blew her a kiss. "I'll be sure to tell Arline that Corbin said hi."

The blood drained from Edna's face, though Cordelia was certain Corbin Abernathy wasn't a regular of Arline's. But if the headlights Cordelia had seen that night were Corbin's, they were in big trouble.

Edna rushed away, no doubt on her way to read her husband the riot act. Cordelia might've felt bad for her if she hadn't been so mean.

Daisy shut the trunk and dusted her hands together. "That'll teach her."

"You know . . ." Cordelia glanced at Edna's retreating back.

"We might not want to go around poking bears. I did see headlights that night."

"Ain't no one going to believe them." Daisy tucked a stray lock of hair behind her ear. "Everyone knows the Abernathys are as dirty as they come, and they'll say anything to get their hands on the Chickadee. Don't pay Edna any mind."

"Fair enough." Daisy knew this town better than she did, and if she wasn't worried, then Cordelia wouldn't worry either.

They'd just finished putting the eggs, bread, and other fragile foods in the back seat when Archer Reed-Smythe strolled up to them. Cordelia's pulse kicked up to an erratic beat as his eyes locked on hers and he gave a slow grin.

He chewed on the end of a toothpick, same as the ex-smokers would do outside the church where her momma attended AA meetings. Cordelia released a small, involuntary squeak and his mustache twitched. Trouble. This man was so much trouble. Try as she might, Cordelia couldn't go on thinking of him as the vile little boy from next door who took pride in how much of the alphabet he could belch.

He tipped his hat. "Ladies."

Daisy immediately began to fuss over him, such was her way. "You poor dear. Sad news all around. How are you and your momma holding up?"

"As good as we can be." He crossed his arms, and Cordelia's treacherous gaze skimmed over the way his shirt tugged against his biceps. "I've got to be honest with you, it was a surprise to find him working that night. Didn't you say earlier that day he had plans to see you?"

Daisy twisted her fingers together and glanced away. "He never showed up. He must've changed his mind and gone into work instead."

Archer raised his brows. "Gone into work on a Friday night

instead of spending his free evening at the Chickadee with you? Come on, now. I find that hard to believe."

His voice was like hot butter over fresh biscuits. Downright mouthwatering. But his line of questioning was too practiced. The glint in his eyes too aware. Like a hunter setting a trap for a rabbit. Cordelia's urge to run kicked up a notch.

"It's been known to happen a time or two." Daisy's voice grew thinner with each word.

Cordelia didn't like where this was going. Alarm bells were ringing in her ears. "Why are you interrogating Miss Daisy?"

"I'm not interrogating." He paused, his gaze darting between the two of them. "Yet."

"'Yet'?" Cordelia placed her hands on her hips. She'd always channeled the short fuse she'd inherited from her momma into more practical endeavors, such as cleaning the grout in her shower with a toothbrush or balancing her checkbook, but it seemed as though Sarsaparilla Falls brought the spitfire out in her. Must be all that South Texas heat. "What do you mean by 'yet'?"

Shadows crossed Archer's expression and Cordelia felt the pinch of regret for being so stern with him. She was protective of Daisy, but he just lost his daddy and deserved a little grace. Cordelia loosened her rigid posture and tried to appear more open and inviting, but when he cocked an eyebrow, she gave up and resumed her natural, straight-faced expression.

"I might as well tell you now." Archer rubbed his jaw where a thin layer of stubble had started to grow. "We had an autopsy done. My father didn't die of a heart attack like everyone is saying. He was poisoned."

Chapter Eight

DAISY WOBBLED AND GRIPPED CORDELIA'S ARM. "NO. THAT CAN'T BE right. I—"

"We're so sorry for your loss." Cordelia ushered Daisy into the passenger seat before she could either confess or faint, giving them both away. "If you'll excuse us, I do believe Miss Daisy has a touch of the heatstroke."

"Sure thing." Archer stepped to the side, his gaze steady and unyielding as he watched Cordelia walk around to the driver's side. "I know you only just got here, but it wouldn't hurt to remind you it would be a bad idea to leave town right now."

Cordelia tripped over the heel of her shiny black flats as she stepped off the curb. A betrayal of nerves that damaged her pride more than anything else. Ever since she'd come in second place in the President's Fitness balance beam exam in the fifth grade—no small feat for a girl who was all limbs and no grace—she'd put clumsiness firmly in the same category as messiness and meanness.

"I have no intention of running." At least for another week. Cordelia yanked her car door open. "No matter how bad you're itching for the chase."

He gave her a full grin, that infuriating toothpick still dangling from his mouth. "It hasn't been the same around here since you've been gone, Delia. I'll be seeing you."

She wasn't sure if that was a promise or a threat. Neither option stopped the goose bumps from raising on her arms. Daisy sat in the front seat mumbling affirmations of encouragement to herself, but Cordelia didn't want to stay in town trying to sort her out. She'd wait until they got back to the Chickadee before asking her questions about poison.

Once they passed the gas station and hit the dirt road, Daisy seemed to snap out of the catatonic state. She turned her big brown eyes on Cordelia, pleading for her very life in their depths. "I swear, I didn't poison the pastor."

"Of course you didn't." Cordelia waved her off. She didn't know Daisy well, but she knew her well enough to know she wouldn't hurt a fly if it bit her riding horse. "You're the one who told me not to pay any mind to Edna Abernathy."

"Yeah, but Archer . . ." Daisy nibbled on her lower lip as she stared out the window, staining her teeth with her bright-red lipstick. "He knew his daddy was coming to the Chickadee that night. That's why he stopped over. He's not going to let this go."

"He can't prove anything." They'd been careful. Cordelia was certain the only person who had seen them had been Corbin, or else the news would've been all over town by now. "He can be as suspicious as he wants, but it's not like he can launch an investigation."

"Actually, he can." Daisy tapped her fingernails on the center console in a staccato rhythm. "He's a detective for the South Texas branch of the FBI."

"He's what now?" Cordelia slammed on her brakes hard enough for the seat belt to dig into her chest. Her heart beat wildly against her ribs. "Since when?"

"Since always? He was an early recruit, fresh out of college. His daddy was so proud." Daisy sniffled as tears began to well in her eyes. "He said if his son wasn't going to serve God, at least he was going to serve the law, which to him was the next best thing."

"That's a problem." Cordelia didn't mean to sound so insensitive when Daisy was in the throes of an emotional moment, but this wasn't the appropriate time for reminiscing. "Do you have any idea how the pastor might've been poisoned?"

Daisy shook her head.

"Do you think maybe his wife knew he was coming to the Chickadee and put something in his dinner before he left the house that night?"

Daisy gasped. "Stella would never. She might not have loved her husband the way a wife typically does, but she didn't hate him. And she really didn't mind him spending his time at the Chickadee. It freed her up to have crochet nights with her gal pal Gladys."

"I'm just examining the angles, not accusing anyone of anything." Cordelia backed away from the pastor's family. She trusted Daisy's judgment of character, if only because she seemed to dislike the same people as Cordelia. "Did he have any enemies that you know of? Anyone he might've mentioned?"

"Oh, no." Daisy's eyes widened in horror. "Everyone in Sarsaparilla Falls loved Pastor Reed-Smythe. He was sweet as stolen honey, salt of the earth and all that."

Cordelia's momma hadn't much cared for the pastor, but seeing as she was no longer in Sarsaparilla Falls, she figured Sherilynn didn't count.

"We ought to make a list." Cordelia worked best when she had a list to organize her day, and she figured a murder investigation wouldn't be any different.

"No offense, Miss Cordelia, but why is it on us to do anything?"

"Because it's only a matter of time before Edna starts crowing all over town once word gets out that the pastor was murdered, and Archer Reed-Smythe is already giving you the eye. As much as I'd like to believe otherwise, he doesn't strike me as a fool."

Daisy sat back in her seat with her arms crossed. "I didn't do anything wrong, except protect his family's peace by moving him to someplace more respectable."

Cordelia softened and patted her shoulder. "I know that, but if we don't want suspicion pointing your way, we need to come up with an alternative suspect."

"I see what you're saying." Daisy sniffed. "I just don't like to go around accusing innocent people of wrongdoing."

"We're not accusing anyone yet. Just making a list."

Once Cordelia and Daisy returned to the Chickadee and filled Arline and Belinda Sue in on everything that had happened in town, the four of them decided to put their heads together to come up with some reasonable suspects. Belinda Sue mixed up a batch of appletinis, which was really just a jug of water, a frozen can of apple juice concentrate, and a handful of single-serve vodkas she'd gotten for ninety-nine cents at the H-E-B checkout line. As the chicks sipped on the tart concoction, they began naming everyone in town who came to mind. Thankfully, Belinda Sue had been on board with Cordelia's way of thinking, so Daisy relented on building a list.

Everything Cordelia learned about investigating a murder had come from reruns of *Father Dowling Mysteries* and *Murder, She Wrote* and whatever else her momma would watch between the jewelry and skin-care hours on QVC, which put them at a significant disadvantage considering Archer's position. But the one thing they had on their side was knowing Daisy didn't do it. While he was busy wasting his time looking into her, they could get a few steps ahead of him by looking into everyone else.

By the time they'd finished their first drinks, they had only three suspects. At the top were Corbin and Edna Abernathy, who had the most to gain from setting up Daisy, and Honey Stevens, who got put on the list by Daisy for her *Fatal Attraction* tendencies.

And Cordelia secretly added Stella Reed-Smythe to the list, on account of the spouse being the most common killer according to *Dateline*, even though the chicks insisted Archer was the only hell she ever raised. Thus far, she had no motive. Daisy had assured her she knew all about the pastor's visits to the Chickadee and didn't mind one bit. And she had a fair point. Plus, now that he was gone, the church deacons were voting on whether she'd even get to keep her house, so being without him didn't do her any favors.

Daisy puckered her lips and reapplied her lipstick. "How are we supposed to go about investigating the Abernathys when they'd call the sheriff the moment we set foot on their land, especially after Cordelia told off Edna today?"

Belinda Sue's green eyes sparked with mirth. "Wish I'd gone into town with y'all after all, just to see that go down."

"It was glorious." Daisy released a happy sigh.

"I could bring her a pie and an apology," Cordelia said.

"Hush now." Daisy sat up so fast, apple juice slid over the rim of her glass and splashed on the concrete. "You'll do no such thing."

Cordelia stared down at the glass in her hand. She had yet to take a sip of the appletini and wished she hadn't asked Belinda Sue to make her one. "I'm not normally like that."

While Cordelia couldn't deny Edna had deserved her tongue-lashing and then some, she still regretted the way she'd spoken. She was starting to understand what her momma had gone through when she'd wake up after a nasty bender and go on an apology tour with half the town. Maybe feeling bad about things was just in her DNA.

"Don't worry about the pie. It's gonna take a lot more than that to get you in." Belinda Sue tilted her glass toward Cordelia. "Edna wouldn't scratch her own momma's fleas, and Corbin's apple fell off the same branch as his daddy. That whole family is rotten."

Cordelia bit her lip, more than a little troubled that good manners couldn't see her out of a bad situation. "What do you propose we do, then? Wait for Archer to show up and start handing out arrest warrants?"

"I knew my ears were ringing on the way out here." At the sound of that voice, equal parts rough and smooth, Cordelia about jumped out of her skin. "Now what makes you think I just go around handing out arrest warrants without provocation?"

Archer had rolled the sleeves up on his shirt, and Cordelia was certain he'd done that on purpose. A man with forearms that nice didn't go whipping them out without just cause. And he had the nerve to toss around the word "provocation."

Daisy had gone pale, still not over her last encounter with Archer, but Belinda Sue popped right up. Her cold efficiency was a welcome balm under the heat of Archer's gaze. "We figured you'd be by sometime to ask your questions, but I'm afraid we won't be much help as we hadn't seen the pastor in over a week."

Archer tipped down his sunglasses so he could look Belinda Sue square in the eyes. "That's not what Edna Abernathy is saying."

Belinda Sue wagged her finger at him like he was a misbehaving child. Though to her, he probably still was nothing more than a rambunctious boy with more energy than sense. "Did Edna also tell you our madam made her look like a fool on Main Street? Or is heresy and petty gossip how they run investigations these days down at the FBI?"

Archer raised his eyebrows at Cordelia. "You don't say?"

The way he looked at her, like he was surprised his little lizard grew up to have crocodile-size teeth, made her skin prickle all the way down to her toes. "If you recall, I used to have no problem putting you in your place."

"I think about that at least once a week." He winked at her. Winked! The utter gall of this man could not be surpassed.

"Good. Then you shouldn't have any trouble remembering that I have no interest in being a source of amusement for you."

"Believe me, Delia, you're the source of a lot of things for me, but amusement isn't one of them."

He turned to Daisy. "But I'm here on business. If you don't mind, Miss Daisy, I'd love to have a look at your trash."

Daisy opened her mouth to respond, but all that came out was a thin squeak of air.

"Absolutely not." Cordelia held out her hand for emphasis, as if halting him would come any easier than knocking down a building. "The Chickadee is *my* property, and you're not searching any of the rooms without a warrant."

"That's fine." Archer pushed his sunglasses back up, shielding his eyes. "I'm not out here in an official capacity. I just thought you'd like to clear your name. But if you'd rather wait for the sheriff to beat down your door, that's your prerogative. This will be his jurisdiction, and he's not near as polite as me."

"You're calling yourself polite?" Cordelia snapped. "I've seen better manners from a fox in a chicken coop."

"I'm going to take the compliment and be on my way now. Y'all try to behave yourselves." He walked away with his hands in his pockets, whistling a jaunty tune like he'd really done something. At least he wasn't investigating. Yet.

Cordelia rolled her eyes at his back, then helped Daisy to her feet. "Come on, let's have a look-see at what's in your trash."

The four of them filed into Daisy's bubble-gum-pink room, and their eyes couldn't help but stray to the bed where Pastor

Reed-Smythe had taken his last breath. The last time the four of them had been in this room together had been to move a body. It felt like a bad omen.

"I don't know how you manage to sleep in that bed." Belinda Sue shuddered.

"It's real easy," Daisy said. "I just lay my head on the pillow and close my eyes. It's only a matter of time before I'm drifting off to dreamland."

"That's not—" Belinda Sue closed her eyes and breathed in deeply through her nose, her nostrils flaring like a bull. "Never mind."

Cordelia picked up the pink trash can with a petal-shaped lid and removed the top. Inside were several tissues, foil wrappers, empty makeup palettes, an aerosol can of hairspray, a few Diet Coke bottles, and a half-empty bottle of wine. She held the trash out for Daisy to examine, internally squirming at all the germs that must be crawling across her fingers. Her industrial-strength hand sanitizer burned a hole in her pantsuit pocket.

"There ain't nothing of note in there," Daisy said.

Cordelia set it to the floor and Arline peered over her shoulder to take in the contents. "Since when do you drink wine?"

"That's not mine." Daisy turned her pert nose up at the bottle. "Even if Miss Penelope is gone, I'm not risking a haunting by breaking her strictest rule."

At Cordelia's questioning look, Belinda Sue said, "No drinking on the job."

Cordelia raised a skeptical eyebrow. "But you've had cocktail hour by the pool every day since I've arrived."

"Men aren't invited to cocktail hour." The snap in Belinda Sue's voice made Cordelia want to drop and give her twenty. "That's our time. We aren't on the clock then."

"Where did the wine come from?" Cordelia asked.

"The pastor brought it," Daisy said, shrugging.

The room went deadly quiet for one beat. Two. Then they exploded.

"Did he buy the wine himself? Was it open when he arrived?" Cordelia asked.

"Good Lord, girl, why didn't you tell us from the jump?" Belinda Sue asked.

"It's always the religious ones with the drinking problem," Arline said. "Why is that?"

"This is Sarsaparilla Falls, you can't throw a stone without hitting a man of God round these parts, that don't mean religion has anything to do with drinking." Daisy crossed her arms as she glared at Arline for making unkind insinuations about a man not yet cold in the grave. "He said the wine was a gift someone had given him on the way over to see me. He offered me a taste, but of course I turned it down. I don't know where he got it from, and I didn't say anything because I didn't think of it."

"That's not a surprise, considering you don't do much thinking at all," Arline said.

"You're one to talk," Daisy said. "We wouldn't even be in this mess if you hadn't broken the glass at the church and stolen from the pastor's office. What do you need a stapler for, anyway? You don't have papers in your room."

Cordelia pinched the bridge of her nose. "Everyone, quiet down for a second."

Much to her surprise, they instantly fell silent. Cordelia couldn't even get this much respect from her houseplants. It was an unusual feeling, being heard.

"I think . . ." Cordelia trailed off, gathering her thoughts about her, plucking ideas out at random and trying to make sense of them. "The wine is the only lead we have so far. We need to figure out a way to get it tested."

"We could take it to Archer," Daisy said. "He's got access to all sorts of labs at the FBI."

Cordelia shook her head. "Too risky. He must be suspecting something like this. Why else would he want to search your trash?"

"I have an idea," Belinda Sue said. "But it's going to require distracting Archer, and we have to get the timing right or it won't work."

"And just how do you plan to do that?" Cordelia asked.

Daisy pressed her fingers to her lips as she looked between Belinda Sue and Arline, who both gave her nods of confirmation. She released a short squeal as she bounced on the balls of her feet. At once, the chicks turned to Cordelia with matching Cheshire cat grins stretched across their aging faces, and a lead weight dropped in Cordelia's stomach. Whatever they had planned, Cordelia had an inkling that she wasn't going to like it. Not one bit.

Chapter Nine

"YOU CAN COME ON OUT, MISS CORDELIA. WE WON'T BITE," DAISY SING-songed.

"Not unless you ask nicely," Belinda Sue added.

Cordelia stepped out of her bathroom, took one look in the mirror, and nearly fainted dead away. The ladies had teased and curled her pin-straight golden brown hair to within an inch of its life. It now rose high on her head like a crown of tangled cream puffs. Daisy had done something to her eyes to make them ten times larger and a deeper blue than she thought possible. Like staring straight into the ocean. Her full lips had been painted bright red, designed to stand out and grab a man's attention, but the outfit really took the cake.

Belinda Sue had packed Cordelia into a black bustier that had her small breasts spilling over the top with mystery cleavage she'd never in her life seen before. She paired it with the tiniest scrap of lace she claimed was underwear, but Cordelia was certain it was just a tissue held together with two strings. A garter holding up sheer black stockings completed the look.

Arline provided a trench coat that had two designer watches hanging from the inside. Arline quickly plucked the watches free, burying them in the pocket of her floral caftan and shooting Cordelia a look that suggested she was *not* invited to ask questions.

"I don't know about this, y'all." Cordelia stood before her partners in crime, wringing her hands and trying not to chew all the lipstick off her mouth. "You don't think he's going to take one look at me and laugh himself hoarse?"

"Honey." Daisy put a hand on her shoulder. "Ain't a red-blooded Texas man alive that would take one look at you and do anything other than sink to his knees and beg for mercy."

Belinda Sue nodded. "She's got that right. You know your books and your lists and how best to organize a closet, but trust that we know men."

An emotion Cordelia couldn't quite identify, but one she was certain she'd spent her whole life avoiding, squirmed in her stomach. She wasn't fit to be any kind of temptress. There had to be another way to distract Archer that didn't involve her looking like a burlesque dancer, but she didn't know men. She'd just have to trust their judgment.

Arline gave her a detailed outline of Archer's office, including where to find the tamper-proof bags, his passcode for the lab, and the exact time the courier would empty his outbox. It was anyone's guess how Arline came by this information, but she wasn't interested in sharing anymore than she'd been willing to explain why she had a trench coat with designer watches dangling from the inside flap. All she'd said was that she made it her business to be familiar with the FBI's comings and goings.

Belinda Sue stuffed a wad of leather into Cordelia's coat pocket, along with a plastic tube filled with leftover wine. "Now, remember, don't enter the building until 5:45. That gives you fifteen minutes to work your magic."

"Right."

"You don't need to be so nervous, Miss Cordelia." Daisy fluffed and picked at Cordelia's sky-high hair. "You've got plenty of feminine wiles."

Cordelia had about as many wiles as a honey badger in a beehive, which Arline had no trouble pointing out, but she was all they had, so she'd have to do.

They went over the plan one last time, then the three ladies under her care waved her off, beaming like proud momma birds who had just shoved their baby from the nest. Cordelia's heels clicked on the blacktop as she walked across the parking lot to her car. She didn't usually wear heels—her fear of bunions was right up there with her fear of mold—but her impeccable balance saved her from looking like a fool.

She drove into town with one heel kicked off on the mat, her stocking-clad toes wiggling against the gas. The closer she got to the FBI field office, the more her shoulders scrunched up against her neck. Daisy had been so sure that Archer looked at her a certain kind of way, but he'd also been the boy who'd told her she was every pirate's dream because of her sunken chest. If he so much as cracked a smile at her getup, she could forget worrying about jail. She'd drop dead of embarrassment right then and there.

The parking lot to the field office was empty and the building dark, save for a single light in the front right window she knew to be Archer's office. Thinking about him sitting in there alone with his head in his hands, trying to piece together what happened to his daddy, sent a twinge of guilt through her. She didn't like manipulating people, and she knew what it felt like not to have any answers where a father was concerned. But it wasn't her place to ease his mind in that regard. She'd already committed to protecting Daisy by any means necessary.

At exactly 5:45, Cordelia wiped her palms against her hips and pushed open the door to Archer's office. The plain white box had a steel desk that covered the length of a wall. Whiteboards and corkboards decorated the room, with various notes and pictures attached. Her eyes got stuck on his suspenders, a weakness, before her gaze fell to the outgoing tray, the drawer with the plastic lab bags, and a plain black-leather journal that held all his notes and passwords.

Right where Arline had said they would be.

Archer's head shot up and he stood. A blank look crossed his face before a slow grin creased the corners of his mouth, like he wasn't about to admit she'd taken him by surprise, though his eyes roved over her made-up face. "After that huff I left you in earlier, I thought you'd go out of your way to avoid me."

"I didn't want to give you the satisfaction of thinking you'd gotten the better of me."

"Darlin', I don't doubt you'd make me work for every inch of that satisfaction, but I'm guessing that's not why you came by."

"Not exactly." The pounding in Cordelia's chest, ears, throat picked up an erratic tempo. No more stalling. She opened her trench coat and let it fall and dangle from the crook of her arms.

His grin halted.

This was a mistake. She should pull up the coat now and leave while there was still a microscopic amount of dignity she could scrape off the floor. Yet she froze, rooted to the spot. Unable to move or breathe or think. She suddenly understood why deer just stood in the road while a car came barreling straight for them.

All the air seemed to evaporate from the room as his pupils drowned out his irises. He took her in from head to toe. "Damn me to hell. Why do I feel like I'm about to be the punch line on one of those hidden camera shows?"

Cordelia bit back her fear and sauntered forward. Where was that famed balance when she needed it? She stumbled, but righted herself before her heel slid out from under her. "Do I look like a joke to you?"

"No, ma'am." He swallowed. Hard. "In fact, I'm a little worried this might be a dream and I'm going to wake up any second now."

"Do you want me to slap you just to be sure you're awake?"

He cracked a smile at that. "Belinda Sue teaching you a thing or two?"

"Ugh." She made a face. "What do you know about Belinda Sue's specialties?"

"It's a small town. People talk." He reached behind him and pulled the blinds closed. "You're probably trying to distract me because y'all know I'm looking into Daisy in connection to the poison, but I would like to state for the record that I have no issue with your methods." His arm wrapped around her waist, and he tugged her against him.

A flash of liquid heat pooled in her stomach. This was all going horribly wrong. Distract, disrobe, disarm. Drop off the sample they'd collected from the wine and get out before he noticed. That had been the plan.

She wasn't supposed to *feel* things.

"I—" She cleared her throat. "I'm not sure what you mean."

"Come on, now." His big, calloused hand stretched across her rib cage, and she released an involuntary gasp. "That's what you're doing, right? Playing games with me?"

She rubbed her hand against his chest, her fingers curling against him on instinct, like a satisfied cat giving a good back stretch. The warmth of his skin sizzled through his shirt, the heat of him igniting her palm. "What if I said I showed up like this because I find you irresistible?"

He laughed, low and deep, as he nuzzled her neck, his lips brushing the tender skin beneath her earlobe. "I'd call you a damn liar."

This was too close. Too much stimulation. Cordelia specifically avoided these situations, knowing how easy it would be to lose her head. Hadn't she watched her momma fall into this trap time and time again? The thought ran like ice through her veins.

She pushed out of his embrace and backed up, giving herself the space she needed to find her equilibrium again.

As she hopped up on his desk, her legs bumped against the drawer holding the lab bags. The chill of the metal surface made her skin pebble. "Maybe I'm just having a bit of fun."

"You're in the right business for fun." He moved closer. A skilled predator stalking unpracticed prey. "Lucky for both of us, I don't mind playing a few games myself."

He reached for her again, but she held up a hand to stop him. "If we're going to do this, eyes open, shouldn't we start on even ground?"

Archer rubbed his jaw over the shadow of late-day stubble. "Little late for that, considering we haven't been on even ground since we were ten and you stole my shorts at the swimming hole and threw them up in a tree."

She pulled the leather banana hammock out of her coat pocket. When he frowned and shook his head, she giggled. The sound—and feeling—were foreign to her. "I thought you said you liked games?"

His expression turned pensive, but she blinked, and his playful demeanor returned. She didn't know where his mind had gone, but that had not been the reaction she'd been expecting when she pulled out the leather underwear. Was he actually going to do it?

"My momma used to ask me why I couldn't be more like that little West girl next door. If she could see you now." He snatched the banana hammock from her. "Those ladies at the Chickadee are a bad influence."

"I wouldn't say that." Cordelia pouted as she slid off the desk, the gesture pulling the lingerie up tight, exposing more of her. "But if you really feel that way, I could always leave."

She turned toward the door, unable to suppress her smile at his sharp intake of breath. She'd just reached for the handle when his arm came over her, pressing firmly against the door. The rough cotton of his starched shirt rubbed against her bare back. Heat radiated off him in waves. She was in so much trouble.

His fingers circled her wrist, spinning her around and pulling her back against his chest. "I don't believe I said anything about wanting you to go."

"I'm not doing this unless I can be assured you're as vulnerable as I am right now."

She stared up at him, blinking rapidly in a move she hoped would pass for a flutter. Seduction was not her forte. She just needed him to leave the room before he discovered she was way out of her depth. His fingers trailed the shape of her face. A touch so gentle, so tender, she felt like she'd left her body altogether and stepped into someone else's life. Someone who inspired long looks and sweet words. The kind of woman she'd always guarded herself against becoming. Her tense muscles relaxed as she melted into his touch.

"All right." His expression softened, though a smile was now playing around his mouth. "We'll do this your way."

He stepped into the bathroom adjacent to his office, and Cordelia immediately got to work. The courier would be arriving in two minutes. She had no time to spare.

She located the lab bag and tossed the wine sample in there, then buried it in his outbox under a batch of other papers. Next, she flipped open his leather-bound journal and began taking pictures of every page. She didn't have time to be careful. The sound of a motor humming outside caught her attention, and she peeked out the blinds.

The courier had arrived. Cordelia shook her hands as she glanced around the office to make sure she hadn't missed anything.

"I hope you know," Archer said through the door, "I wouldn't do this for just anyone."

Without responding, Cordelia slipped out the door. She passed the courier as she was belting up her trench coat, and he gave her a knowing look. Like he knew what kind of outfit she had on underneath. Or maybe that was just her imagination working overtime.

Shame burned her cheeks as she rushed out to her car and peeled out of the parking lot without looking back. There was a solid chance Archer would be hopping mad when he came out of the bathroom and realized he'd been had, but she couldn't think about that yet. As soon as they got those lab results in hand, they had no choice but to go looking for who had poisoned the pastor before Archer, the sheriff, and the town started looking too closely at the Chickadee.

Chapter Ten

PALYTOXIN. THAT'S WHAT SHOWED UP ON THE LAB REPORT.

Two days ago, while Archer was getting acquainted with a leather thong, the courier had taken a sample of wine from Archer's outbox down to the FBI's lab for testing. For two days, Cordelia had been checking the results hourly, worried that Archer would be clued in to the results before she could get to them. And now she could breathe a sigh of relief. She punched in the code to have the results wiped from the system and the sample destroyed.

He would never know she'd used him to find out what had killed his daddy.

Her insides squirmed as she thought about how she'd left him. Thus far, she'd avoided going into town. She wasn't looking forward to the day when their paths would inevitably cross again. She could only hope he'd be too embarrassed to mention it, though that was unlikely.

"Palytoxin?" Daisy scratched her head and the whole of her hair moved with the motion. It was only then that Cordelia realized she must've been wearing a wig. "I'm not sure what that is, but that don't make no sense. The whole town is saying arsenic."

"The pastor might've had arsenic in his system from who knows what, but the palytoxin is what killed him." Belinda Sue's nose scrunched as she brought her tablet close to her face, then moved it away again. Trying to find that perfect balance between her near- and farsightedness. "Nasty business, this palytoxin. Can only be found on certain soft corals that grow in saltwater. You can't buy this stuff on the eBay. Poisoning can mimic a heart attack."

"Why didn't they find that on his toxicology report?" Cordelia asked. The results of the autopsy were top-secret police business, so, naturally, the whole town knew.

"They probably weren't looking for it," Belinda Sue said. "Arsenic is a much more common poison. They might've seen that and quit digging. But make no mistake, the palytoxin in that wine is what ultimately did him in."

"And we're the only ones who know it," Daisy said.

"Should we tell the sheriff's office?" Cordelia asked. When the three of them looked at her like she had too many cobwebs in her attic, she held her hands out. "I'm not saying we point the finger at ourselves, but we could call in an anonymous tip."

Belinda Sue shook her head hard enough to crack a nut. "Nope. Out of the question. If we bring up palytoxin in any way, shape, or form, it's only a matter of time before they link that poison back to the wine he drank in Daisy's room."

"I don't want to go to prison, Miss Cordelia." Daisy's timid plea sealed it.

"Fine." Cordelia crossed her arms. "It was just an idea. I'm not sure if we're equipped to solve a murder."

"Two weeks ago you weren't sure if you were equipped to be a madam," Belinda Sue said. "But look at you now."

This did not set Cordelia's mind at ease, given that she still didn't consider herself a madam. She longed for the days when she thought the worst thing she'd have to do was chase an unruly client off the property with a shotgun.

"Any ideas on how we go about solving this?" Daisy pulled

a folded piece of paper from the back pocket of her hot pants. "Should we add more people to our suspect list?"

Belinda Sue smacked her palms together. "Well, would you look at that? Daisy is turning out to be a regular Sherlock."

"We ought to do research first," Cordelia said. "We need to know more about this palytoxin and where it might be found here in Texas. Anyone up for a trip to the library?"

The sky turned the color of a fresh bruise, and the clouds bloated with much-needed rain. The air snapped with the scent of copper and wet rock. Cordelia couldn't help but think it was a sign of things to come, even if she wasn't prone to believing in such nonsense.

Belinda Sue didn't want to be left out of the fun this time around, so only Arline stayed behind while the rest of them piled into Cordelia's car. They stopped to get gas on the way into town. The pimple-faced kid behind the counter, who couldn't have been a day over nineteen, wagged his eyebrows at her.

"I didn't realize the Chickadee had younger ladies now." He didn't take his eyes off her as he made change for her twenty. "Might have to stop by sometime."

"I wouldn't mess with this one, son. She's got a real mean streak." At the sound of Archer's rough-road, biscuits-and-honey voice, she wanted to collapse in on herself like a dying star. She hadn't seen him since she slipped out of his office, and hoped she could go on avoiding him until the end of her days. "Rumor has it she likes to string young men up by their toes and laugh at their genitals."

The tips of the boy's ears turned red. "That can't be true."

"I'm afraid it is," Cordelia said. "You should've seen how much I laughed at Mr. Archer Reed-Smythe just last week. He's got the funniest little—"

"All right now, that's enough." Archer slung an arm over her shoulder and covered her mouth with his hand. "Don't go scarring the boy before he's old enough to have his first drink."

He maneuvered her toward the door, and she bit his palm the minute they stepped outside. Shoving out of his embrace, she whirled on him. "I wasn't finished making my transaction."

Archer loomed over her, his shadow casting a long line of shade across the boiling asphalt. "I think you were more than finished in there."

"That's not for you to decide." Cordelia would've stomped her foot on his boot if she wasn't certain he was wearing steel toes. "Why don't you just go on and mind your own business? We don't have any reason to cross paths."

"You know that's not true." He leaned in closer, and the piney scent of his aftershave made her breath hitch. "I think you at least owe me an explanation of why you skipped out on me the other night. Do you have any idea how much I had to pay the courier to keep the sight of me in a leather banana hammock to himself?"

Cordelia laughed, realizing a second too late that was the wrong move, when his expression turned blacker than the clouds moving in from the horizon. The sky rumbled overhead just for good measure. She cleared her throat. "Looks like a storm is moving in."

"A storm's coming, all right." His grim expression had her backing up a step. The amusement that normally twinkled in his eyes had guttered. "You've really got nothing to say for yourself?"

"I changed my mind." She lifted her chin. "Don't tell me that was your first time experiencing a woman saying no to you."

The twitch of his mustache suggested it might've been, but he lifted a finger. "I've got no problem with the word 'no.' And I knew from the get-go that you were likely messing with me. What I have a problem with is squeezing into a costume you insisted on, then you not even having the courtesy to tell me you were leaving."

"You survived."

A muscle in his jaw twitched.

Cordelia's momma didn't hand out practical advice very often, but she was fond of saying a person could catch more flies with honey than vinegar. Taking a deep and calming breath, she schooled her features to look less confrontational. "I'm sorry."

Those two words cost her about a pound of pride, but it was the right thing to do. She'd been using Archer. He'd known it, but he hadn't known she would leave him high and dry. Something about him just made her want to argue. No one else brought out that side of her, not even her momma when she'd fallen off the wagon for the sixth time in a year after endless promises to quit drinking.

"Sorry for leaving?" A spark of mischief lit his eyes. "Or sorry you missed the show?"

Heat rose to Cordelia's cheeks. "Maybe a bit of both."

He shook his head, his gaze dipping to her lips. "What am I going to do with you?"

"Nothing I'd be interested in."

"We'll see about that." He wrenched his eyes away from her mouth, tipped his hat, and strolled away, just as casual as could be.

As soon as he turned his back, Cordelia had a strong urge to say something mean, just to light that fire under him again. What was wrong with her? She didn't do confrontation, but Archer was just . . . walking away. Minding his business, like she asked. So why did it make her feel like she'd ruined something she never knew she wanted?

Cordelia slid into the driver's side, half dazed. Daisy poked her head between the seats from her spot in the back. "What was that all about with Archer?"

Cordelia started her car. "He just wanted to clear the air, is all."

"He doesn't know about us using his passwords for the lab, does he?" Belinda Sue asked.

"No, he didn't mention it." Cordelia drove off, doing her best to keep her eyes straight ahead and not let them trail to where Archer still sat in his truck in the parking lot.

An unease followed her into town, thicker than the incoming storm, which promised to be a doozy. An ache on her heart that pulsed below the surface, like a sore tooth that hadn't fully healed. It must've been the weather bringing down her mood. She refused to pin any of her current feelings on Archer Reed-Smythe.

By the time they arrived at the library, the sky had opened up. Sheets of hard summer rain sizzled as they hit the sun-soaked sidewalk. Daisy and Belinda Sue hollered when rain pelted their wigs and made the synthetic strands melt from their heads like cheap wax.

From underneath the awning, Daisy shivered as she tried to pile her wet beehive into a respectable twist, but there was no saving it. She looked like a drowned rat with bright red lips and too much rouge.

"I'm not going in there looking like this." Her mouth hardened into a stubborn frown. "Call it vanity if you like, but lookin' good is my business and I've got a reputation to uphold."

"Who's going to see you?" Cordelia asked.

"Anyone might," Daisy said. "If old men can't sit outside and gossip, they go to the diner or the library to gossip. Ain't no place safe in this town in a rainstorm."

"She's right." Belinda Sue bobbed her head and her wet victory curls flopped down her neck. "We're not showing our faces in there lookin' the way we do."

"I've got a sewing kit on me." Cordelia opened her purse and began rooting around in the side pockets. "Pretty sure I got some spare bobby pins in there."

"You're a regular Boy Scout, Miss Cordelia, but I don't think bobby pins are going to save this." Daisy held her wet wig with one hand and covered her face with the other.

"I guess you can wait in the car." Cordelia held out the keys. "But one of these days we're going to discuss why I'm the one getting stuck doing all the investigating."

Belinda Sue snatched the keys before she could blink, and the two of them hustled back down the walkway and ran to the car. Shaking her head, Cordelia pushed open the doors to the library and stepped inside.

The familiar scent of books was the first thing that hit her. There was nothing quite like the hardback, paper, glue combo to set her soul at ease. She could hardly believe she hadn't made the time to visit here yet. She had an abundance of romance paperbacks in her apartment, thanks to Great-Aunt Penelope, but it wasn't the same as having every genre at your fingertips at once.

She spotted a woman behind the counter, near her age with thick, curly hair, warm brown skin, and a wide smile that crinkled the corners of her eyes.

Cordelia browsed the aisles and soaked in the comforting familiarity of being in a library. If she was back in Dallas, she might've been doing this exact thing in a different location. The routine of it soothed her, but that's all it was. Routine. A nagging little voice at the back of her mind kept reminding her that this wasn't her home. She didn't belong here. It unsettled her to realize the only place that really felt like home was the Chickadee.

What did that say about her?

It wasn't until she'd wandered into the marine biology section that an idea occurred to her. Libraries were the main hubs of both gossip and information in town. Grabbing every book on coral she could find, she brought them up to the desk and greeted a woman with dark curls shaping a round, friendly face. "Hi. I'm sort of new in town, my name is—"

"Cordelia West." The woman offered her a hand. "You took over the Chickadee when Miss Penelope passed, God rest her soul."

"That's right." Years of living in Dallas had made Cordelia accustomed to anonymity, so it still took a minute when strangers not only knew her name, but her business.

"I'm Martina Ruiz, pleased to meet you."

"Pleased to meet you too." Cordelia set her hand on top of the stack of books. "Do you know anyone in town with a saltwater tank? Specifically, who would know what kind of soft corals would be best to keep in them?"

If Martina was surprised by the question, she didn't let it show. Though Cordelia knew from experience it couldn't have been the strangest thing she'd been asked this week. "I can't say I know anyone around here who might. The local pet store doesn't carry anything that exotic."

"It was worth a try." Cordelia glanced up at the ceiling. It had been a while since she'd conversed with like-minded individuals, and she missed talking books. "I actually work at a library in Dallas."

"You don't say?" Martina's wide smile brightened.

Cordelia nodded. "I'm on vacation, but I love it. Or I did, until all those lunatics raised a stink trying to ban books. I can't say I love them."

Martina's expression darkened. "I know a thing or two about that."

"I figured you would. A small town in Texas can be a tough

place to defend the free flow of information." Cordelia paused, weighing her next words carefully. "Has any of that calmed down for you since the passing of Pastor Reed-Smythe?"

"Unfortunately not." Martina's lips pinched tight as a fiddle string. "The pastor had started the fire and fanned the flames too high. A right hypocrite, seeing as how everyone knew how much time he spent down at the Chickadee. No offense."

Cordelia held out her hands. "None taken."

"It was fine for him to use the tithing that paid his salary to step out on his wife, but heaven forbid a child reads a book about two boys kissing. I thought it might let up, but there are plenty of deacons around here who believe the same, or worse."

"I'm sorry to hear that." Cordelia rested a hand over Martina's, feeling a kinship she didn't experience with many people outside her momma and the chicks. "Stay strong. You're doing a good thing, protecting books for the next generation."

Martina gave her a look sad enough to bring a tear to a glass eye. "It's worth it, even if some days it doesn't feel like it. Though I'm not the only one in town who has to put up with the deacons. Vinner Mendez over at the Orb has his fair share of issues too."

"I'll bet he does." And the Orb would be the next place they'd be visiting. The more information they could collect, the better.

Cordelia returned her stack to the shelves and left the library. She'd be back though, if only to talk to someone who understood the parts of her that liked the quiet stability of books. She might not have found out anything about where one would acquire palytoxin, but if the pastor and his deacons were hassling people over morality issues, they might have a few more suspects to add to their woefully short list.

Next stop, the Orb.

Chapter Eleven

"OOH, I KNOW THE DEACONS MISS MARTINA IS TALKING ABOUT." DAISY fluffed her wet curls, slapping them over each other in a make-shift braid, making her look more like a drowned hen with ruffled feathers. "I bet it's Mack and Dean giving her grief. I'll talk to them."

"And say what?" Cordelia asked. "That you'll quit providing them services if they don't leave the library alone?"

"As a matter of fact, that's exactly what I plan on saying." Daisy gave up on her hair and tied a cloth bandana around the whole thing. "I'm a patron of the arts."

"Daisy chipped in on the children's wing of the library when Miss Penelope donated to have that section built." Belinda Sue's chest puffed with pride. "And she's provided over five thousand books to date to the children of this county. She's a big advocate of literacy."

"That's amazing." Cordelia went as soft as a two-minute egg. Just when she thought she had the chicks figured out, they went and showed her another side.

"I had trouble reading anything outside real basic stuff, until Miss Penelope told me I had to get my GED. Helped me study for it and everything," Daisy said. "It was the hardest thing I'd ever done, and I don't want any child in this town having to struggle the way I did."

Cordelia smiled at her in the rearview mirror. "You're a gem, Daisy. Rare as hen's teeth."

Turning into the near-empty parking lot of the Orb, Cordelia slid into a spot near the door and shut off the engine. Only two motorcycles took up space on the otherwise empty slab of cracked asphalt. The dry scrub grass poking up alongside the plain brown exterior held a fine collection of cigarette butts, broken glass, and a one-eyed babydoll. The very air stank of day drinkers and hopelessness. It reminded her of her childhood home.

"I'm not doing this one alone." Cordelia took out her sewing kit. "So the two of you need to decide who has the least offensive hair, because I need backup."

Belinda Sue took the bobby pin Cordelia offered and stuck it between her teeth. "If you give me a minute to get these curls in order, I can go in with you. I've got some business I need to clear up with Trent Baker anyway, and if I'm not mistaken, that's his bike out there."

"What kind of business?" Cordelia asked.

"Nothing you want to know about," Belinda Sue said with grim determination.

Belinda Sue and Cordelia slipped on their sunglasses and walked into the Orb, shoulders back, strides in rhythm. They weren't professional investigators, but they sure did get a kick out of playing the part.

The first thing that smacked Cordelia in the face was the smell. Cheap beer, sweat, and a two-week-old ashtray. The Orb had never been a classy establishment—most people preferred to do their drinking at home or at barn parties—but it looked like it hadn't seen the soapy side of a rag since the Reagan administration.

Peanut shells littered the concrete floors. A flat square of inlaid wood at the center of the room made up the dance floor, empty now on a weekday afternoon. Two men in leather jackets shot pool at one of the tables in the back, cigarette smoke hovering around them like burned toast. Belinda Sue didn't waste any time making a beeline for them. The one with the salt-and-pepper beard and John Deere hat stood up a little straighter as she approached.

Shaking her head, Cordelia took a seat at the bar. Vinner Mendez had owned the Orb for as far back as anyone could remember and had always been right around sixty. No one knew his actual age or how long he'd actually owned the Orb. He was one of those mainstays of Sarsaparilla Falls who didn't much like change since he never participated in it himself.

His thinning gray hair was pulled back in a ponytail at the base of his neck, and his tongue poked through the hole of his missing front tooth as he smiled. "Miss Cordelia. I heard you were back in town and running the Chickadee to boot. How's your momma?"

Cordelia stiffened at the mention of Sherilynn. She'd been a regular at the Orb. There had been more than one time when Cordelia had to walk down here in the dead of night and help her home when she'd overindulged, because no one in town was willing to drive ten blocks to drop her off. The memory of it burned like bile at the back of her throat.

"She's fine. On the wagon twenty years now." Cordelia pretended to look at the drink menu on the chalkboard so she wouldn't have to answer any more questions about her momma.

"To what do I owe the pleasure of your fine company this afternoon?" Vinner asked.

"Belinda Sue said she had some business to handle." Cordelia glanced at Belinda Sue, who had the man she assumed to be Trent Baker on his knees, holding a cube of chalk dust between his teeth as she rubbed the tip of her cue into it. "Seems like she might be a while."

"Can I get you a drink?" Vinner rested his meaty forearm on the bar. "On the house, for all those nights you had to walk your momma home."

Her expression turned frosty, like the furnace blew out behind her eyes, but she didn't need to remind Vinner he was just as guilty for what she had to endure as a child as every other adult in town. Those days were dead and gone. She had a new purpose for being here, and once she'd done her duty, she'd never have another reason to step a foot into the Orb.

Cordelia tapped a finger to her lips, then nearly retched when she realized the unwashed bar was the last place she'd touched with her bare hands. Digging out her trusty bottle of hand sanitizer from her purse, she rubbed in a couple of drops while she pretended to contemplate the drink menu. Even though she already knew what she was after.

"Do you happen to have a brand of wine by the name of Dew Valley?" The wine the pastor had been drinking the night he was poisoned. "They have a Cabernet I'm fond of."

Vinner's impressively large forehead wrinkled. "We got Boone's Farm in the back, but I couldn't tell you how old it is. I don't get a lot of wine drinkers round these parts."

"No, that's okay. I'll just take a Coors Light." She paused and glanced at the rack of glasses with dull brown streaks running down the sides. "In a bottle if you got it."

"Sure thing, Miss Cordelia." Vinner grinned as he pulled a bottle from the mini fridge. "Anything for the new madam."

She let the title go without bothering to correct it. It didn't even make her pause anymore. Cordelia sipped her beer as she watched Belinda Sue force Trent Baker to lick the toe of her stiletto. If he didn't have an excited glimmer in his eye, Cordelia might've thought she was torturing the poor man. But he was every bit the willing participant.

When she'd finished her pool game with Trent's partner, she took a wad of bills from Trent, stuffed them in her bra, and told him she'd finish with him later. Then she sauntered over and hopped up on the stool next to Cordelia. "Did you find out anything good?"

"Just that Vinner hasn't heard of any wine outside Boone's Farm." Cordelia took a sip of her beer and set it aside without even finishing half. "I haven't asked about the deacons."

"We can't just leave here with nothing. Vinner is a lot smarter than he plays most of the time. He's gotta have some kind of use." Belinda Sue lifted her hand and waved the bartender over. "What do you know about the pastor's death?"

He took his time walking over and stopped in front of them, arms crossed as he leaned against the back counter. "I know they're saying he was poisoned by arsenic."

"We heard the same." Belinda Sue pointed her thumb at Cordelia. "Seems kind of strange though, don't it? Wouldn't whoever did it be worried about damnation?"

"Killing is killing," Vinner said. "Don't matter if that man was a pastor or the local garbage man. It ain't right, no matter who it is."

"Didn't you have some trouble with the pastor?" Cordelia asked, and Belinda Sue kicked her under the bar. She winced and rubbed at the knot on her calf.

Vinner narrowed his eyes. "I've had trouble with damn near everyone in town who blames me for their loved one's alcoholism." He gave Cordelia a pointed look that had her shrinking in her stool. "That's the burden of owning the only bar. That don't make me a killer."

"Of course not." Belinda Sue shot Cordelia a look implying she ought to zip it before she got both of them thrown out. "The madam wasn't suggesting you had anything to do with it. She's just wondering if someone might've taken your cause into their own hands."

Vinner frowned. "I know the people who drink in this bar. They can get rough and tumble from time to time, but they're good country people. If the sheriff wants to look into me or anyone else I'm associated with, he's more than welcome, but I'm willing to bet the call on the pastor's life came from inside his own home."

"He means the church," Belinda Sue whispered out of the corner of her mouth.

"I got that," Cordelia said, wondering why they hadn't put any members of the church on their list sooner. Aside from Honey Stevens, who was only there because Daisy had a personal grudge. "Have you heard about any of the congregation being mad at him?"

"Well." Vinner picked up a glass and began polishing it with the filthiest rag Cordelia ever set her eyes on. A mischievous grin tugged his lips. "They might not have liked how much time he spent down at the Chickadee with Miss Daisy."

Cordelia gave him a tight smile. "Noted."

"You've been a big help, Vinner." Belinda Sue stood and poked at Cordelia's back to indicate she should do the same. "We appreciate your hospitality."

"What's your interest in this case, anyway?" Vinner asked. "He died after a break-in at the church. That don't seem like it has anything to do with you ladies."

"Arline don't get out much these days and she likes her gossip."

Vinner chuckled. "Fair enough. Tell her I said hi."

"We will." Cordelia rushed out the door faster than double-struck lightning before Vinner could ask more questions and start connecting dots.

If he was already suspicious of why they were asking after

the pastor, it probably hadn't been a good idea to ask him outright about the wine, but he didn't know about the palytoxin. He wouldn't put two and two together. Hopefully. At least their visit into town hadn't been completely worthless. Both he and Martina had pointed them in the direction of new suspects.

"You were about as subtle as a fox in a henhouse. It'll be a wonder if Vinner doesn't call the sheriff on the two of us," Belinda Sue said.

Cordelia threw up her hands. "I'm doing my best here. And the trip wasn't a total waste. He had some good ideas about where to look next."

"I know what you're thinking," Belinda Sue said. "But we didn't come here to open up a whole can of suspects. We just came to gather some additional information, but I don't know why we're not putting all our efforts into investigating Corbin and Edna."

"Because he made a good point about the members of church being more likely suspects. They had direct access to him, and whoever gave him that wine must've been someone he trusted, or why else would he accept it?" Cordelia asked.

"Ain't no one in the congregation going to murder the pastor because he enjoyed Daisy's company. Half the men in that church enjoyed Daisy. That's not a good enough reason for murder."

Cordelia trod carefully with Belinda Sue as they got back in the car and pulled out of the parking lot. Daisy peppered them with questions, but they decided to wait until they got back to the Chickadee so they wouldn't have to tell it twice. Cordelia had some thoughts, but she wasn't ready to voice them yet. Not until Belinda Sue had a drink in hand and loosened up some. The rain had slowed to a dull drizzle, but it was still too nasty for cocktail hour by the pool. They'd have to settle for tea in Cordelia's apartment.

As they pulled onto the dirt road leading to the Chickadee,

several large trucks passed them in the opposite direction with the words O'LEARY DEVELOPMENT printed on their sides. Rocks and other roadside debris pinged against Cordelia's car in the cloud of dust they kicked up. All the vehicles carried large metal structures out to the small piece of land Corbin had managed to purchase before being shut down by Penelope for the rest.

Belinda Sue kept a beady eye on the trucks. "What's that snake up to?"

"Whatever it is, he best keep it to that spit of land he calls his own," Cordelia said. She might've been willing to bargain with Corbin before she found out what his family did to Belinda Sue's father, but she'd sooner bed down on a mattress from the side of the road than give him an inch. "If he steps a toe over the property line, I'll sue him into oblivion."

The ghost of a smile played over Belinda Sue's face, pinkening her pale cheeks. "I still think we'll get him another way. This is far from over yet."

Arline was already waiting inside Cordelia's apartment when they returned. How she entered was anyone's guess since Cordelia kept her place locked, but it wasn't important enough to make it an issue. They shared what they'd learned at the library and the bar.

"That wine label looked expensive," Arline said. "I could've told you Vinner wouldn't have anything like that on hand at the Orb. I'm surprised he even had Boone's Farm."

Cordelia paced, restless as a cat in a tin barn during a rainstorm. "I thought it was necessary to make sure. We did go there with the intention of finding information."

Arline picked up her tablet. "I tried out the Google while y'all were gone, and Dew Valley wine can only be bought at a market up in Bramble Park. They sell it by the crate to restaurants. Individuals can't buy single bottles."

"Google. That's a good one." Belinda Sue gave Cordelia an accusatory look. "Shouldn't you have thought of Google?"

Cordelia bit her tongue to keep from saying that being the only person under the age of sixty didn't automatically make her a tech guru. But Belinda Sue didn't mean to be so thorny, that was just her rosebush way, and Cordelia accepted it.

"We could take a picture of Honey and whoever else to Bramble Park and see if the store owners recognize her," Daisy said.

"That sounds like a fine plan," Belinda Sue said. "We'll take a picture of Corbin and Edna too. I think there was one in the local paper a few months back. Those two stand out like crows in a cornfield. Anyone should be able to recognize the murder on them."

"About that." Cordelia stopped pacing and faced the chicks, who sat on her couch in a row, Arline and Belinda Sue on the ends, and Daisy—the peacemaker—between them. "I was trying to think of a gentler way to say this, but I should probably just say it."

"Go on, then." Belinda Sue flicked her wrist like she already knew she wasn't going to like whatever Cordelia was about to say.

"I don't think y'all should get so wrapped up in your personal grudges that you're not willing to look at other suspects." Cordelia looked Belinda Sue and Daisy square in the eye to ensure they both understood she meant business. "The most important thing we need to do is clear Daisy's name. Would it be great if we could hang our personal grudges out to dry? Sure. But that's not the objective here."

"We know that." Belinda Sue's lip curled. "I think Corbin and Edna did it because they've got the best motive. Am I wrong about that?"

"You're not wrong, but Honey's got motive too," Daisy piped up, bouncing slightly on the couch cushion. "She's real territorial, and I wouldn't be surprised if she slipped him a little palytoxin thinking it would just make him sick enough to go to the hospital, not knowing it would kill him."

"Honey's a nurse," Belinda Sue said. "She can't be that stupid about poison."

"And Corbin and Edna are regular CSIs?" Daisy fired back, her pert nose scrunching as if readied for battle. "What makes you think they even know what palytoxin is?"

Cordelia rubbed her brow. "This is what I was talking about."

Managing the chicks was like herding cats. The infighting wasn't going to help keep Daisy out of jail, but they were as stubborn as mules with a mouthful of cockleburs. They didn't know how to let things go, even if it was to their own detriment.

If they didn't solve this soon, the authorities would close in on Daisy, and they would all be put away for being accessories.

"The only way we're going to get answers is if we go to Bramble Park and find out who bought the wine," Arline said. "Until then, all the two of you are going to accomplish is raising hell and annoying me."

Belinda Sue and Daisy fell quiet, and Cordelia shot her a grateful look.

And in the silence, while Daisy and Belinda Sue stewed, Cordelia started coming up with ideas of what to do next if Bramble Park turned out to be another dead end.

Chapter Twelve

"I DON'T KNOW WHY YOU'VE ALWAYS GOT TO RIDE SHOTGUN," DAISY grumbled from the back seat. She had the window down and her hair protected by a sheer scarf.

"Because I'm an old soul and you're young at heart," Belinda Sue said.

Arline grunted, and Daisy shot her a dirty look. "Don't tell me you like it back here any more than I do."

"I don't care where I sit, so long as we get where we're going," Arline said.

Daisy was in a right foul mood, and Cordelia had no doubt it was due to none of them taking Honey Stevens as a suspect seriously. And while Belinda Sue's narrow focus on the Abernathys was also based on a grudge, Cordelia had to admit they were the most likely suspects. They had the best motive, and it was suspicious as all get-out how they happened to be on that near-empty stretch of prairie at just the right time to watch them drive the pastor's car and body back to the church. But so far, no one had the means or opportunity. Except Daisy. Which made it that much more imperative that they link the wine to someone else.

Bramble Park was an hour and a half from Sarsaparilla Falls, but it might as well have been another world away. Nestled close enough to the Gulf of Mexico to be a beach town, it was all high-end homes and boutique shops. A charming facade. The kind of place that would have no tolerance for aging sex workers and a reluctant madam.

"Ooh, look, they have an ice cream shop." Daisy pressed her face against the glass, her eyes big and full of wonder. "I bet they sell fudge. Can we get some fudge while we're here?"

It amazed Cordelia how fast Daisy could flip from crotchety old granny to a child trapped in a senior body, but if a little fudge was all it took to cheer up her, she'd buy a trunk full.

"Sure." Cordelia gave her a patient smile, even though all she wanted to do was nail down their suspect and head back to Sarsaparilla Falls, where things felt familiar.

Funny how quickly the town had become a part of her again, and how uneasy she felt being anywhere else. Like she'd never really left, just stepped away for a while before she could go back home. Even her more unpleasant childhood memories were beginning to fade, the edges growing dull and soft, like a photo left in the sun.

Cordelia parked her car in front of a fancy brass meter with a green patina. She dug a few quarters from her purse and fed the machine while the chicks got out of the car and stared, slack-jawed and stupefied, like they'd never been to a tourist town before.

The buildings all came in candy colors like pink, peach, and baby blue. Iron lamplights with electric bulbs lit the sidewalks at night. The cobblestone streets were kept clean with sections roped off for plastic tables with striped umbrellas, and big pots spilling flowers of every hue were spread along the walkway.

"You could eat off this sidewalk," Daisy said.

"Some people already are." Belinda Sue nodded to a couple seated on the curb, balancing plates of pizza on their bare knees. "I ain't ever seen anything like this."

"You've never been to the Gulf?" Cordelia gave the three of them an incredulous look. "How is it you've lived in Texas your whole lives and never been to the Gulf of Mexico?"

"We've got a watering hole just outside Sarsaparilla Falls," Belinda Sue said. "And a real nice pool at the Chickadee. What do we need to go to the Gulf for?"

Cordelia had to concede that she had a point. And really, who was she to judge? She'd only ever been to the Gulf once herself, when one of her momma's boyfriends promised them an all-expenses-paid trip to Galveston, only to stick them with the hotel bill before the week was up. Sherilynn had to take up a second job for six months just to break even again.

"Look at these little knickknacks." Daisy tapped on the glass of a storefront with her overly long nail, drawing a few side-eyes from tourists. "Have you ever seen anything so useless and adorable in your life? They even got a stone hippo. Miss Penelope would've loved it here."

"We can look around later if you want, but we should probably take care of the business we came here to do first." Cordelia consulted her phone in search of the market.

A bell chimed over the shop, and Cordelia looked up in time to see all three chicks disappear through the door. She supposed it couldn't hurt to let them have a little fun first.

Sighing, she moved to join them when she spotted Stella across the street with a woman who was quite a bit taller, long and lean, like a living strand of ivy. She wore her strawberry-blond hair short, and her pointed features and tweedy academic style of dress gave her an Ichabod Crane look. Cordelia locked eyes with Stella, who widened hers in return. Stella immediately whispered something to the woman in her company and the two of them hustled up the street and out of sight.

Odd. Did Stella recognize her after all these years? And if so, what was she so afraid of?

Cordelia entered the store and tapped Daisy on the shoulder, who jumped and nearly dropped the snow globe she was holding. “I just saw Stella.”

“No kidding?” Daisy passed the globe off to Arline. “Did you say hi?”

Cordelia shook her head. “I couldn’t say anything. She was across the street with another woman. As soon as they spotted me, the two of them ran for the hills.”

“Probably Gladys, the two of them are thick as thieves.” Daisy picked up a crystal duck and tapped its beak. “That’s weird, though. Stella is normally real friendly. Maybe she thought you’d judge her for taking a vacation when she’s supposed to be mourning her husband.”

“Maybe.” She nearly laughed at the idea of Stella Reed-Smythe being worried about Cordelia West judging her. Times sure had changed. “We should get going.”

Pulling Daisy away from every store they passed turned out to be a Herculean task. Every time she saw something cute, she had to stop and coo over it. A purse shaped like a frog. A fountain made of hand-blown glass. Clay Christmas ornaments molded to look like Norman Rockwell figurines. Everything in the town had been built to be cute.

It took half an hour to reach the brick facade of Val’s Vino, a charming wine shop that boasted a vine-covered courtyard for tasting parties. The owner, Val Kirkland, greeted them with a warm smile that dimmed significantly as she took in the chicks. While Cordelia had opted for her usual attire of a pencil skirt and cream shell top, the chicks had dressed in their usuals: hot pants for Daisy, skin-tight leather for Belinda Sue, and a floral caftan for Arline. With their big hair and makeup, they looked like they were auditioning for a rodeo sideshow.

"Are y'all here for the tasting?" Val asked, a clear note of hesitation in her voice.

"We sure are." Cordelia stepped forward and offered her hand and her most professional smile. "My . . . um . . . aunts and I have heard such good things about this place."

Belinda Sue snickered at being referred to as an auntie, and Cordelia shot her a look over her shoulder.

"Okay." Val didn't look convinced, but she led them toward the back anyway.

The store had that shabby-chic style that some Texas women went gaga over. It was how her momma's business became so profitable. Val's Vino even had crackle-paint shelves and gray oak floors, right out of a stylish farmhouse magazine. Little seating areas with mismatched chairs that still went together perfectly held hand-embroidered pillows.

"It looks like a spa in here," Daisy said.

"You don't know what a spa looks like," Belinda Sue said.

"Sure I do." Daisy rolled her eyes at Belinda Sue's need to always be contrary. "I got cable, don't I?"

"Would you two knock it off?" Cordelia hissed under her breath. "You've been picking at each other like hens over the last ear of corn all afternoon. I'm one wheel down and my axle is dragging. Give it a rest already."

Cordelia rarely snapped at them, and even though it was in Belinda Sue's nature to start a fight in an empty room, they respected her position and let it go.

Val opened a set of French doors that led out to the prettiest little brick courtyard. A fountain of marble cherubs sat at the center, with black wrought-iron tables covered by red umbrellas spread around the open space. Ivy climbed the walls and the Texas sun beat down from where it rose high in the sky.

"This is lovely, thank you." Cordelia took a seat. "I'm really looking forward to trying your Dew Valley Cabernet. It's getting rave reviews."

"Yes, that's a popular one," Val said. "People drive in from all over for it."

Cordelia opened her mouth to ask if anyone had driven from Sarsaparilla Falls recently for a bottle, but she took one look at Belinda Sue and closed her mouth again. The knot on her calf where she'd gotten a swift kick the other day was still tender enough to keep her quiet.

A young girl with a slick, dark ponytail and an all-white uniform brought out the first round for tasting. A Chardonnay from the coast of California. Considering Cordelia wasn't much of a drinker, she barely managed a sip. Arline, on the other hand, downed her serving in one gulp and stuck the glass in the pocket of her caftan.

"This tastes like pure sunshine." Daisy licked her lips. "I feel real fancy sitting here like this, drinking wine like a lady."

If Cordelia had proper girlfriends, this might've been something they would do together, but she'd never really been part of a friend group. She had a habit of keeping folks at arm's length, afraid that if they got close enough, they'd see her roots. The parts of herself she tried to hide behind neat clothes and a cautious manner.

They tasted a few more samples before the server brought out the Dew Valley Cabernet. Arline excused herself to find the bathroom, leaving Cordelia alone with Daisy and Belinda Sue, who were still sour with each other. Arline didn't talk much, but she made a good buffer.

"This has been a nice little escape, but when are we going to start asking questions?" Cordelia shifted in her chair. She wanted to feel like she belonged here, but the truth of it was the environment made her restless. It was too stuffy, and they were too . . . Sarsaparilla Falls. She was just waiting for them to be found out at any moment.

"That owner is coming back around. The one who looks at us like something her dog threw up," Belinda Sue whispered under her breath. "Let me handle this one."

Val stopped back around their table to check on them. "Is the Dew Valley to your liking?"

"Very much so. Would we be able to buy a bottle ourselves?" Cordelia asked.

"I'm afraid not." Val didn't look the least bit sorry. As if letting the likes of them be seen carrying a bottle of her wine would devalue it. "Dew Valley isn't for public sale."

Belinda Sue narrowed her eyes as she exchanged a look with Cordelia. "Are you sure about that? Because some friends of ours from Sarsaparilla Falls just bought a bottle last month."

Belinda Sue pulled up the picture of Corbin and Edna on her tablet. Val frowned at the photo and shook her head. "I get a lot of customers on a weekly basis, so I wouldn't be able to say for sure if they were here, but I can say they most certainly didn't buy a bottle because it's only for sale at the five restaurants I have a contract with."

Daisy watched the exchange like a ping-pong match until she saw her opening and dove in. She pulled up a picture of Honey on her phone. "What about this woman? She said she bought an individual bottle here too."

"That's not possible." Val pressed her lips together, clearly losing patience, but not wanting to cause a scene. "And I'd appreciate it if you kept your voices down. Dew Valley is known for its exclusivity, there are only five restaurants that serve it, and I won't have unfounded rumors tainting the brand."

"Can we at least get a list of the restaurants that serve it?" Cordelia asked.

Val hesitated. "Sure. Just give me a moment to get that together."

Val hurried away to retrieve the list, but Cordelia had a strong suspicion she wouldn't be back. Her suspicions were confirmed when the dark-haired waitress informed them they had another party coming in and would need the seating, despite there being several open tables.

Cordelia slumped back in her chair. "What a waste of time this turned out to be. I guess we can load up on fudge to make the trip worthwhile."

Cordelia still didn't believe Val when she said the wine wasn't for individual sale. The pastor had gotten the bottle from someone, and it wasn't anyone from Bramble Park.

They stood, ready to leave before the last round could be served. Daisy swiveled her head. "Where did Arline get off to?"

Just as they got ready to track her down, she came rushing into the courtyard, holding her stomach like she had the hounds of hell pressed against her colon. "We need to go. Now."

"We're coming. Hold your horses." Belinda Sue took her sweet time, only because she knew Arline was champing at the bit and she was in the mood to pick a fight.

Halfway back to the car, Arline ducked into an alley between a toy shop and an antique store. She pulled a large rectangular book out from under her caftan. "I knew that uptight hussy wasn't going to tell us nothing. You could see it on her face, plain as day when we walked in, not looking like we reeked of money. So I stole her guest book."

"Arline!" Belinda Sue snatched the book out of her hands.

"You were always smart as a whip. Don't let anyone tell you different."

Cordelia knotted her hands together, torn between fear and awe. "She's going to know it was us. She's got my credit card on file."

"She can't prove nothing." Daisy took the book from Belinda Sue and began flipping through the pages. "We just need a name is all, then we can leave the book on the sidewalk. Someone will return it to her. No harm, no foul."

Cordelia closed her eyes and whispered a prayer under her breath, even though she wasn't the praying type. "I hope you're right."

The three of them gathered over Daisy's shoulder as she flipped back through the last month, looking for a familiar name. Nothing in the last month. Or two. No single purchases of Dew Valley wine from any customers. Maybe Val hadn't been lying about the exclusivity.

"This is starting to feel like a lost cause," Daisy said. She'd gone back six months already and not a single recognizable name had popped up.

"Hold up." Belinda Sue laid her palm flat on the book. If it hadn't been for Daisy's nimble reflexes, she would've smacked it to the ground. "Would you look at that?"

The three of them leaned in closer. In a fine-point squiggly black scrawl was the purchase of a single bottle of Dew Valley Cabernet. But the name of the purchaser ended up opening a larger can of worms than they'd been prepared for. Because of all the people they'd suspected of poisoning the pastor, this one would've been last on the list.

Written there in ink near seven months old was a name they all recognized. Mr. James Reed-Smythe. The pastor himself.

Chapter Thirteen

"I'M GOING INTO TOWN." CORDELIA LEANED AGAINST THE POOL FENCE. The chicks were drinking mint juleps, which were really just shots of bourbon with a few sprigs of mint from Arline's windowsill herbs. The smell of it reminded her too much of her childhood. "Do any of y'all need anything?"

"Yeah. You can find us some men," Arline said.

Daisy sipped on her drink. "All three of our clients canceled tonight. Weird, right?"

A small smile played on Cordelia's lips. "Is that why y'all are drinking gin?"

"Might as well make the best of a bad situation." Belinda Sue held up her glass in a mock toast, already wobbling a bit in her beach chair.

"Y'all have fun." Cordelia shook her finger at them. "And try to stay out of trouble."

Over the last week, their investigation had ground to a halt. Ever since they found the pastor's name in Val's guest book. They combed through every page, and the pastor was the only one who'd ever bought a single bottle of Dew Valley Cabernet. The name next to the sale only appeared once as well, which led them to believe whoever had sold him the bottle had been new, done so on accident, and had been let go as a result.

Daisy swore up and down he said it had been a gift. He had

bought it a long time ago and didn't know single bottles weren't for sale. It was possible he'd gifted it to someone, who then gifted it back to him unaware. But even in that far-fetched scenario, they had no way of knowing who'd been in possession of the bottle when it had been drugged with palytoxin.

Cordelia couldn't leave when things were still so up in the air, but if she didn't come up with a plausible suspect within the week, she could kiss her life in Dallas goodbye. She could only be away for so long before her boss would have no choice but to replace her.

Cordelia pulled into town and slowed her car down to thirty-five, a respectable five miles over the speed limit. As she passed the Orb and the dollar store, she could've sworn people on the sidewalks stopped their business to watch her drive by. Strange.

Goose bumps prickled the back of her neck as she turned onto Park Street, and this time her imagination wasn't playing tricks on her. People stopped walking their dogs or pushing their kids on the swings so they could stare her down. Was she going too fast? She eased her foot off the gas and brought her car down to the posted limit.

Just as she was about to turn on the street that would be a straight shot across town to the H-E-B, the sheriff pulled out from a side street. This definitely wasn't normal. The inside of her car suddenly felt hotter than blue blazes, and she fiddled with the air conditioner, to no avail. Sweat beaded Cordelia's brow as she kept a real close eye on her speed, not wanting to give him a reason to pull her over. This would be fine. She wasn't doing anything wrong.

But she didn't make it more than another block before the sheriff flicked on his lights. The inside of her mouth felt as if it had been swabbed with rubbing alcohol. She tried to swallow, but her tongue felt swollen and heavy. She made it a point to keep her record cleaner than her apartment and had no experience in dealing with the law.

The sheriff approached, a swagger in his step as he twirled a keychain branded with O'LEARY DEVELOPMENT. She rolled down her window to greet him. "Good afternoon, Sheriff Maynard. I don't think we've seen each other since I was knee-high to a grasshopper."

Back when the sheriff was a deputy, he'd stuck her momma in the drunk tank more than once. The first time it happened, Cordelia had dug up the mason jar in the backyard and taken the crumpled bills down to the courthouse to get her released. He thought it was the funniest thing. After giving her an honorary plastic sheriff's badge and a sucker, he told her to sit tight in his office while he went and collected her momma.

He wasn't laughing now though.

Sheriff Maynard leaned into her window, the scent of cheese and cheap aftershave wafting off him like stink on a beetle. "Real interesting story in the paper this morning."

Cordelia's pulse pounded in her throat, making it hard to breathe, but she schooled her features to remain neutral. "I'm afraid I haven't had a chance to read the paper today."

"Edna Abernathy gave an interview about some of the strange things she's witnessed in recent weeks when checking on her husband's property in the dead of night." His grin sent a shudder of panic racing down her spine. "Like you and the other ladies at the Chickadee driving the pastor's car off the property the night he was poisoned."

Cordelia's blood burned hot enough to fry pork crackling. Edna had no idea who she was messing with. Cordelia wasn't the socially awkward daughter of the town drunk anymore, and she wasn't about to be bullied by the likes of that woman. "I didn't realize it was the sheriff's job to pull people over for unsubstantiated rumors."

"We're investigating a murder here. We'll look into all leads, unsubstantiated or not." He straightened and knocked his fist against the roof of her car. "I'll be by the Chickadee tomorrow to have a chat with Daisy."

"You do that," Cordelia said. "Then you'll see we've got nothing to hide."

"I certainly hope that's the case. The Chickadee may be an institution in this town, but there ain't nothing more important than the church." The sheriff walked back to his car whistling Reba's "The Night the Lights Went Out in Georgia."

"We're in Texas, fool," Cordelia muttered under her breath as she drove off and pulled into the H-E-B parking lot.

She took a few moments to steady herself before getting out of the car and grabbing a cart like all eyes weren't on her. Walking calm as could be into the grocery store, she held her head high and her eyes straight ahead. Let them talk. It's not like she'd never weathered the storm of town gossip before. It would only be a matter of time before someone slept with someone else's wife or someone put ground turkey in a potluck chili and a whole new controversy would start. She just had to survive this week.

Most people shopped by aisle, but Cordelia preferred to do her shopping by size and weight of the items on her list. Heavier stuff at the front of her cart and lighter in back. That usually meant a whole lot of backtracking and going up and down aisles several times, but she'd never once had a cracked carton of eggs.

That was how she'd ended up running her cart smack-dab into the she-devil herself, Edna Abernathy, in the baking aisle. Cordelia thought about plowing into her again for good measure. Especially when Edna gave her that little smirk, like she'd pulled out in front of Cordelia on purpose. Cordelia had never met someone she hated on sight. Until now.

"If it isn't the madam of the Arsenic and Old Lace motel." Edna's mole stretched across her temple as Edna smiled at Cordelia like they were old school friends chewing the fat. "I would've thought you'd be too ashamed to show your face in town after what y'all did to the pastor."

Cordelia's spine stiffened, as she became aware of all the people who slowed their carts in the outside aisles hoping to catch a show with their dinner. "I'm surprised you'd be so bold as to lie to the newspaper. Didn't they teach the meaning of libel in school?"

"It ain't libel if it's true." The smug jut of Edna's chin sharpened her already harsh features. "And now the whole town knows y'all ain't so high and mighty."

"Does the whole town also know the only reason you went to the paper with those false accusations is because you're mad that Corbin is spending all his free time with Arline?"

A buzz of chuckles and titters swept through the adjoining aisles as word about Corbin's nonexistent extracurriculars went around. Edna's cheeks flushed with color. "Corbin would never take up with that kind of trash."

Cordelia shrugged. "It's my word against yours."

"And you're an accomplice to murder who was raised by a drunk who spent more time on her back than she ever did upright taking care of her family." Edna looked around, making sure she still had the right amount of attention. "It's no wonder your daddy abandoned her."

Edna thought she'd won that round, and it was clear there was no level low enough for her to sink, but Cordelia had been raised in the shadow of her daddy's abandonment, and it fit her like a wool coat. A little itchy and uncomfortable at times, but it was hers and she'd done just fine for herself living with it. It was only a weapon to Edna because she wasn't a survivor and she'd never be able to cope with a life like Cordelia's.

The thought bolstered her. "Those kind of petty remarks aren't doing you any favors. Everyone knows you and Corbin got your sights set on Great-Aunt Penelope's land, but I'd sooner do business with the devil himself than sell you a single square foot. Haven't you cheated enough people in this town? Maybe you ought to cut your losses now."

That sent the aisles whispering again, but this time the buzz sounded angrier. Like wasps before a swarm. Edna swiveled her head in panic, knowing she was losing the crowd. As if everyone was just reminded of the fact that they didn't like the Abernathys any better than someone accused of killing their beloved pastor. They'd swindled too many good folks out of their hard-earned legacies.

Edna's expression grew darker than a black bear stuck in a smokestack. "You have a lot of nerve saying I should cut my losses when you've hitched your wagon to a murdering old whore who isn't worth the piping on the sewer she crawled out of."

Cordelia squeezed her fists tight enough to raise a blister. She'd had about enough of Edna disrespecting Daisy when she wasn't half the woman. She took a step forward. It gave her a sick sense of satisfaction to see Edna pale to a sickly yellow, like mustard without the bite. If she wanted to crow about murder, Cordelia would've been more than happy to show her a murder.

The clang of metal and squeaking wheels screeched in the air as folks who'd crowded the baking aisle to watch the confrontation began to make room for a fight.

"I've got ten on the new madam," Vinner Mendez hollered.

"I'll take that bet," a man with a braided beard said. "Abernathys don't fight clean."

Shouts filled the air as people began pulling bills out of their change purses and pocketbooks. Cordelia would've found it amusing if she weren't intent on making Edna pay. Not only had she publicly accused Daisy of killing with no evidence, but she'd been trying to cut her down as a woman. There were few things Cordelia hated more than a bully.

"Whoa, there." Before Cordelia could take more than two steps, Archer appeared and laced his fingers with hers, bringing her to a halt. "Let's step outside and cool off for a minute."

Cordelia's hand jerked in his. Was this a joke? Just who did Archer Reed-Smythe think he was? This was her fight and he had no right to step in where he wasn't wanted.

"What are you doing?" The crowd parted as Archer strode out of the aisle, and, with his hand still firmly holding hers, Cordelia had no choice but to trot along beside him. "I wasn't finished with her yet."

"You sure about that?" He continued to keep a grip on her hand, though she was reticent to admit she could've let go anytime she wanted. The fight had already gone out of her, but the principle of it remained.

Once they stepped outside, the hot Texas air blowing through the thin linen of her trousers like an oven baking an eye of round roast, she brushed her hands down her front and straightened the lapels of her jacket. Wisps of honey-brown hair got tangled in her eyelashes, and she batted the loose strands away with her hands.

Doing her best to look every part the unflustered schoolmarm, she narrowed a single eye on him. "Just who do you think you are dragging me out of the store like a sack of feral alley cats?" She shoved her hands against his chest, but she might as well have been pushing at a brick wall. "You humiliated me."

"We both know that wouldn't have ended well for you."

"I could've taken her."

"Of that, I have no doubt." He crossed his arms over his

chest, and his amusement infuriated her. Did he possess another expression, or did he just consider her to be his personal jester? "But do you think if you'd given Edna the right hook she was frankly asking for that she wouldn't have found a way to spin it in her favor?"

"I don't care." Cordelia stuck out her bottom lip, knowing she was pouting like a toddler, but she couldn't seem to stop herself. "Did you hear what she said about Daisy?"

"Daisy's a grown woman who can hold her own, but if you'd gone off and walloped Edna, you think she wouldn't have sued the socks off you?" He put both of his enormous hands on her shoulders, shooting warmth straight down to her toes. Looking her square in the eye, he said, "Come on now, darlin'. You're supposed to be smarter than that."

Now that her temper wasn't running as thin as a thrift-store rug, she could see his point. It still chafed that Archer Reed-Smythe, the boy who would glue pennies to the sidewalk just to watch people try to pick them up, was now giving *her* a lesson in maturity. "I scc your point. That's all you'll get from me. Now I need to finish my shopping."

As she passed, he gently grabbed her elbow and pulled her back to him. "You could do that. Go back in and face all the whispers. Or we could do something else."

She ignored the way her skin tingled under his touch and eyed him with suspicion. No good could come from that kind of glint in the eyes of a man born for trouble. "What did you have in mind?"

Chapter Fourteen

LETTING ARCHER TALK HER INTO THE MIDDLE OF LAKE ODESSA ON A two-person dinghy certainly wasn't the worst decision Cordelia had ever made. This month, anyway. It didn't occur to her until they were a good hundred yards from shore that she didn't have an escape if he wanted to start prying and asking questions she didn't want to answer. Plus, she'd never learned how to swim, but that was the least pressing of her current worries.

The pads of her fingers dug into the thin plank of wood that made up one of the bench seats. "What do you plan on doing with me now that you've got me out here?"

"I have so many options." He gave her a roguish grin. "Might be hard for me to decide."

If he was thinking of pushing her in the water as some kind of joke, she'd take a chunk of him with her on the way in.

"Please try to be serious for once in your life," she said.

Undeterred, he reached into the thin plastic box lining the inside of the boat and pulled out two rods. "I thought we could do some fishing."

"Fishing?" Cordelia held the rod between two fingers, like it might bite her if she brought it any closer. "What would we want to do a thing like that for?"

"Because it's relaxing." He chewed on the end of a toothpick as he baited his hook and cast his reel into the water. "I can show you how if you need help."

"I most certainly do not." Cordelia sniffed.

She'd never actually been fishing—dirt and worms represented everything she stood against—but she'd be a June bug in a chicken coop before she ever let Archer Reed-Smythe think he'd gotten the better of her.

She pulled a worm from the dirt cup and tried not to gag as it curled its fat, slimy body around her finger. The worm wriggled around her hook, and she dropped her line before he could change his mind and crawl off. She'd save casting for another time. Unfortunately, the worm immediately lost his hold on the hook and sunk to the bottom of the lake, but that was all right. She didn't want to deal with the horror of catching something.

Archer peered over the edge of the dinghy, his gaze landing on her empty hook, but he didn't say anything. He just gave her that grin.

"Oh, bugger off," Cordelia said.

Archer laughed. "I knew this would be a good idea."

After several extended minutes of silence, Cordelia bobbed her line up and down on the water and drummed her fingers against the metal hull of the tiny two-person boat just to break the tension in the air. She'd always been comfortable with the quiet. It was the only time she could ever hear herself think. But being out on the water with Archer and the gently lapping waves wasn't the same kind of quiet as alone quiet, and it made her want to fidget just to fill the space where there ought to have been words.

"Any thoughts on this heat we've been having?" Cordelia asked. Talk about the weather was about as basic as one could get, but she had to fill the void somehow.

"It's summer in Texas." He didn't elaborate beyond that.

"How about the Cowboys? Think they'll have a good year?"

Archer raised an eyebrow, knowing damn well she didn't give a hoot about football. "Are you trying to chase the fish away on purpose? I'm not sure if we'll have a prayer of catching anything if you keep making this much noise."

She shifted on the wood bench. "I'm not usually like this."

"I get it. I make you nervous, don't I?" He winked at her from under the brim of his Stetson. "Sorry I wasn't born uglier."

She choked on the laugh that bubbled up without her permission. "I think you get a rise out of baiting me. You make me nervous, but not for the reason you're thinking. I'm just waiting for you to toss me overboard."

"My momma raised me better than that." He took their fishing poles and packed them up, resigned to the fact that he wouldn't be catching anything other than hell today.

"She tried her best, anyway." Cordelia tilted her head as she studied him. "Did you really bring me out here to fish?"

"Yes and no." He leaned forward, resting his forearms on his knees. "I thought we could use some time away from the prying eyes of the rest of the town to clear the air."

"If you're talking about what happened in your office—"

He held up a hand. "I consider that matter closed. I wasn't lying when I said I have no problem with the word 'no.' But there is still the matter of my father's death between us."

Cordelia gulped on the cork that tried to clog her throat. "I'm not sure if that's a thing that's between us, seeing as I hadn't seen your daddy since I was half as big as a minute. Don't tell me you're listening to Edna."

"This ain't about Edna. Everyone knows the Abernathys are so crooked they'd spit up a screw if they swallowed a nail." He lowered his voice as if the fish had ears. "But I know he was with

Daisy that night. She done told me she was expecting him that day. He wouldn't have changed his mind, and he never wrote sermons on Friday evenings."

"You're barking up the wrong tree." Cordelia shifted her gaze to the water. "Daisy didn't kill your daddy. She wouldn't even kill a fly if it landed in her oatmeal."

He sat back, his eyes clouding over like he was disappointed, but what did he expect from her? If she told him about the wine, he'd go to the sheriff and they'd be done for. "I'm not saying Daisy is a killer. She's like an inappropriate auntie to me. But I think y'all know something and you're not saying what it is. Who are you protecting?"

That was too complicated a question for her to ever answer honestly. "Can we just head back? I've still got my shopping to do."

He paused for a beat. Two. Then he shook his head. "All right. I can take you back to your car. Do you mind if we stop by my office first though? I just have to check on a few things."

"Sure. No problem."

The drive back to town was awkward at best. Archer kept turning the radio off and on, like he didn't know if he wanted to fill the silence or not. Maybe he just didn't want Cordelia to ask him any more inane questions. Eventually, he settled for silence.

He turned to her, his arm stretching across the back of the bench seat so that his fingers dangled precariously over her shoulder. "Can I ask you something?"

She pursed her lips. "You've been asking me things all day, not sure why you're bothering with permission now."

"Did you really think I'd toss you in the water?"

The question took her aback. Of all the things she expected him to have a serious moment over, this fell near last on the list. "It's something you would've done once upon a time."

"When I was ten?" His brows pinched, like this news upset him as much as the Cowboys missing the playoffs. "Do you honestly think I haven't changed at all in twenty years?"

"No." Not exactly. Though she'd changed plenty in the last twenty years. Hell, in the last twenty days. So why couldn't she give Archer the same benefit of the doubt? "It's like . . ." She twirled her wrist as she collected her thoughts. "When I left this town, everyone in it kind of stayed frozen in my mind. I left and changed and did other things, but when I came back, it's like I expected everyone else to be the same. Even if that's not how it works."

"That's fair. It must've been hard, leaving the life you knew."

She faced the window. "Not really."

Starting over when you had nothing to lose wasn't quite the same as losing what you had and starting over. She never mourned Sarsaparilla Falls. Every bit of trouble she'd ever had here was on account of her momma and her ghosts. And while Cordelia had inherited the trauma as surely as she'd inherited the Chickadee, there was only so much haunting someone else's ghosts could do to a person.

She thought setting herself up to be someone entirely different from Sherilynn was a much better use of her time. Though the older she got, the more she began to realize that you could only stray so far from your roots. They had a way of dragging you back, eventually.

Archer cleared his throat, and when Cordelia glanced at him, he rubbed his jaw. "What if I said I wanted to take you on a proper date?"

She would say it was unexpected, if she'd been able to say anything at all.

She wasn't a fool; she understood Archer found her attractive. But she also understood he was the sort of man who liked to keep his life casual, while everything about Cordelia, down to her linen pantsuits and well-organized lists, screamed high maintenance. They were about as compatible as a rattlesnake and a jackrabbit.

Hoping to cut the tension vibrating against her bones and lighten what felt like a serious change in the nature of their mildly contentious relationship, she gave him a cheeky grin. “How long did it take you to work up the nerve to ask me out?”

“Since the first time I saw you again at the pool, after two decades of not seeing you.” He glanced at her. “Why are you looking at me like you want to punch me on the shoulder and call me champ?”

She frowned. “I was trying to keep things casual.”

“Not a good fit for you, is it?”

“I’m not the one making this weird.”

“Darlin’, you changed the game when you walked into my office wearing nothing but a trench coat and a few scraps of lace.” He gave her a teasing grin. “I still can’t properly look that courier in the eye. My outbox is a mess.”

Her face flamed with the memory, and she grasped for a quick subject change. “Have you ever thought of shaving your mustache?”

“No. Why?” The corner of his mouth twitched. “You don’t like it?”

As she drank him in, her eyes tracked each individual hair on that thick brush over his full lips. His mustache would probably feel like sandpaper on her skin, but she didn’t find the visual unappealing. She bet he had real soft lips. Cordelia had always been a sucker for gentle kisses. They made her stomach dip, like she was floating.

“I hate it,” she whispered.

He held her gaze, his voice low and rougher than the dirt road leading to the Chickadee. “If that’s how you look when you hate a man, I think Saint Peter himself would be willing to crawl through a den of sin if it meant reaching you on the other side."

She pulled her hair over her shoulder, letting the thick curtain of it shield her reaction to him. That was just his way. A natural-born flirt. That didn't mean he was getting to her. She was smarter than that, more careful. Always had been. It kept her safe.

Archer pulled up in front of his office and parked his truck. "You're welcome to come in. I promise it will be much less eventful than last time."

Lord, help her.

He came around to the passenger side to open the door and help her out like a proper Texas gentleman. She tripped, pitching forward, and he held her arms to steady her. Staring up at him, close enough to share a breath, she once again studied the curve of his lips and thought about how nice they would feel pressed up against hers.

"Delia." He said her name like a beggar asking for mercy. Slowly, as not to startle, he reached up and traced the line of her jaw before tucking her hair behind her ear.

This was it. She was going to kiss Archer Reed-Smythe. The boy who had terrorized her as a child and grew up to be more man than she could possibly handle.

Her eyes fell closed. She pushed up on her toes. An open invitation. He cupped her face, a gentle slide of his calloused palms against her cheeks, and sucked in a quick breath. She swore she could get drunk on that sound. Of him wanting her and being just a little bit scared of her too. There was power in being a woman.

"Oh my God. The pastor's son and the madam of the Chickadee?" The grating, high-pitched voice sent Cordelia stumbling backward right before Archer was about to kiss her. "I guess that apple didn't fall too far from the tree."

His arms fell to his sides, letting her go, but there was no mistaking the irritation in his gaze as it landed on their intruder. "Honey. What are you doing here?"

Honey Stevens swished her hips as she crossed the parking lot, eyeing Archer like he was a hog roasting on the spit and she'd brought her own fork. "I came by to see if you'd found any more information on your poor daddy."

He ground his teeth. "As I told you before, I'm not in charge of this investigation. It's a local matter, and it would be a conflict of interest in any case."

What he didn't say, but was heavily implied, was that even if he was at all involved in the investigation, he wouldn't be telling her squat. Honey seemed to take the hint though. Her expression turned cold as she eyed Cordelia. "I'm surprised to see you associating yourself with a suspect. Aren't you worried about what people will think?"

"Can't say I give a damn." Archer aggressively chomped on his toothpick, snapping it between his teeth. He spit the ends out. "If that's all, we're going to—"

"Wait." Honey gripped his arm, and Cordelia's eyes narrowed as her hold lingered, her fingers flexing over the cut of his biceps. "I didn't want to say this in front of present company . . ." Again, she eyed Cordelia like she was an egg-sucking dog, and Cordelia had to remember the good breeding she'd never had just to keep her temper in check. "But word on the street is that someone called in an anonymous tip to the sheriff's office about a large stock of arsenic up at the Chickadee. He's headed there now."

The blood drained from Cordelia's face. She knew it wasn't the arsenic that killed the pastor, but no one else knew that. Of course they'd gotten rid of the wine bottle, but it hadn't occurred to any of them to check the motel for arsenic. It wouldn't be out of the question for Great-Aunt Penelope to have kept some on hand. Rodents could be a problem out in the country.

Without another word, she left Archer and Honey behind as she ran the two blocks back to the H-E-B and peeled out of the parking lot, tires still smoking and the echo of Archer's voice calling for her in her wake.

Chapter Fifteen

CORDELIA PULLED UP TO THE CHICKADEE, ROCKS PINGING OFF HER tires as she squealed to a stop behind the sheriff. She expected to see Daisy being led away in handcuffs, but what she came upon instead was a scene straight out of Copacabana.

Sheriff Maynard had his boots propped up on a beach recliner, enjoying a dollar-store version of a tequila sunrise, poured for him by Daisy. His deputy sat in another recliner, enjoying a similar treatment from Belinda Sue. Except she made him balance his glass on his head, like an end table, before she'd let him have a drink.

Hot air blew in from the wide plains, kicking up dust and gently lapping the clear pool water. The sheriff rested a hand on his stomach, patting it in the way only a fully satisfied man could as he grinned at Daisy, who swarmed and coddled him like a salesman at a used-car lot.

"Cordelia." Daisy jumped off the sheriff's lap and came rushing to the gate. "You're back. What took so long? Where are your groceries?"

"I didn't get around to getting them. . . ." Cordelia trailed off, distracted by the thoughts of arrest and ruin still buzzing in her mind. "What's going on here?"

"Oh." Daisy brightened, like the sheriff's presence was a good thing. Of course, she didn't yet know how he'd pulled Cordelia over earlier and not-so-subtly threatened her. "The sheriff got some kind of silly tip about us having arsenic on the property. We let him have a look around and he didn't find anything, so we offered him a drink and a little break before he had to get back to work. We're in the hospitality business, after all."

Cordelia lowered her voice. "Are you sure Great-Aunt Penelope didn't keep arsenic on hand? Just in case rodents wandered in from the brush?"

"Nah." Daisy waved a hand, dismissing her. "The only thing that ever wanders in here from the brush is a random snake, but we also happen to be in the business of handling those."

Daisy snorted at her own joke, and Cordelia shook her head. All that fuss for nothing. She'd torn out of town like a bat out of hell, left Archer hanging on his dinner invitation, and for what? To watch the chicks play nursemaids to the Keystone Cops of Sarsaparilla Falls?

"Shouldn't they be moving along?" Cordelia asked. "Considering they've got a real murderer to catch and they're not going to find him out here?"

"There's nothing wrong with making the sheriff feel welcome at an establishment that's not altogether legal," Daisy said out of the corner of her mouth. "If you can't play nice, you should just let the rest of us handle this one."

Cordelia had never been scolded by Daisy before, and she had to admit that it didn't sit right with her. Plus, Cordelia couldn't argue with the fact that Daisy was right about the sheriff. The Chickadee wasn't a strictly legal operation, and it didn't hurt to help the lawmen in town see the value of it anyway.

"You're right," Cordelia said. "I'm just in a mood. Had a bad run-in with Edna at the H-E-B, and another one with Honey outside Archer's office."

"Edna thought she was being slick by going to the local paper.

She's so rotten, salt couldn't save her." Daisy gave Cordelia a mischievous glance. "I heard you put her in her place though. And got escorted out of the store by Archer."

"Gossip sure does travel fast," Cordelia muttered.

"Sweetie, this is Sarsaparilla Falls. Not even the wind can move as fast as small-town gossip." She looped her arm through Cordelia's. "What did Honey Stevens want? I'm assuming she was hanging all over Archer like cockleburs on a mule."

"She's the one who told me the sheriff was heading out here to make arrests."

Daisy snorted. "Of course she did. I wouldn't be surprised if she'd called that tip in herself. She's the kind of woman who'd eat up that half-cocked lie Edna fed the papers."

"Could be."

Cordelia didn't elaborate because she knew how quick Daisy was to latch on to Honey as a suspect, but it felt more like Honey had been throwing personal barbs outside Archer's office rather than just being her usual unpleasant self. As if she wanted to get one over on Cordelia, and possibly anyone associated with the Chickadee in general. It was something she'd have to think on later, when she had time to catalog the entire interaction and piece together why it felt so off.

"The boys are about to leave," Daisy said. "Why don't you join us for cocktail hour?"

Cordelia patted her arm. "Why not? I can always go grocery shopping tomorrow."

Cordelia didn't recognize this free-wheeling version of herself who put off chores for poolside gossip, but she liked who she was becoming. Maybe this was who she could've been if she and her momma had been taken in by Great-Aunt Penelope when they were low. Or maybe she wasn't ready to embrace this side of herself until she'd done things the opposite way first. Either way, for the first time in her life, Cordelia was beginning to understand what it felt like to be comfortable in her own skin, and there was something very freeing in that.

Cordelia stepped into the Sarsaparilla Falls library and waved to Martina, someone she'd come to admire and respect. It wasn't easy being a librarian in a small Texas town that had more backward thinkers than you could shake a stick at, but she handled the role with grace and class. The more visits Cordelia made to the library, the friendlier they became. It had been a long time since Cordelia had gone out of her way to make friends, and it filled an emptiness in her that had been so hollow she hadn't even known something was missing.

The familiar scent of ink on paper and a hint of carpet cleaner still brought her comfort, but it no longer felt like a part of her. Now, when she thought about the scents that made up her world, it was Love's Baby Soft and cheap tequila. Heavy musk perfume and makeup palettes. She was living on borrowed pizazz and redefining the word "home" for herself.

The sheriff hadn't made any arrests in the last few days, but he'd also stopped tailing Cordelia around town, so she considered that a win. Since the H-E-B incident with Edna, the town had taken up sides, with most of them falling on the side of the Chickadee due to all the goodwill they'd built up over the years, and on account of Edna's sour disposition. She wasn't an easy woman to like. But business hadn't picked back up yet. The men in town might've claimed they weren't chickens, but they had their henhouse ways.

Added to that, Edna had a mean streak, and she didn't like being bested by a bunch of women she thought were so far beneath her, they had to look up to see hell. Which meant she'd strike again, unless Cordelia could wrap up this investigation first and knock out the only leg she had to stand on right from underneath her.

Cordelia sat down at one of the computers near the back of the room and booted it to life. Belinda Sue had a tablet, but the fewer suspicious searches that showed up on her browser history, the better it was for all of them. The wine had been their best lead, but it wasn't the only one. They could still try to track down the palytoxin.

"You have a real interest in coral, huh?" Cordelia jumped at the sound of Martina's voice, biting the inside of her cheek and drawing blood.

"It's something I'm thinking about getting into." Cordelia closed her tabs with a shaky hand, grateful she hadn't been looking up anything more incriminating than nearby pet stores that dealt in tropical saltwater aquariums.

"You should ask the hospital where they get their supplies from," Martina said. "They're not exactly in town like you asked before, but they've got a huge tank in their lobby, all kinds of seahorses and anemones and whatnot in there."

"The hospital . . ." A prickling sensation tickled the back of Cordelia's neck. Like all the synapses in her brain were firing at once. "The one between here and Three Oaks?"

"Sure." Martina gave her a funny look. "It's the only hospital you're going to find around here for at least fifty miles in either direction."

The hospital where Honey Stevens worked. Cordelia leaped to her feet so fast, Martina took a step back to avoid getting hit with the chair. "Thank you so much." Cordelia pumped her hand, much to Martina's bemusement. "You have no idea how helpful this has been."

Cordelia rushed out of the library faster than a scalded

cat, not even bothering to reshelve the books, which definitely wasn't like her. But if she could wrap this murder up by the end of the day, then she could get on with figuring what her new normal would look like and decide if she even wanted to go back to Dallas.

She took the steps at such a brisk pace, she didn't see Archer until she was nearly chest to chest with him on the sidewalk. "Oh." She halted, her bones rattling from the vibration of her sudden stop. "Hi. How are you?"

That could not be any more awkward. She hadn't spoken to Archer since she lit out of his office parking lot. Since he'd asked her on a date and almost kissed her. Then nothing. He hadn't stopped by or made any move to seek her out, and she wondered if he'd changed his mind about her, seeing as she'd ditched him twice now without a goodbye.

"I'm fine." The glint in his dark eyes held a note of teasing. "And you?"

"Fine. You know." She brushed her hands down her neat A-line skirt. "Staying busy."

"I hadn't heard about the sheriff making any arrests out at the Chickadee, so I assume all is well out there?" His mustache twitched, and she wondered why he always had to look at her like he was on the verge of laughing. Did he really find her that funny?

"Yes. Well. It turns out he had a nice time by the pool after he searched the property and didn't find any arsenic. So. It appears the investigation has moved in another direction."

"That's good. Glad to hear it."

"Are you?" If she'd had a wad of cotton in her hand, she would've stuffed it in her mouth just to shut herself up. What was it about Archer that got her tail up? One minute she was thinking about kissing him, the next she was thinking about shaving his mustache in his sleep just to get a reaction out of him. It was enough to tie her up in knots.

His brows pinched. "Of course I am. You can't honestly think I want my inappropriate auntie to be responsible for my father's death?"

"No. I suppose not," she muttered, as if his belief in Daisy's innocence was just as offensive as his belief in her guilt. "I just wish the sheriff would get around to arresting someone so I could stop looking over my shoulder, waiting for Edna's next hare-brained scheme."

"This ain't Dallas," he said. "Things take a little more time around here. But Sheriff Maynard is capable enough. I'm sure he'll lock this down before too long."

"And are you staying out of things?"

He rolled his eyes. "As much as I can."

"Okay." She hesitated, waiting for him to bring up the date again, but when he didn't, she had no choice but to leave with her dignity intact. "See you around, I guess."

Maybe he was waiting for her to say something, seeing as how she was the one who'd run off the other day, but when it came to taking risks, she'd move five dead bodies before showing her hand to a man like Archer Reed-Smythe—though her heart and her mind couldn't seem to get on the same page. As she headed toward her car, she glanced back and was pleased to discover he was watching her walk away. He wasn't trying to hide it either. Tipping his hat, he let that grin play over his rugged features. Her stomach did a flip, a gentle kisses kind of flip, and she pressed a hand to it just to calm the butterflies.

The drive to the hospital took less than twenty minutes, flying down country roads with the radio turned up and a billow of dust blowing behind her tires. Cordelia couldn't think of the last time she'd felt so light. Like all her missing pieces were finally falling into place.

Creekside General, the local hospital, wasn't like the one she'd been to in Dallas when she'd had to have her appendix removed. Creekside was smaller, with only a dozen beds and a staff of five. While it served three counties, if anyone needed more serious treatments, they got referred to the bigger cities. Mostly they tended to minor gunshot wounds and birthing babies.

The doors to the lobby swooshed open, dousing Cordelia with a shot of cool air. Aside from an older woman sitting in the corner dozing off, with her knitting needles in hand, the lobby was empty. There wasn't even a person manning the front desk.

The fish tank gurgled at the center of the open room. Just as Martina had said, it held a variety of seahorses, anemone, bright rocks, and a few clownfish. But no coral. It could've been removed, but wouldn't someone have noticed it missing? Whoever cleaned the tank?

Unless Honey was the one who cleaned it.

"Can I help you?" A woman wearing cactus-print scrubs approached the front desk. Her hair was thrown into a haphazard bun with shorter tufts sticking out on the sides. She did *not* look like someone who suffered foolishness.

"Has this tank ever had coral in it?" Cordelia tapped the glass and withdrew her hand when the fish scattered like the Newman brothers from a bar of soap.

The nurse squinted at the tank like it was her first time seeing it. "Not that I recall."

"Is there someone I can talk to? About your fish tank and whether or not it ever held coral?" Cordelia tried to smile, but she was certain her right eye was twitching too much for her to come off as casual. "Martina Ruiz from the Sarsaparilla Falls library directed me here."

"I know Martina." The nurse tucked some of her loose hairs back into her bun. "The doctor set up the tank. It's a hobby of hers, but I'm afraid she won't be available to talk. It's a little crazy around here right now."

"I can come back another day. Or call ahead." That would've been the polite thing to do, instead of showing up out of the blue asking strange questions about coral.

Cordelia turned to leave when a commotion from down the hall caught her attention. A crash and shouting, followed by tears and pleading. The nurse glanced at Cordelia, resignation in her eyes. Like this wasn't the wildest thing she'd experienced this week. Cordelia could relate. She worked at a public library in Texas, after all.

The doors between the waiting area and the rooms burst open, and Cordelia's jaw dropped as she locked eyes with Honey Stevens.

Who was being led away in handcuffs by Sheriff Maynard.

Chapter Sixteen

GETTING INTO HER CAR, CORDELIA DROVE AIMLESSLY FOR AN HOUR before pulling up to the jailhouse. She couldn't have said what brought her there. Maybe it was the nurse at the information desk letting her know their saltwater tank had never had coral in it. Or maybe it had been the look of pure terror in Honey's eyes as she was led away in handcuffs. Cordelia was familiar with that look. She got the same one every time she had to deal with a tub of moldy food that had gone overlooked in her fridge.

The deputy noted her name and did a double take. "Miss Cordelia. What are you visiting Honey for? You looking to bail her out?"

Cordelia glanced around as if she expected him to be speaking to someone else. "I'm sorry. Have we met?"

"No, ma'am." He tipped his hat. His brown uniform hung limply off his thin frame, like he'd borrowed it from his dad. "But everyone in Sarsaparilla Falls knows you."

"Right." It unnerved her when people treated her like a minor celebrity. She was still getting used to the notoriety that came from the Chickadee. "Pleased to meet you."

"I'm sure we'll be seeing each other." He glanced around and lowered his voice. "I've been a regular of Miss Arline's for the last year."

"Well, now. Isn't that something?" That was information she

never needed to know. He looked like he'd been a few years behind her in grade school. "Can I see Honey now?"

"Sure thing." He took her to the back room.

Two cells had been built into the wall, separated by three feet of space, with a cot and a dingy metal toilet in the corner of each. The memory of her momma drying out on the other side of those bars flashed through Cordelia's mind. The fear and shame rose in her, clear as the first time it had happened. Sometimes she'd swear she could still smell the sour stench of her momma sweating gin through her pores while she held a glass of water with shaky hands.

An empty desk faced the cell with a mix of files and photos scattered across the surface. Three video cameras were positioned at various angles. The deputy pulled a folding metal chair to the second cell, where Honey sat on a cot, ankles crossed, facing the wall. Her neon-pink scrubs lit up the room like Christmas lights in March.

"Thank you." As soon as the deputy left, with the promise that he'd be right on the other side of the door, Cordelia pulled back the chair and took a seat.

"Why are you here?" Honey still hadn't turned around, choosing to speak to the brick wall. "If you came to gloat, you can just turn yourself around and leave."

"I don't see anything to gloat about." Cordelia folded her hands in her lap. "I'm just trying to understand how you ended up here."

Honey finally faced her. Her red-rimmed eyes and puffy cheeks gave away just how hard she'd been crying on the ride over. "Betty Jean. She told Dr. Lin that the pastor and I had an argument the day he passed, and she's swearing she personally saw me give him arsenic straight from my own purse."

Of all the things she'd been expecting Honey to say, that

never entered her mind. She knew Honey was probably a few pickles short of a barrel, but she had no idea her territorial ways took such extremes. "Is that true?"

"Of course not. Why would you ask me such a thing?" she screeched. Glancing at the camera, then back at Cordelia, she lowered her voice. "I'm a nurse. I took an oath to heal."

"Why were you fighting?" The more Cordelia learned about the pastor, the less she thought of him, but she still couldn't see him getting into a public squabble with a woman who fancied him in an unrequited way.

"He had pneumonia a few months back, that's no secret, and when he came in for his wellness check, I might've said some unkind things about Daisy knowing it was Friday and he'd likely be on his way to see her after his appointment. Betty Jean must've been watching from the hall like a sneak, but having words don't make me a killer."

"What about Betty Jean's claim that she saw you giving pills to the pastor?" Cordelia clicked her tongue. "I think you're leaving out a few details."

"I gave him Tylenol." Honey's flat, unaffected expression reminded her strongly of Arline. "If I'd given him the pills from the hospital's supply, it would've cost a hundred and fifty dollars. I was trying to do right by him since we were close."

"That's unfortunate." Honey had been about as close to the pastor as Texas was to Australia, but Cordelia didn't think it would be prudent to point that out right then.

And while Cordelia should've been relieved to get a break from the town's scrutiny and the sheriff's suspicions, Honey's story checked out. It sounded suspicious as all get-out, and it likely wouldn't hold up in court. Cordelia also knew full well that Honey didn't kill the pastor. Whoever put the palytoxin in his wine did, and her conscience wouldn't let Honey take the fall.

"I don't know how they intend to make these charges stick. I know how the law works. Their case is flimsy at best," Honey said, and attempted to throw Cordelia a smug look, an effect that lost its luster on account of her wobbling bottom lip.

"I suppose that's between you and the judge." Cordelia took in her electric-pink scrubs, smeared lipstick, and lopsided hair. Honey wouldn't last a day in prison. "Why would you fight with him over Daisy though? They weren't in a relationship. He was a married man."

"I would've done everything she'd done for him for free." She stuck out her bottom lip. A petulant toddler who'd never learned the meaning of the word "no."

"Maybe he liked the fact that his arrangement with Daisy was strictly business."

Honey had nothing to say to that. The toilet in the empty cell gurgled and emitted an inhuman belch that left a powerful stink in the air. Cordelia discreetly covered her nose with the collar of her shirt. Honey eyed the unruly toilet like she was wondering how much worse it would get before she'd be let out. It was a cruel situation for anyone to be in.

Though Cordelia's empathy for Honey could only go so far—she was meaner than a rattlesnake on a bed of coals, and she had no business getting into the pastor's personal business when he was just there for a wellness check—she didn't kill the pastor. It would always come back to that. Someone else had put the palytoxin in his wine.

"I know you're sitting there judging me." Honey picked at her chipped nail polish. "And I'm just wondering where you get the gall, considering your reputation is trash."

A month ago, hearing someone speak so callously about her reputation would've sent Cordelia into a fit of damage control. Before the chicks swooped into her life being every bit themselves without apology and living life on their terms. They got respect because they didn't need it or want it from anyone but themselves. And the more time Cordelia spent in their company, the less she felt that pressing, constant need for approval.

"I'm not judging, I'm just thinking," Cordelia said. "Did you happen to see the pastor with a bottle of wine that day?"

"You're kidding, right? It was a wellness check. Not even the alcoholics bring liquor to the doctor's office with them." Honey gave her a pointed look.

Cordelia ignored the clear jab at her momma. "I'm not saying he brought the bottle in with him, but did he mention getting a gift, or had anyone given it to him at the hospital?"

She narrowed her eyes. "Why are you asking me this?"

"I'm not interested in seeing you hang for a crime you didn't commit."

"I knew it." Honey jumped to her feet. "You know something."

Cordelia sighed, eight shades over these tiresome games. "I know as much as you."

"No, you don't. You're asking funny questions about wine, and you're certain I didn't kill him even though you don't like me and have no reason to believe otherwise. Why?" She wrapped her hands around the bars, tightening her hold like she would've rattled them if they hadn't been bolted into the ground. "What do you know?"

Cordelia stood, realizing her mistake a bit too late to take it back. "I've got to go."

"What do you know?" Honey yelled at her as she retreated. "You can't leave me in here. I didn't kill anyone."

Cordelia exited the room and pressed her back against the door, hand on her chest to catch her breath. It had been stupid to come here. She couldn't do anything for Honey without putting Daisy in harm's way. And if Honey started wagging her tongue about the wine, it could spell trouble for the Chickadee. Especially if there were still people who believed Edna's story. Cordelia should've just left well enough alone.

If only she could find the real killer before anyone else got caught in the crosshairs.

Promptly after leaving the jailhouse, Cordelia pulled out her phone, her thumb hovering above her boss Betsy's number. Word of Honey's arrest would spread quickly. The heat would be off Daisy and the chicks would soon be busier than ever. Now was as good a time as she'd ever get to tell them she wanted to return to Dallas.

But she couldn't do it. Not only was Honey innocent, leaving a real murderer to go free in Sarsaparilla Falls, but Cordelia felt more like herself at the Chickadee than she ever had in Dallas. There was really only one thing she could do.

She pressed call on her boss's number.

"Hello? Betsy?" Cordelia paced beside her car. "I'm afraid I won't be returning to Dallas. Please consider this my notice. I'm sorry I didn't get in touch with you sooner."

That was all it took. A two-second conversation to end the life she thought she'd always wanted. And the only thing she felt bad about was that she didn't feel bad at all.

Her phone buzzed, and she answered without looking at the screen. "I know I put you in a tough spot, Betsy. I'm so sorry, but I can't leave Sarsaparilla Falls."

"I know my hearing ain't what it used to be, so please tell me I misheard you and you're not in that town?" The loud screech coming through the line most definitely wasn't Betsy. Cordelia pulled the phone away from her ear in horror.

Only to see her momma's number on the screen.

"Momma, listen." Cordelia gripped her hair at her nape. "Before you freak out."

"*Before* I freak out?" Her momma's pitch could set off dogs from twenty miles away. "I'm way beyond freaking out. Just what in the hell are you doing in that town?"

She couldn't even say the name. Twenty years away and nearly that many years sober, and she still couldn't stand to speak the name of the place that had driven her out of her mind. Cordelia knew she was going to have to have this conversation with Sherilynn eventually, but she'd hoped to do it in person. In public. Where there were witnesses.

"You know how I told you I was exploring other job opportunities?" Cordelia just had to bite the bullet and come clean to her momma. "As it turns out, I inherited a motel."

Silence. "A motel? What motel?"

"Um." Cordelia clenched her teeth. Sarsaparilla Falls only had one motel, and her momma knew it. Squeezing her eyes shut, she forced out the words in a rush. "The Chickadee."

"Oh my God." A muted bounce like a tree branch hitting a trampoline came through the line. If Cordelia wasn't used to her momma's histrionics, she would've thought she'd fainted dead away on her couch. "And just how did a thing like that happen?"

"You know how Daddy told you all his relatives were dead too, and that's what the two of you first bonded over? Welp, surprise. It turns out he was lying. Miss Penelope was his aunt."

"I'm not concerned about the lies of a known liar." Sherilynn's voice sharpened. "What concerns me is why you seem to be taking after him by not telling me."

Cordelia bristled. She wasn't anything like her daddy. Unlike him, she wasn't lying to her momma on purpose. She'd just been put between a rock and a hard place and chose the rock for the time being. "I was going to tell you eventually. I was just working up the courage to do so because I knew this was how you'd react."

"Oh, sure. Blame me."

"I'm not—"

"My only daughter, running a cathouse." Sherilynn groaned. "Where did I go wrong?"

"Is that a rhetorical question, or . . . ?"

Her momma released a long-suffering sigh fit for chaise longues and smelling salts. "I'm coming down there."

"No. Please don't." The last thing Cordelia needed was to add her momma to the list of senior women she was in charge of minding. "This really isn't a good time."

"Why? What's going on?" Her momma could dig up dirt from a soap factory.

"I'm still getting settled and figuring out my way around things." She could hardly tell her momma she was trying to solve a murder that had happened on her watch. "How about I call you when things settle down?"

"I guess that would be okay." Sherilynn West wouldn't be deterred forever. She was born and raised in Texas, and the stubborn gene came part and parcel, but Cordelia hoped she could put her off for just a little while longer. "But if you don't call me regularly, I'm going to assume something terrible has happened and then I'll have no choice but to scurry down there."

"Yes, Momma. I understand."

Cordelia hung up, blowing out a breath of relief as she leaned against her car. That could've gone much worse. Of course, her momma hadn't actually shown up in Sarsaparilla Falls. If that happened, all hell would likely break loose, but that was a problem for another day.

With her job and her momma settled, Cordelia headed back

to the Chickadee to share the news. The chicks were overjoyed she was staying, though they pointed out that they never thought for a second she'd leave. Belinda Sue served up the day's drink special: Dirty Shirley Temples. Which were really just Sprite and Absolut Cherrys. Cordelia once again abstained.

"Honey belongs in jail." Daisy raised her glass like she was about to shoot out the lights, but there was nothing about Honey's situation worth celebrating in Cordelia's opinion.

She needed to get them back on track. "She's not a nice person—"

"And she sounds like a lousy nurse," Belinda Sue said.

"Yes," Cordelia said. "Bad at life and her job. But that doesn't make her a killer."

"So?" Arline said. "If the sheriff thinks she did it, why is that our problem? We don't owe Honey Stevens our time or effort."

Cordelia closed her eyes and breathed in deeply through her nose. Her sense of right and wrong was being tested daily. She didn't care about Honey any more than the rest of them, but they were holding a key piece of evidence that could absolve her in an instant. As far as Cordelia was concerned, that meant they had an obligation to see this through.

"We're not letting Honey hang for the crime someone else tried to pin on Daisy," Cordelia said. "My momma was a careless drunk, and she still raised me better than that."

"Fine." Arline crossed her arms, a sour expression etched into the hard lines of her face. "It was just a suggestion."

"What should we do then?" Daisy asked. "We're not the sheriff. There's only so much investigating we can do on our own without authority."

"That's because we've been playing it safe so far," Cordelia said. That instinct she'd been fighting her whole life, the one that tried to encourage her to be a little more fearless, try something a little more dangerous, reared up in her. Maybe it was finally time to let her out of the box. "We only have one suspect now."

"Corbin and Edna." A grim light of determination entered Belinda Sue's eyes, like she'd been born to dish out punishment, and not the fun kind she used on her clients.

Cordelia nodded. "Edna's been walking around town like she don't put her pants on one leg at a time like the rest of us. If you ask me, she's wearing that confidence like a fake fur. As if she knows she didn't earn it."

"It's too bad we'll never get near her house," Daisy said. "All we would need is one peek inside to see if they've got a saltwater tank."

"That would be a start," Cordelia said.

They would still need to connect them to the Dew Valley wine, and the point where they handed it off to the pastor. But finding out they had access to palytoxin would go a long way toward building a case. They already had the motive. They just needed the rest to fall into place.

"Ladies." At the sound of that strong, sure voice, Cordelia's bones melted like butter. She hadn't even looked at him yet, and Archer Reed-Smythe was already having his way with her.

"Oh, Lord. Archer, what did you do to your face?" Belinda Sue asked.

Startled, Cordelia spun around and her jaw about hit the floor. Archer rested his powerful forearms, sleeves rolled up, on the gate to the pool. His mustache was gone. Shaved clean off, leaving his face bare and nearly unrecognizable.

"You shaved." Cordelia was stating the obvious, but she was too dumbstruck to say anything else. "Why?"

Archer shrugged, looking unsure of himself for possibly the first time in his life. "You said you hated it."

"I changed my mind," Cordelia said. "Grow it back."

Archer laughed. "I'm afraid I can't pull off something like that on command."

"I didn't say you had to do it now." She averted her gaze, finding it hard to look at him. She wasn't a facial hair person by any means, but Archer was proving to be the exception to every one of her rules. "Sometime this week would be fine."

"Delia." Ooh, the way that voice made her toes tingle. That kind of chemical reaction deserved to be studied in labs. "I was hoping you'd given some thought to going out on a proper date. I'd like to take you to dinner."

Daisy sighed like she'd collapsed on a fainting couch. Cordelia pinched her lips together. She did not want an audience for this conversation. It was awkward enough trying to keep a straight face when Archer looked like a sheep without its wool.

Smoothing her hands over her lap, brushing away the wrinkles in her skirt, she nodded stiffly. "I have given it some thought, and I've decided to accept your invitation."

Daisy squealed, and Cordelia shot her a look to quiet her down.

"If"—Cordelia held up a finger—"you grow your mustache back before then."

His lips twitched with amusement. "Consider it done. I'll pick you up next Friday."

As soon as he left, all the chicks faced Cordelia, looking like cats who had the mouse cornered. Cordelia picked a piece of invisible lint off her skirt, ignoring the fiendish stretch of their jack-in-the-box grins. She wasn't anyone's form of entertainment.

"Archer shaved off his mustache for you," Daisy said, like he'd presented her with a diamond ring. "He's never done that before."

"Probably because deep down he knew he'd look ridiculous without it."

Belinda Sue rapped her knuckles on the metal frame of her beach chair. "Don't go acting like that's not something special. That boy's had a mustache since the seventh grade."

"The madam and the pastor's son." Arline cackled and slapped her knee. "I couldn't write the script on this if I tried."

"Well, you can just cap your pen, because it's not a thing." Cordelia huffed. "We're just having dinner, not getting hitched."

"But it could lead to that." Daisy's voice had gone breathless as she fanned herself. "You and Archer would have the cutest babies."

"They most certainly would," Belinda Sue said. "With a whole pack of aunties just waiting to spoil them."

Cordelia held her hands out. "Y'all are getting way ahead of yourselves. No one is having babies. I'm not even sure if I want babies."

Babies were the epitome of messy, with their diapers and spit-up and floppy heads. The thought of trying to keep something alive with so many needs made Cordelia break out in a cold sweat. She could barely manage the three fully grown functional adults under her care.

Belinda Sue opened her mouth to make a point Cordelia intended to dismiss when her phone buzzed. Putting the conversation on hold, Belinda Sue answered the phone, her stern expression brightening as she informed the person on the other end of the line that she did have openings for the evening, and scheduled them into her tablet. Seconds later, Daisy's and Arline's phones went off as well. Word of Honey's arrest had gone public.

And just like that, the Chickadee was back in business.

Chapter Seventeen

WITH THE CHICKS ENTERTAINING MEN AT ALL HOURS OF THE DAY NOW that Honey's arrest had fully discredited Edna's story, Cordelia found herself with a lot more time on her hands. She spent it in the library, hanging out with Martina, and telling off the occasional patron who tried to make a fuss about children's literature containing satanic messaging. Since she wasn't actually employed by the library, she got to use all the good curse words in her lexicon to tell them exactly what she thought about their preaching. Just because the town was down a pastor didn't mean they were looking for any random person off the street to fill the role.

She'd set herself up at a computer near the back, doing a deep dive search of all the restaurants that served Dew Valley wine. They'd let their only solid lead go once they'd found out the pastor had bought the only bottle that had been individually sold, but that didn't mean he couldn't have gotten another bottle from someone else. Someone who knew his preferences.

If only Arline hadn't stolen that guest book from Val's, then she could've called her for the list and saved herself the trouble. As it stood, she hoped Val would never cross her path again. She had her nose so high in the air she could drown in a rainstorm, and Cordelia had enough arrogant women who thought they were better than her right here in Sarsaparilla Falls.

The sound of two women giggling together in the Local Interest aisle caught her attention. She nearly ducked and hid when she realized it was Stella Reed-Smythe. Archer's momma. She recognized the academic woman at her side as the one she'd seen her with in Bramble Park the day they went to Val's Vino. The two of them stopped short when they caught sight of Cordelia openly staring.

"Oh. Hello, Cordelia." Stella stepped forward and offered her hand, which was limp and cold, not unlike a dead fish. "I heard you were back in town."

"For a few weeks now." Cordelia ran the toe of her ballet flat across the threadbare carpet. Stella Reed-Smythe had always made her as nervous as a long-tailed cat in a room full of rockers. Like she could smell imperfections on people. "I moved back when my Great-Aunt Penelope passed on."

Stella laid a hand over her heart. "Penelope was a good woman. One of a kind."

"I'm sorry about your loss as well," Cordelia said.

"It's been hard, but I'm getting on okay." The woman next to Stella shifted, and she turned to her. "This is my friend Gladys Murphey. She's been a big help."

"Pleased to meet you," Cordelia said.

"I remember when you were just a bean sprout," Gladys said. "You probably don't remember me, but I used to work with your momma at the dentist's office."

Cordelia squinted at Gladys like she was trying to remember, but seeing as she didn't recall her momma ever working at a dentist's office, the odds of her having any memory of Gladys were slim. "No, ma'am. I'm sorry, but I don't."

"As expected. She stopped working there when you were about two or three." Gladys might've said her momma stopped working there, but the implication that she'd been fired for drinking or stealing or calling off too often for a hangover hung in the stilted air between them.

And Cordelia, falling back on her old pleasing habits whenever her momma's behavior got called into question, pasted a sweet smile on her face. "Momma's doing well now. Living in Dallas and running a consignment shop. Been in the AA for near twenty years."

"That's good to hear," Gladys said, the tension in her shoulders visibly relaxing.

People had funny ways of talking about her momma. Like she was the elephant in the room they were all trying to ignore. The way her legacy had extended well past her years in Sarsaparilla Falls would probably amuse Sherilynn nowadays.

"Are you reading up on coral?" Stella tilted her head and examined the stack of books piled up on the table next to the computer. "Isn't it so fascinating? I saw some for the first time on my honeymoon and absolutely fell in love. It's such a unique living species."

"I've been doing some research on it lately." Cordelia did *not* add that it was in relation to her deceased husband's murder. "Biology is a side interest of mine."

"Beauty and brains," Gladys said. "No wonder Archer is so smitten with you."

"Oh." Cordelia's face flamed a brighter red than Stella's scarf. Unlike her momma, she didn't enjoy the spotlight. "He's not . . . We're just acquaintances, that's all."

"Everyone is talking about how he shaved his mustache for you." Gladys gave her a wicked grin. "And then you told him to grow it back."

If a sinkhole had opened under Cordelia's feet right then and swallowed her whole, she wouldn't have minded one bit. This was one part of small-town life that fit like a pair of heels two sizes too small. Why had she decided to leave her anonymous life in Dallas behind again? Her old neighbors didn't know her name, let alone her business.

Stella laughed and smacked Gladys's arm. "Leave the poor girl be. She doesn't need you giving her trouble when she has her hands full enough with my son." Stella winked at Cordelia and she could instantly see where he'd gotten his charm. "I appreciate you encouraging him to grow his mustache back. He looked like a caterpillar without the fuzz."

"Ain't that just a worm?" Gladys asked.

"It suits his face," Cordelia said.

"Just like his daddy." Stella patted Cordelia's arm. "It was lovely to see you. I've been telling Archer to bring you by so I could say hi, but he said he didn't want to scare you off. Like I could ever do such a thing."

Right. As if Cordelia weren't currently aware of all of her extremities and exactly what they were and weren't doing. But through the fog of white noise playing inside her mind on repeat, she felt vaguely annoyed that Archer knew her well enough to make that kind of call. She'd purposely been keeping him at arm's length.

After Stella and Gladys bid her farewell, she turned back to her computer to finish her research, but didn't feel much like continuing to follow Dew Valley's trail. Perhaps running into Stella had caused a tendril of guilt to sneak into her subconscious. But it didn't feel right investigating the murder of her husband when they were sharing the same space. Especially when Cordelia was holding information that could potentially help the sheriff.

She waved goodbye to Martina and stepped outside to call her momma.

"Is this my darling daughter, Cordelia?" Sherilynn's overly enthusiastic greeting made the muscles of Cordelia's back clench.

She only did that when she was gearing up for a lecture. "Because I thought she'd been kidnapped."

"You can't kidnap adults, Momma. 'Kid' is literally in the word." That wasn't actually true, but it sounded good when she said it.

"Fine." Sherilynn blew out a puff of air. "Abducted, taken, what have you. It's been a week since you dropped that bomb on me then disappeared into the ether."

"Five days," Cordelia said.

"As good as a week! Do you know what that's done to my blood pressure?"

Cordelia couldn't imagine it had done any worse than those licorice ropes and salty chips she liked to eat by the bag, but being a good Texas daughter, she rarely sassed her momma. "I'm sorry I haven't called sooner. Things have been a little wild around here."

"Wild how?" When her momma took that tone, the one suggesting that the person on the receiving end better not think of lying, she could make a freight train take a dirt road.

"Nothing I can't handle." Cordelia injected a brightness into her voice she wasn't altogether feeling to keep her momma from prying too deep. "Figuring out the logistics of moving and navigating a new job are all difficult prospects."

"You could just move back here."

"Momma."

"I know, I know. You're an adult, living your own life, which somehow ended up including the running of a cathouse, but I don't judge. I do worry though. Have you met anyone nice?"

The hopeful note in her momma's tone made Cordelia cringe. She might've raised Cordelia in an unconventional manner, but she was still a Texas momma through and through. The fact that her thirty-year-old daughter hadn't settled down with a gaggle of kids yet was a serious point of concern for Sherilynn.

"I've met lots of nice people. Small towns are full of them."

"Don't give me lip, Cordelia Mae. You know what I meant. I swear you can be as obtuse as your daddy." It had been a few years since Sherilynn had brought up her no-good abandoning ex without prompting, and while Cordelia's warning signals went on high alert, her momma didn't mention him with the same anger and bitterness of her childhood. Sometimes progress took a few decades. "I meant have you met any nice gentlemen." A pause. "Or ladies."

It had taken Sherilynn a minute to understand the meaning of the word "bisexual." She hadn't been hateful or upset about it, just out of touch. She often became awkward around the subject, unsure of how to phrase things without accidentally saying something offensive out of ignorance, but her heart was always in the right place.

"No, I haven't met anyone yet." Cordelia pointedly did not mention Archer. She'd already had enough of that during her run-in with Stella. "I'm still getting settled."

"I think I ought to come visit you."

Cordelia's heart dropped to her stomach. "No, Momma. It's really not necessary."

"Nonsense. I was already feeling some type of way when you lied to me about Sarsaparilla Falls. I don't trust that town. If I could see how you're faring for myself and make sure people are treating you right, I think I'd feel much better about you being there."

"Now is really not a good time. I'm still getting myself sorted, and you know how much of a bear I can be when I'm out of sorts. Not to mention how busy you must be with the store."

"I got a part-timer now. I can take a few days off. Why don't we plan for next month?"

"Sure." Cordelia pressed her finger and thumb against her

eyes as she attempted to thwart her growing headache. "We can see about next month."

Cordelia hung up with her momma and rested her back against the stone hedge that separated the public sidewalk from the library's front lawn. She didn't want her momma anywhere near Sarsaparilla Falls, but it was becoming evident she wouldn't be able to keep her away forever. And maybe it wouldn't be so bad now. Cordelia was so used to protecting her momma's fragile psyche that she never really learned to let go and trust her momma could fully take care of herself now. Near twenty years sober, and Cordelia still worried the littlest things could send her momma flying off the wagon.

Putting the unsettling call behind her, Cordelia stood to head into town. There was a little dress shop at the corner of Main that had been a video rental store twenty years ago. It was rare for Cordelia to wear anything other than a pantsuit or a proper A-line skirt and shell top, but she didn't think either of those would be appropriate for a date with Archer. Of course, she still had to see how the mustache was coming in.

Voices from down the walk a piece had her ducking behind the hedge. She'd be able to pick out Edna's shrill tone with two bits of cotton stuffed in her ears, but she didn't recognize the gentleman she was arguing with. He had wide-set eyes, hair as black as Edna's soul, and a bald patch that shined under the midday sun. His ill-fitting suit was the color of oatmeal, and he had three gold rings on each hand. He didn't look local. There was an air about him. Her momma would call it a polished turd. Bad vibes. They wafted around him like heat off a ghost pepper.

Cordelia moved around the other side of the hedge, letting the stone facade conceal her as she inched closer to Edna and the mystery man.

"I already told you it's going to take more time," Edna said.

Cordelia flattened her back against the hedge and slid down until her rear hit the short grass of the library's lawn. "The untimely passing of Penelope West put a wrench in the plans."

The man responded, but his voice was so low and raspy, he might as well have been talking through a paper tube on the other side of the street.

"We tried another angle, and that fell through too." Edna tried to keep her voice down, but a flock of seagulls screeching over a discarded hot dog made less noise. "Corbin is working on the county tax collector, but even that's taking more time since his daddy's contact retired. He's having to start from scratch. We need another two weeks. At least."

The man responded again, and Cordelia risked lifting her head to get her ear above the hedge, but it was no use. This seedy man in Edna's company was clearly someone accustomed to not wanting to be heard, and knew just how to go about it.

"I'll tell Corbin." Edna's voice had gone from shrill and pleading to downright despondent. Whatever the man had told her wasn't sitting right with her, but she still deferred to him. The red flags rose a little higher on the pole.

Cordelia would bet dollars to donuts the other angle they had tried to get their hands on the Chickadee was framing Daisy for the pastor's murder. Edna's certain guilt only solidified itself in Cordelia's mind. Now she just needed to figure out who this apparent accomplice was.

At the sound of footsteps fading away, Cordelia stood and straightened her skirt. The mystery man had disappeared, as if he'd been conjured from a portal to another dimension, but the bad vibes lingered. Cordelia rubbed her arms against the chill. Whoever he was, Edna and Corbin were in deep with him, and it appeared they'd made some promises regarding the Chickadee they couldn't possibly make good on.

Edna had picked up a brisk pace and had just rounded the corner, but Cordelia still had time to catch up if she hurried. Running along the grass, she hit the stairs and took them two at a time until she reached the sidewalk. From there, she traced Edna's steps until she caught sight of her again, standing outside the bank, exchanging heated words with Corbin.

Cordelia pulled her sunglasses out of her purse and slipped them on. Edging in closer, she peeked around buildings and slipped under awnings. Once she reached the hardware store, she hid in the alcove that marked the entrance.

"He's not giving us more time," Edna said. "You need to move on the Chickadee now."

Move on the Chickadee how? Just what were these two sneaks up to? Corbin had obviously tried his daddy's tactics and failed, much to Cordelia's relief. She wouldn't let the Chickadee go without a fight, but she was hardly up-to-date on tax laws either. The only thing she could do was suss out their plans and hope she could slap them with a murder charge before they made good on whatever deal they had made.

"I'm doing my best. We just need to put him off a little longer." Corbin glanced down the street, his puckered eyes squinting at passersby. Cordelia pressed herself farther against the wall of the hardware store entrance. "Come on, let's get inside."

They disappeared into the bank, and Cordelia moved to follow when a big set of hands clamped down on her shoulders. A short scream got stuck in her throat. Swinging around, she plunged her hand into her purse, ready to retrieve her pepper spray, when Archer's amused grin stopped her in her tracks.

It had only taken him five days, but he'd fully grown his mustache back.

Chapter Eighteen

WHEN ARCHER SAID HE WAS TAKING HER ON A DATE, CORDELIA DIDN'T know what to expect. Archer wasn't what she'd call a predictable sort. He was just as liable to take her to a possum roast in a barnyard hayloft as he was to bring her to a five-star restaurant with all the fixings.

Since he didn't give her a dress code, she ended up going with a cotton sundress she'd gotten from Tilly's Closet, the dress shop on the corner of Main. The owner, Tilly Gomez-Esteban, had been a grade ahead of Cordelia and spent a few years living in Austin before coming back to Sarsaparilla Falls to care for her father. She made polite conversation with Cordelia, but it was clear she didn't remember her from school or approve of her current position at the Chickadee. At least she wasn't nasty like Edna.

Cordelia ended up walking out of the shop with a butter-yellow dress that hit just below her knees, with little white flowers embroidered into the gauzy fabric. It was the softest piece of clothing she owned, and she wondered if wearing it would send the wrong message. She didn't want Archer to start thinking she was the kind of woman who picked wildflowers in an open field with a baby on each hip. Her professional attire was a much more comfortable fit for her personality, but it didn't feel right for a date, so here she stood in her apartment, wringing her hands and second-guessing all the poor decisions that had led her up to this point.

Daisy had come over earlier to help Cordelia with her hair and makeup, and it turned out Daisy had a deft hand for a natural look; she just preferred the big hair and bright lips that had become her signature over the years. The result of her subtler work left Cordelia stunned. She'd worried she'd end up looking like she had on the night she'd shown up at Archer's office in a trench coat and not much else, but Daisy had curled her hair into loose flowing ringlets and touched up her eyes just enough to make them shine a little brighter.

"You're going to have that man eating out of your hand by the end of the night, Miss Cordelia." Daisy dashed a light layer of blush over Cordelia's cheeks. "I don't think you even realize what kind of power you wield."

"I think I'm beginning to learn."

Cordelia had never considered herself particularly powerful or standout in any way, but living with the chicks had changed something in her. It gave her a whole new level of respect for women who knew their worth and lived on their own terms. She didn't even realize she'd built her entire sense of self around the expectations of others until she broke from the mold she'd created to cope with her past and started a new life outside of society's definition of pleasing.

Daisy kissed her on the cheek, then scolded herself and removed the lipstick stain before giving her a hug and exiting her apartment. Leaving Cordelia alone to stew. She'd just talked herself out of the whole date idea when Archer knocked on her front door.

He handed her a bouquet of pink carnations. "These always reminded me of you."

"Carnations remind you of me? Why is that?" Both surprised and delighted, Cordelia set the flowers near her sink to tend to when she got home.

"Their scent. A little sweet. A little spicy." His mouth ticked up on one side in a crooked grin. "I sent you a letter with a picture I'd drawn of them when you moved away, though you probably don't remember that."

"Those were carnations?" Cordelia choked on a laugh. Unbelievable. All those years she thought he'd been comparing her to a pile of garbage.

"Okay, that's a fair question." He rubbed the back of his neck. "My art skills weren't the best at ten. I guess that explains why you didn't write me back? Broke my heart."

"I thought you hated me." Everything she ever thought she'd known about Archer Reed-Smythe had just gotten turned on its head. She wasn't sure how to process it. "You always said the meanest things, and you were such a troublemaker."

"I'd like to blame that on being a dumb kid." He gave her a look. "But I'm still known to cause trouble from time to time."

Cordelia pursed her lips. "I don't doubt that."

"Pretty sure I've been in nothing but trouble since you've come back to town." He offered her his arm like a proper gentleman in a black-and-white movie.

Milkmaids couldn't dream of churning butter as smooth as Archer. She wasn't used to dating people with moves. Most of her past lovers had about as much charisma as a ream of printer paper. They were easy to manage. Uncomplicated. Neutral.

Archer wasn't any of those things.

They passed by Belinda Sue's room, and three sets of eyes peeked through slats in the closed blinds. The chicks would be expecting company of their own any minute, now that the Chickadee was busier than ever, but they cleared their schedule to watch their madam leave on her first date in years like a pack of protective aunties. This must've been what all those other people who had big, meddling extended families felt like, and she'd be lying if she'd said it didn't feel nice to have someone looking out for her for once.

Archer opened the passenger side for Cordelia, and warmth bloomed over her face as his gaze lingered on her bare legs before he closed the door. As they drove into town, he talked about a case he was working on involving a high-profile criminal named Sean O'Leary, who was trying to control the oil fields in the area by taking over the small towns that made up a county voting bloc. Archer couldn't say too much on account of official business, but if Cordelia was to read between the lines, it sounded like Sean O'Leary had his sights set on Sarsaparilla Falls.

Twenty minutes outside of town, near the town of Cherry Hill, Archer pulled up to a Mexican restaurant with open patio seating and twinkle lights threaded through the lattice panels that sectioned off the space. The drone of cicadas hummed in the air. While the restaurant looked as though it had popped up in the middle of nowhere, they couldn't be that far from town. The parking lot was packed and the sound of conversation and laughter filtered out the open doors.

"La Mariposa Plateada is the best-kept secret in Cherry Hill." Archer took Cordelia's hand as he helped her out of his truck, his eyes once again drifting to the places where her bare skin was exposed to the cool night air. "It's owned by Martina Ruiz's family."

"I didn't know her family owned a restaurant." Cordelia had spent plenty of time in Martina's company at the library, and she never mentioned it.

"It's not something she makes public anymore. People used to suck up to her, hoping to get special treatment or reservations on certain holidays."

Cordelia pursed her lips. "Is the food that good?"

"The best I've ever had. And lucky for me, Martina is invested in you having a good time tonight, so she pulled a few strings."

"Lucky for both of us then."

Cordelia was not used to the princess treatment, and it made her vaguely uncomfortable in a way she couldn't put her finger on. Like she hadn't done anything to earn it. It didn't occur to her that being treated well didn't have to come with conditions. All her exes had been raised on concrete and only knew the city life of moving from one point to another as fast as possible, leaving behind anyone who couldn't keep up.

The host led them to a quiet table at the back of the restaurant with soft lighting and the illusion of privacy, thanks to the hundred-gallon saltwater tank that formed a barrier between the intimate tables in back and the noisier ones at the front of the house.

A baby-faced waiter with a chin pimple promptly headed over to take their drink orders in a polite and practiced voice. Cordelia pointed to a random item on the menu, not even bothering to check if it was nonalcoholic. Her focus was glued to the fish tank.

Cordelia had point-blank asked Martina about local pet shops, coral, and the care of saltwater tanks, and Martina had sent her to the hospital to find answers. Why? She must've known her family owned a restaurant with a much more impressive tank than the one in the hospital lobby. Unless she didn't want Cordelia to know about it, but then why would she allow Archer to make short-notice reservations?

Cordelia's head swam in more circles than the tropical fish chasing one another around the gently swaying seaweed. None of it made sense.

"It's something else, isn't it?" Archer nodded to the tank.

"It sure is." Cordelia's eyes roamed over the tiny ecosystem at work.

Seahorses, clownfish, and brightly colored species she'd only ever seen in movies danced around one another. Plants dotted with a bioluminescent glow swayed in the bubbling water. A charming castle with a thick patina created hiding holes for the more timid fish. And scattered along the bottom were round lumps of coral with thick neon-green fibers growing off the individual spores. Palytoxin. The only sample of the neurotoxin Cordelia had been able to find within a fifty-mile radius.

And it was located in the restaurant owned by Martina's family. Martina, who had a very public feud with the pastor over books. Someone Cordelia had never considered a suspect, never questioned, because she'd been helpful and friendly and forthcoming. And because she acted as if she knew nothing about coral or saltwater tanks.

"Is everything okay?" Archer asked. "You seem distracted."

Cordelia cleared her throat and tried her best to smile. She couldn't tell Archer what was bothering her without spilling all the details about the wine, moving his father's body, tricking him to gain access to his labs. Suddenly, this date had become a lot more complicated.

While Archer tried to engage her in conversation, she kept sneaking side glances at the tank. The waiter set a frothy drink with a pineapple garnish in front of her, and she took a sip, nearly gagging as the acidic burn of fruity vodka hit her throat. She quickly ordered water and hoped Archer wouldn't notice the way she'd pushed her other drink to the side. She needed a clear head and as many wits about her as she could keep for the evening.

Cordelia opened the menu. "What would you recommend?"

"We have to get the guac and chips. The apple straws are a turnoff for some people, but one bite and you'll swear you've never tasted something so good in your life."

"I'll take your word for it." Cordelia flipped the menu over to figure out which drink she'd ordered, and her heart stopped. There, at the top of the wine list, was Dew Valley Cabernet.

Cordelia's hands started shaking so badly she dropped the menu. "Excuse me, I'm just going to run to the ladies' room. Can you order for me?"

She didn't care what he picked. Her stomach rolled so hard, she didn't have a prayer of keeping any kind of food down. Val had said she had an exclusive contract with five restaurants. Cordelia had only found two at the library before she'd run into Stella and given up for the day. What were the odds of palytoxin and Dew Valley sharing the same space? The poisoned wine had to have come from here. It was too coincidental.

"Are you sure you're okay?" Archer stood as she did, concern etched into every feature on his ruggedly handsome face. "If this place is too much . . ."

"No." Cordelia's voice cracked, prompting her to take another drink of the pineapple monstrosity. Her throat burned and her head became fuzzy around the edges. "No, this restaurant is lovely. I'm just"—what could she say?—"having female problems."

In a manner of speaking.

Before Archer could say another word, she grabbed her purse and rushed to the back of the restaurant, nearly ramming into their waiter on his way back to the table. She had Daisy's number pulled up and ringing as she pushed the door open. La Mariposa Plateada was fancy enough to have a waiting room in the restroom. Cordelia sat on the edge of the white leather couch, tapping the toe of her sandal on the ground as her phone continued to dial.

Daisy's voicemail picked up, so she tried Belinda Sue next. Arline didn't believe in cell phones, so there was no point in trying to reach her. She rang Daisy three more times in a row before she finally picked up. The gruff sound of an older man laughing in the background filtered through the other end of the line.

"Miss Cordelia?" Daisy's breathless voice hitched with worry. "What's going on? Did your date go sour?"

"Not yet." Cordelia glanced at the door as it swung open, bringing in two tipsy women and the scent of apple body spray. "I'm just not sure how I'm supposed to sit through dinner and act like everything is normal when we're seated next to a saltwater tank with palytoxin growing on the coral and Dew Valley Cabernet on the menu."

"No." Muffled static crackled in Cordelia's ear as Daisy placed her hand over the receiver and told her client she needed to step out for a minute. "Okay. Dill is going to take a breather. Where are you?"

"At La Mariposa Plateada." Cordelia glanced around again and lowered her voice. "A restaurant owned by Martina Ruiz's family."

"Ooh, the stew is thickening." The click of Daisy's heel against the concrete came through the line. "What should we do with this information?"

Cordelia rubbed her thumb over a hangnail. "I was hoping you'd have some ideas."

"I'm not the ideas gal, that's more Belinda Sue's thing, but I just heard a whip crack and Bradley Wipple begging for his life in her room, so I'm not inclined to go tapping on her door at the moment."

Cordelia squeezed her eyes shut to block out the image her mind conjured. "Do you think I ought to come home early?"

"Absolutely not." Daisy shrieked as if it were her evening in jeopardy. "There's nothing we can do about this tonight, so you might as well go on back to dinner and enjoy yourself. I'd stay clear of the wine though. Just in case."

Cordelia hung up with Daisy and washed her hands. Staring

at her drawn reflection in the mirror, she patted cold water over her cheeks. How had this date gone so far off the rails? Archer could already tell she was twitchy, and she couldn't tell him it had nothing to do with him without giving away what was really going on.

Pulling herself together, Cordelia pushed open the restroom door and headed back to the table. But instead of finding an appetizer waiting, Archer stood next to their table like he was ready to leave. Cordelia approached cautiously, not saying anything, just giving him a curious look. She didn't want to manifest bad vibes and ask if he was calling off the date.

"I just took an interesting phone call." The grim set of Archer's expression didn't bode well for Cordelia, but she kept her expression neutral and her hands knotted behind her back.

"Oh?" She tried not to blink too much as her thoughts cascaded over one another, giving rise to intrusive, panic-stricken scenarios. "From who?"

"From the lab in Dallas. It seems like they received a toxicology sample from me the night you showed up at my office in that trench coat and left as soon as the courier arrived. Funny thing." He gave her a long look. "I didn't submit a toxicology sample to the lab."

Cordelia glanced between the saltwater tank and Archer. Sweat pooled at her spine. Feeling trapped and borderline claustrophobic, she did the only thing a reasonable woman in her position could do. She turned around and ran.

Chapter Nineteen

"JUST HOLD ON A SECOND." IN THE PARKING LOT, ARCHER WRAPPED HIS arms around her waist and pulled her tight against his broad chest. "Where did you plan on going?"

In hindsight, Cordelia could see it had been a mistake to run. She had no car, she didn't know the area, and she couldn't see any lights other than those surrounding the restaurant. Her flight-or-fight response had kicked in though, and she'd always considered herself a pacifist. That didn't leave her a lot of choices as far as nature was concerned.

Now, her pride offered her no option other than to see this through. She elbowed Archer in the stomach. He released a short grunt, but that didn't loosen his hold. Were the man's arms made of iron? How was it possible he could hold her so tight without hurting her?

Trying another tactic, she went limp. "You win."

He laughed against her ear and the vibration of it sent a shiver all the way down to her toes. Pressed this close together, there was no hiding her reaction to him. He released her and turned her around before he embarrassed them both.

"Why in the hell are you running?" He crossed his arms over his chest, and Cordelia lost a few shreds of dignity staring at the impression that made with his sleeves rolled up.

"It seemed like a good idea at the time."

Archer blew out a frustrated breath. "What did you submit to the lab? And how did you get my passcodes to delete the results? Just so you know, if you plan on pulling a stunt like that in the future, the FBI does surprise audits of our systems every month to ensure we're not compromised."

Cordelia would walk over hot coals before she'd betray Arline. "I'm not sure what you mean. I didn't submit anything to the lab."

His amused expression turned hard. The look in his bourbon eyes chilled her down to the bones, despite the air hovering at a balmy eighty degrees. "Don't toy with me, Delia. Tampering with the FBI is a federal offense."

"Are you going to arrest me?"

"I should," he muttered. Pacing back and forth in front of her, he ran his hands through his dark hair, causing the curled ends to stand up at unruly angles. Cordelia wished the effect had been a little less appealing. "Just tell me what you submitted."

"I'm afraid I can't do that."

He stopped in front of her. "Why not?"

"Because I didn't submit anything."

"I swear to God." He raised his eyes heavenward, as if praying for patience that had no intention of being delivered. "You could drive a man to drink."

"If you need help with that, I know people in the AA."

He held up a finger, walked away, paced a few feet, then returned. "I think I'm going to drive you home now."

"That's probably a good idea."

Without another word, they headed back to his truck. Ever the Texas gentleman, Archer still opened the door for her and offered her his hand so she could boost herself into the seat.

Cordelia tried to ignore the way her skin tingled when they touched. It was just chemistry. No big deal. That didn't mean they were compatible in any other way.

They drove back in silence, Archer tapping his fingers on the steering wheel to a beat only he could hear. Cordelia stared out the window, watching the open plains scroll by. It wouldn't be the worst thing in the world to confide in Archer. He'd probably listen in that open, honest way of his, and she didn't think he'd actually turn her in to the sheriff. But it was too late to start over. She'd chosen to deceive him and she wouldn't sell out Arline to make it right.

He pulled up outside the Chickadee and opened the passenger door for her, helping her down. Frustration and annoyance vibrated off him like a fiddle string pulled taut, but he didn't push her further, understanding his efforts would've been futile.

She turned to walk across the parking lot when he stopped her. "Delia."

She turned around. "Yes?"

With his tense stance and his hat pulled low enough to shield his eyes, he looked every part the detached FBI agent. "I'm going to find out what you submitted to the lab, and if I find out Daisy played a hand in my father's death, there will be hell to pay for the Chickadee."

With that, he got into his truck and drove away.

Cordelia blew out a long breath. Archer would make good on his threat, of that she had no doubt. But she also had a solid lead to chase for the first time and a limited amount of time left on her hands before everything came crashing down. Not wasting another second on regrets as far as Archer was concerned, she went back to her apartment and fired up the internet.

It was time to get to the bottom of just how closely the pastor was linked to Martina Ruiz.

Cordelia passed the pool to find the chicks already gathered for an impromptu happy hour. Despite it being close to ten at night, Belinda Sue passed around mimosas made up of Minute Maid orange juice and Five O'Clock vodka. Thinking of Archer's words just an hour earlier, about how she could drive a man to drink, Cordelia once again abstained.

"How did your date go?" Daisy asked.

"Not well." Cordelia filled them in on the details. "If he finds out about the palytoxin, I'm scared he's going to point the sheriff in this direction again."

"He's not going to find out." Belinda Sue smacked her palm hard enough to make Cordelia jump. "We'll wrap this up before he gets the chance."

"What do we know about Martina other than she works at a library, her family owns the best Mexican restaurant in three counties, and she don't like book banners?" Daisy had a pink notebook and fuzzy pen balanced on her crossed knee, ready to take notes. The full moon and light from the pool gave her plenty of illumination. "There's got to be something we missed."

"What about that rumor that went around a few years back about her hooking up with Stewart Combs in the World Religion section and nearly losing her job when a board member happened to stop in that day and catch Stewart with his hand up her shirt?" Belinda Sue asked. "Stewart ended up breaking things off because the pastor didn't approve of one of his deacons carrying on with Martina on account of her being agnostic."

"Being agnostic was worse than hooking up in a public library?" Cordelia asked.

Belinda Sue shrugged. "I don't much get the rules of religion myself, but it's my understanding that it's right up there with murder and blasphemy."

"Of all the ridiculous . . ." Cordelia cut herself off. She didn't much understand religion herself, and so made a point not to make too many judgments about it. "I suppose that's a lead we could follow. Should we talk to Stewart first?"

Daisy waggled her eyebrows. "Arline could talk to Stewart."

"We don't do a whole lot of talking," Arline said. "Don't see why we'd start now."

Belinda Sue held out her hands. "Here's what we're going to do. We're going to go to church." When she was met with a collective groan, she gave the three of them a sharp stink eye. "I'm being serious here. We should've been going the whole time. Church is a hotbed of gossip and manners. That's where we'll really be able to suss out who's doing what."

"Or who," Daisy added.

Cordelia couldn't deny that Belinda Sue had a point. One of the reasons she'd always felt on the outside of things growing up in Sarsaparilla Falls was because her momma hadn't been allowed to attend church. It ended up cutting her off from the whole community. Of course Sherilynn's outrageous antics didn't help matters, but being barred from the church cut Cordelia off as well.

There had to be more to a community than religion though. Looking at Daisy, Belinda Sue, and Arline, Cordelia could say that for certain. Community didn't have to be made up of shared beliefs or common grounds. Sometimes it existed in the respect of differences and the desire to have old ways of thinking challenged. No good ever came from standing still.

"I'm with Belinda Sue on this," Cordelia said. "We're not going to learn anything new by sitting around here and making assumptions."

"I'll wait outside and see how it goes." Arline crossed her arms. "If y'all make it past the threshold without turning to ash, I'll consider following you in."

On Sunday morning Cordelia stood outside her car, waiting for the chicks to finish getting ready. Belinda Sue was the only one who had done any churching growing up, so walking through the finer details of appropriate attire had been an exercise in patience. While Daisy made a solid point when she said God wouldn't care too much about what they looked like as long as they showed up, it still wasn't a good-enough reason to walk into the Holy Cross Episcopal Church wearing hot shorts and a halter top.

The three of them ended up raiding Arline's closet, since the floral caftans she preferred were about as close as they were going to get to church dresses. Cordelia wore one of her trim A-line skirts and cream tops with a matching jacket. She looked ready for a business interview, which wasn't much different from any other day.

As they pulled into the parking lot, Cordelia tried to ignore the double takes. The people of Sarsaparilla Falls might've respected the Chickadee, but that didn't mean they wanted to be reminded of their sins when they were trying to pretend to be holy.

"Why's everyone staring at us?" Daisy asked. "Did we wear the wrong thing?"

"Folks in this town prefer to keep their vices and their morals separate, if you know what I mean. Plus, they're probably mad they don't look as good as us." Belinda Sue looped her arm through Daisy's, leading the way into the church. "Come on. Let's give 'em hell."

Cordelia followed, with Arline bringing up the rear, refusing to enter before Daisy and Belinda Sue as promised. The inside of the church was large and open, so different from the maze of halls and doors in the labyrinth beneath the area of worship. Thick maroon carpet blanketed the floor, while the pristine white walls made the space look much bigger than it was in actuality. A large wooden cross stood behind a podium with a microphone, and a stained-glass window depicting Jesus with a lamb allowed a kaleidoscope of colored light to stream through.

The effect was intimidating, but maybe that was what they'd been going for. Her momma used to say half of religion was based on how well a preacher could scare people into trying to buy their way to heaven. Cordelia shuffled into a pew at the back with the rest of the chicks.

"I heard they're bringing in guest pastors until they can hire someone to fill the role," Daisy whispered. "So the person speaking today might not be here for good."

Cordelia didn't much care who was speaking. Her attention was more focused on the odd looks they kept getting as more patrons shuffled in and headed toward the front. A few people waved, but this wasn't like the grocery store. It was clear this was the one place in town where the chicks didn't belong.

Daisy shifted in her seat. "Should we be sitting all the way back here? I feel like people keep looking at us like we're the bad kids in class."

"We *are* the bad kids," Belinda Sue said. "Not much we can do about that."

Stella entered the church with her friend Gladys and stopped short when she spotted Cordelia and the chicks. Offering a tentative smile, she rushed forward and took a seat near the front, not daring to look back. As if she didn't want the parishioners to think she approved of the chicks being in church. Never mind that the entire congregation knew where her dearly departed husband spent his Friday nights.

"I'm not sure how this is going to help us if no one even wants to meet our eyes," Daisy said. "They don't know we eat supper before saying grace."

"Just observe," Cordelia said. "You can tell a lot about people by watching them."

Cordelia meant to follow her own advice, but she couldn't keep her gaze from wandering to Stella and wondering if Archer was going to show up and join her in the front row. Would he be mad that she'd shown up at his daddy's church? Or would he file it away under his building belief that Daisy had done something wrong and Cordelia was helping cover it up?

It wasn't long before the guest pastor took the altar to begin the service, and still no sign of Archer. Maybe he was busy with work, or maybe he'd never gotten in the habit of attending church after his years as a child forced him into it. Either way, he wasn't here, and for that Cordelia could breathe a little easier.

After the service, during which Cordelia had to elbow Arline in the ribs several times when she began to snore, they headed outside. Daisy filled a coffee cup with sugar donut holes while she promenaded around the lot like a Pomeranian at a dog show. Stewart Combs, the man they'd been hoping to question, wasn't anywhere to be seen either. After standing around long enough to fulfill her duty, Arline clomped back to the car.

Cordelia sidled up next to Belinda Sue. "Are you about ready?"

"In a few," Belinda Sue whispered out of the side of her mouth. "That's Edwin Combs Daisy is talking to. I'll bet she's finding out where Stewart's gone off to."

While she waited for Daisy to finish her conversation, Cordelia took in the small clusters and groupings that made up the town's social networks. The handful of ladies whose husbands weren't allowed near the Chickadee stood together in a tightly knit pack, staring down their noses at everyone else around them. Their husbands stood in their own circle talking about the latest high school football game and rehashing their own glory days. Edna and Corbin were among them, which didn't surprise Cordelia in the least.

On the other side of the parking lot stood a larger group of women. The ones who did allow their husbands to frequent the Chickadee. They flitted around the smaller circles they made, laughing louder than was acceptable by the standards of the buttoned-up crowd. Their groups of men and women mingled. In general, they seemed more relaxed. More comfortable in their own skins. Probably because they were all getting what they needed out of life.

And separated from the two groups were Stella and Gladys. Cordelia would've thought that being the previous pastor's wife gave Stella some standing. But it didn't seem like either group tried to bring her into their fold, and she didn't appear to make an effort to gain their favor either. Occasionally, people from the other side would cross the lot and talk to people who had pull in the community, like the bank manager's wife or a councilman, but none of them approached Stella. It was like she was on an island. Cordelia wasn't sure what to make of that.

She'd just taken a step forward to speak to Stella when Daisy grabbed her elbow. "I got the goods on Stewart. Let's get back to the Chickadee before the folks who don't want us here decide to toss us in the river to see if we float."

Chapter Twenty

DAISY REFUSED TO TELL THEM ANYTHING UNTIL THEY GOT BACK TO the Chickadee. They stopped at the H-E-B and picked up a plate of fried chicken, potato salad, and cowboy beans. They wanted to have a proper lunch for surviving their first Sunday at church.

Cordelia wanted to do a picnic and spread a blanket out on the concrete around the pool, but none of the chicks wanted to sit on the ground on account of not being sure if they'd be able to get back up. So they pulled chairs around a table with a pink umbrella and ate in the shade.

Arline tore into a drumstick, lips smacking as she stared Daisy down.

"I'm getting there." Daisy scooped a dainty spoonful of beans onto her paper plate. "Just hold your horses. There's a lot going on in the Combs camp."

"Such as?" Belinda Sue tapped a single bloodred nail against the clear tabletop, refusing to take any food until they had a good handle on their current lead.

"Okay." Daisy draped a napkin over her lap. "Apparently, Stewart and Martina are still very much a thing, and the reason he wasn't there today is because they do a lot of anti–book banning work in San Antonio on the weekends. Not by his choice."

"What do you mean, not by his choice?" Cordelia asked.

"According to Edwin, Mack Baker and Dean Hernandez cornered Stewart at the Orb one night and told him the pastor sent them to say he wasn't welcome at church if he was going to continue seeing that purveyor of porn. That's what they call librarians now. Can you believe that? For giving kids access to books. I'll never understand. Anyway, they told him this a week before the poisoning, and he wasn't in church that first Sunday after the pastor turned up dead."

Arline dropped her drumstick. "What are you saying?"

"I'm not saying anything." Daisy held out her hands. "I'm just passing along info."

"It sounds like we ought to add Stewart to our suspect list." As much as the saltwater tank and Dew Valley threw off Cordelia's equilibrium, she couldn't see Martina as a killer. Much easier for her to picture Stewart Combs, whom she didn't know and had no relationship with.

"Maybe." Daisy tapped her lips. "But I don't think the pastor would've removed Stewart. Mack and Dean like to throw their weight around and act bigger than their britches."

"The pastor wasn't innocent." Mack and Dean didn't sound like good people, but Cordelia couldn't forget how firm the pastor had been on banning her momma from church, never opening his doors or his heart, even when she was struggling to get clean.

"We can talk about this until the cows come home," Belinda Sue said. "But we're not going to solve anything by arguing about the character of a man who is dead and gone. What we need to do is establish Stewart's and Martina's whereabouts the night the pastor was poisoned. Daisy, are you sure he got that bottle of wine the night he came to see you and not before?"

Daisy nodded. "He said he got it as a gift on his way over and thought about bringing it home, but wanted to drink it with me instead. I had to decline, though, because of the rules."

"Why don't you pull up the community events website?" Arline asked. "The church is always doing this and that in town. Find out where the pastor was before he came here and make a list of who would've been with him before that."

Belinda Sue turned to Arline, resting her cheek on her fist. "You really ought to speak up more often. You end up being the smartest of us all."

"And I stay that way by staying quiet." Arline grunted. "Kids these days just want to hear themselves talk. Got no respect for listening."

Belinda Sue, Arline, and Daisy gathered around Belinda Sue's tablet to look into community events, while Cordelia used her phone to go on the library's website. She hoped to find an event that crossed over with the church. Instead, what she found proved Martina's and Stewart's innocence beyond a shadow of a doubt.

"Have a look at this." Cordelia handed the phone to Belinda Sue.

The three of them enlarged a picture of Martina at a national library conference in Oklahoma the day the pastor was killed. She hadn't returned until that Sunday afternoon. A man with a wide grin and thinning hair stood next to her with his arm around her shoulders.

"That's Martina and Stewart." Belinda Sue tapped the screen. "They couldn't have given the pastor the wine. They weren't even in town."

"That's what I figured." Cordelia slumped in her chair.

On one hand, she'd formed a tentative friendship with Martina and was happy she wasn't a killer. But on the other hand, they weren't any closer to clearing Daisy. Trying to sort out small-town scandals from actual clues was like trying to divide oysters and clams.

"So that's that," Arline said. "Where do we go from here?"

"I think we ought to refocus our efforts on looking into Edna and Corbin," Belinda Sue said. "They've had the best motive to date, and the only thing we've uncovered about them is that Edna had a questionable conversation with a shady gentleman near the library."

"I'm not ruling them out, but what do you propose we do?" Cordelia asked. "There's no way they'll answer any of our questions or let us get close enough to find evidence."

"I have an idea," Belinda Sue said. "And you're not going to like it."

"You're right," Cordelia said. "I don't like this."

Cordelia stood next to the card stock at the local drugstore, turning the metal rack as she searched for a professional-looking invitation. Daisy and Arline had insisted on coming along, despite it being against Belinda Sue's better judgment. They ended up causing a ruckus in the candy aisle, arguing over the last bag of Tootsie Roll Pops. At least they managed to draw everyone's attention away from Cordelia and Belinda Sue. Though they weren't exactly inconspicuous either. A sixty-year-old woman in a leather catsuit was bound to stick out.

"Do you really think they're going to buy this?" Cordelia asked.

"Of course they will," Belinda Sue said. "Edna and Corbin like nothing more than feeling important. By the time they figure out the midnight auction is a ruse, we'll be well clear of their property."

It had been Belinda Sue's idea to break into the office building Corbin had built on the speck of land he'd been able to purchase out in the brush country, not too far from the Chickadee. At first, they'd considered waiting until the place went dark, then sneaking over. But it never went dark. Belinda Sue figured

Corbin must've been sleeping there, because no matter what time they drove by, the lights were on and Corbin's truck was parked at the end of the long, dusty driveway leading up to the outpost he'd set up.

He had to have been protecting something important if he put that much effort into keeping the space guarded like that.

So Belinda Sue had come up with a plan to lure Corbin and Edna out of town with a fake midnight auction in Crystal Creek, an exclusive event attended by local leaders in business. It took at least an hour to drive to Crystal Creek, and another hour to drive back once they figured out it was all a hoax.

Cordelia had a bad feeling about the whole thing, but Belinda Sue's confidence in the plan gave her a boost to push forward. And at this point, they were out of other options. It would only be a matter of time before Honey was cleared, Archer's suspicions would boil over, and all eyes would be on Daisy again.

"None of these are fancy enough." Belinda Sue frowned over the display of cards. "We've got to be convincing if we're going to make this work."

Cordelia's phone buzzed. Daisy had stopped fighting with Arline long enough to text her that Archer had just entered the store. "Dang it. I don't need this right now."

"Need what?" Belinda Sue asked.

"Nothing." Cordelia pointed to a YOU'RE INVITED card off the rack with a fancy wooden mandala carved into the thick stock paper. "This one will work."

Cordelia power walked down the aisle, hoping to make a quick getaway, and ended up running smack-dab into Archer. Because of course she did.

"Archer." She tipped her chin. "Good to see you."

"Is it?" He rubbed his jaw. "Because Daisy about passed out

when she saw me, and you look as though you'd rather be anywhere else."

Why did this man insist on testing her? "Fine. It's terrible to see you. Is that better?"

"Honesty is always better." He gave her a long, searching look, but she wasn't taking the bait. "Wouldn't you agree?"

"Yes." She gave him her most prim smile.

"I heard you went to church this week." He leaned in closer, a wicked gleam in his eye and the woodsy scent of his aftershave making her head light. "You're not hoping God will absolve you, are you? Because it's a little late to ask for His help."

"It's none of your business why I was there." Cordelia turned up her nose. "I noticed you weren't present. I'm assuming it's because God already knows you're long past saving."

"One of these days, Delia, who you think I am is going to butt right up against who I actually am, and I hope I'm there to watch that pretty little head of yours explode."

"And I hope you're the one who gets stuck cleaning up the mess. If you'll excuse me . . ." She gave him her back as she walked past, letting her hips swivel only a little.

"Just so you know, I'm still keeping an eye on you," Archer called after her.

She spun around. "That's called stalking. Do I need to file an official report?"

"Not stalking." He looked her up and down, his bobbing Adam's apple betraying his appreciation. "I just have a special interest, is all."

While his obvious attraction to her made her pulse race, he could also fire her up like no one else. Then there was the small matter of being on opposing sides of his daddy's murder. As long as he suspected Daisy, she couldn't give him an inch. His loyalty was to the law, but hers was to the Chickadee, and no amount of chemistry would change that.

"Feel free to shove your interest." Unable to leave on such a sour note, lest he think he got the better of her, Cordelia reached deep into her well of good Southern manners to tack on a "Have a nice day." She marched out of the store, too riled up to wait for Belinda Sue to make up her mind about a card that probably wouldn't fool the Abernathys anyway.

Daisy wandered out next, twirling a gummy worm around her finger as she sucked on the head. "What's got your tail up, Miss Cordelia?"

"Why does Archer have to provoke me every time he sees me?" Cordelia pushed crescent-shaped indents into her palms. "It's like he can't help himself."

Daisy gave her a grin that was a shade too feline for comfort. "He likes getting a reaction out of you. I suspect he's about the only one who can make you throw a fit like that."

"I'm not throwing a fit." Cordelia ground her molars together. "I just don't like to argue and that's all he seems to want to do. No wonder our date was such a disaster."

"I think your date was a disaster because he tried too hard to impress you and ended up fumbling the ball." Daisy nudged her shoulder. "Not that he knew anything about the palytoxin or Dew Valley, but were you feeling comfortable before that?"

Cordelia let her thoughts wander back to that night. The drive over had been good. Easy. Like she could just be herself around him. All that went out the window as soon as they pulled up to the restaurant though. She appreciated the effort he'd taken, but it felt like she'd been asked to dance when she didn't know any of the steps. She clammed up and Archer stopped being himself. It had disaster written all over it from the get-go.

"Welp." Cordelia lifted her hands and dropped them back by her sides.

"Oh, honey." Daisy rubbed her back. "It's not too late to fix this. You've just got to tell him you don't need all them bells and whistles."

"Why don't I? I'm not a simple woman."

"Who called you simple?" Daisy peered around like she expected a culprit to show themselves. "You never got the chance to be comfortable with someone seeing your worth, so you still feel like you need to do something to earn it. Ain't nothing simple about that."

Cordelia gave her a wry grin. "Are you psychoanalyzing me now?"

"Just calling it like I see it." Daisy leaned against the car, chewing thoughtfully on her gummy worm. "Archer's a good egg. You ought to trust him."

Cordelia raised an eyebrow. "Trust him with what really happened to his daddy?"

Daisy shrugged. "I think he might end up surprising you."

Considering it was Daisy's freedom on the line, she should've put more stock in the advice, but Cordelia wasn't willing to take a chance on maybe being surprised by Archer. They'd gone way too far down the rabbit hole, and their only way out at this point was through.

The entrance to the drugstore flew open and Belinda Sue came running up the sidewalk like the devil himself was on her heels. Arline walked casually a few feet behind her. People out for their daily errands turned to stare at Belinda Sue as she frantically waved her arms.

"Go on, now. Get in the car." Belinda Sue dove into the back seat, grabbing Arline's caftan to pull her in, and slammed the door shut. "Let's get a move on."

Cordelia checked her rearview mirror as she backed out.

"I'm going to pretend there's a perfectly reasonable explanation for why we're rushing out of here like the law is on our tail."

"You know how you were going to buy the invitation with cash so there wouldn't be a paper trail leading to us after the break-in?" Belinda Sue asked.

"Yeah?" Cordelia bit her lower lip, already guessing where this was going.

"When you took off on me, I sort of had to steal the card."

"Okay." Cordelia breathed deeply through her nose. "I'll leave a few dollars on the counter the next time I stop in for cough syrup. Anything else I should know?"

"I've been banned from entering Parson's Drugstore for life," Arline said.

"I don't even want to know," Cordelia said.

"It's not the first time." Arline pulled out a cellophane-wrapped box containing a Cherry Blossom body mist and matching shower gel. "And they didn't catch me with this."

"The good news just keeps coming." Cordelia turned toward the dirt road that would take them back to the Chickadee, hoping their plan would work. The quicker they could be done with this nonsense, the quicker she could get back to tracking down what remained of her sanity.

Chapter Twenty-One

NEARLY A WEEK LATER, CORDELIA PARKED HER CAR, HEADLIGHTS OFF, in the middle of the brush country, a mile away from the Abernathy compound. Thanks to a conversation Daisy had overhead between Edna and Beatrice St. James at Tilly's Closet, they knew the fake midnight auction invitation had worked. They just had to sit tight and wait for Corbin to leave.

As soon as the pinpricks of light from his pickup truck disappeared into the vast plains on the way into town, Cordelia moved her car into Abernathy territory. It would take Corbin ten minutes to pick up Edna from his home base, and another hour from there to reach Crystal Creek. That bought them roughly an hour and a half to break in, search for evidence, and make their exit with plenty of time to spare. Hopefully, without Corbin being any the wiser.

Cordelia parked behind the largest building, a giant warehouse with a tin roof and corrugated walls. They had nothing but endless miles of flat plains, scrub grass, and sky at their backs. A safety precaution in case anyone came up the main road by surprise.

Arline's orthopedic shoes crunched on the hard-packed gravel behind the smallest building, a wooden structure that looked like a double-wide storage shed. Cordelia stood beside her with her hands on her hips as she surveyed the property.

None of them had ever gotten so close to the parcel of land the Abernathys protected like rabid dogs. They assumed a workspace of some kind had been built, which accounted for the large, shadowy structure that rose from the earth like the sole tomb in a long-abandoned cemetery. They hadn't been prepared for the smaller buildings that had been camouflaged by the warehouse. Or all the heavy machinery.

"What do you suppose this is about?" Cordelia nodded toward the rows of metal rods lined up on the ground, along with pieces of what looked like a pulley system.

"Oil." Arline sniffed like she could smell it in the wind. "He's got all the pieces for a rig right here. He's probably just waiting for the permits to start building."

"Or access to the right parcel of land," Belinda Sue said, a sneer curling her lip as she stood on Cordelia's opposite side. "I'm thinking this here is the real reason why he wants to get his hands on the Chickadee so bad."

"There's oil on Chickadee land?" Cordelia asked.

"Penelope thought there might be," Belinda Sue said. "Of course, she also thought there was an abandoned gold mine and buried treasure from Gulf pirates too. The Chickadee's got a whole host of legends around it, but none of them have ever been proven."

Cordelia gestured at the scene laid out before them. "Obviously, Corbin thinks some of the legends are true, but he seems to be banking an awful lot on a rumor."

"I don't think this is strictly bankrolled by Corbin," Belinda Sue said. "The Abernathys have always made their fortune in land development. Oil isn't a casual side hobby. This looks like it's got someone else's fingerprints on it."

"Who?" Cordelia asked.

"Only one way to find out." Arline took a step forward, and

Belinda Sue yanked on the back of her zebra-print caftan, dragging her back.

"We're not having a repeat of that whole debacle with the church," Belinda Sue said. "Save your bulling for someone else's china shop. Daisy's got this one."

Daisy came rushing forward, waving a small metal box in her hand. "It's been a minute since I picked a lock, but I'm sure it's like riding a bike."

Cordelia didn't know how Daisy had learned to pick locks, or why she'd needed to use that particular skill often enough for it to become as habitual as bike riding, but that was one of those questions she'd learned not to ask. Nine times out of ten, she regretted knowing the answers.

The four of them approached the warehouse first. Cordelia held her phone's flashlight up, while Daisy went to work on the giant padlock securing a set of chains wound tight around a pair of rolling metal doors. From the Chickadee, this building had looked so squat and unimpressive, but up close it was large enough to house a few planes.

Daisy muttered to herself as she dug around in the lock, waiting for the telltale click. A bead of sweat rolled down her temple. Cordelia chewed on a hangnail, trying not to put too much pressure on Daisy, but every second they spent trying to get into the warehouse was a second of searching time they lost. And they still had three more office buildings to check.

Letting loose an annoyed grunt, Arline clomped around to the other side of the warehouse. The grinding squeal of rusty hinges split the night air.

"If y'all are done playing with that lock, there's an open window back here one of you could climb into," Arline hollered.

Cordelia rushed around the corner with Daisy and Belinda Sue on her heels. Arline stood on a metal barrel and had a window six feet off the ground pushed all the way open. It would require a certain amount of upper-arm strength to pull herself up there, but Cordelia was likely the only one of them who could attempt it. She hadn't forgotten how long it took the four of them to drag the pastor's body to her car.

"Why don't I peek around in here, while Daisy tries the locks on the smaller buildings?" Cordelia offered Arline her hand so she could take her place on the barrel. "If we split up, we can cover more ground and get out of here sooner."

"Sounds like a plan to me," Belinda Sue said.

The chicks left Cordelia with the warehouse while they went off to tinker with the smaller office buildings. She grabbed the sides of the window, wincing as she sliced her finger on a wayward nail. Throwing one leg onto the sill, Cordelia gripped the upper edges of the opening and pushed her arms back. Her muscles tightened, making her skin stretch as she seesawed her way in. Kicking her other leg against the corrugated shell of the warehouse, she tried to find purchase. Her bones burned from the strain, but she managed to pull herself up.

She dropped through the opening. Her ankle bent and her bone smacked the concrete floor as she landed at an awkward angle, but nothing snapped. She remained steady on her feet, with adrenaline keeping pain at bay. Dust particles floated in the air and she sneezed. It took a moment for her eyes to adjust, but a series of high windows and skylights allowed plenty of moonlight to cast a silvery glow on the cavernous space.

Most of the open warehouse was taken up by more machinery, likely related to drilling. Cordelia had never seen land rigs in pieces before, so she couldn't be sure, but the equipment looked new and expensive. Corbin and Edna had money by Sarsaparilla Falls standards, but they weren't rich enough to eat their laying hens. So who was footing the bill?

And what had they promised in return?

Along the back wall, a long metal table built into the structure ran the length of the warehouse. Various papers and receipts littered the surface. Cordelia pulled out her phone and snapped pictures of everything scattered across the desk. She didn't pause to read anything or parse out the relevant from the useless. They'd already burned through at least half an hour and she had no idea if the chicks were having any luck with the other buildings.

Behind a classic car that looked out of place, Cordelia ran across a five-drawer filing cabinet. Three of them were locked, and seeing as how she didn't possess Daisy's picking skills, she had to skip over those. The fourth drawer held old tax forms, while the bottom drawer contained a whole dossier on her Great-Aunt Penelope. A list of the ladies who had been employed by her over the years, where they were now, and what kind of record they each possessed. Arline had a folder three times thicker than everyone else's. Cordelia could only imagine what it held. There were also records of Great-Aunt Penelope's clients, business associates, charity contributions, and taxes.

Torn between wanting to protect the privacy of the chicks and gathering as much evidence as possible, Cordelia snapped pictures of Great-Aunt Penelope's dealings and left everyone else's files alone. It wasn't her business to know that information any more than it was Corbin's, though she figured her great-aunt wouldn't mind the privacy invasion.

Cordelia had just begun to stuff the files back in the drawer when a thin folder came loose from the binder and caught under the cabinet. She picked it up, stopping cold when she came across her own name. They had maybe another fifteen minutes before they needed to hightail it out of there, but Cordelia plopped down right there on the filthy floor, not caring about the dirt for possibly the first time in her life, and read every note hastily scribbled on the papers.

Corbin Abernathy had an entire breakdown of Cordelia's life. Her history with the people of Sarsaparilla Falls, her mother's every indiscretion, her odds of seeing through the terms of the trust, her reception from the locals she'd interacted with, a list of possible enemies and alliances. He'd even managed to learn that she hadn't been honest with her momma about her return to town at first, and he'd jotted down a few notes on how he intended to use that to his advantage.

It didn't look like he knew she'd since told her momma the truth, but he must've had eyes on her in Dallas in a limited capacity. At least enough to know her routines and working hours. The thought of that sleazy snake going anywhere near her momma made her blood run cold.

It was one thing to mess with her—she understood that Corbin Abernathy was not her friend—but to drag her momma into his dirty dealings? After everything she'd overcome? That was a bridge too far for Cordelia. If she'd had a match, she would've been real tempted to light fire to that filing cabinet and watch the whole thing burn.

As it was, she wasn't leaving these notes behind. If Corbin wanted a war, he'd have to stick to her. Her momma had already fought her share of battles and had won them by the skin of her teeth. Cordelia wouldn't allow her to go back. Not to her dark days, when her demons got the best of her, and not to the town that refused to help when she'd been down.

Cordelia stuffed the papers into the lining of her dress where she'd sewn a secret pocket for things like house keys and chewing gum. Knowing she only had minutes left, she debated on taking the chicks' folders, too, just to stick it to Corbin, but the goal had been to get out of there without him ever being aware they'd paid him a visit. So she reluctantly left the filing cabinet behind and hustled back to the open window.

Dragging a sturdy metal stool with a dented seat to the window, she hoisted herself up and worked her way back through the opening. Just as her foot touched the barrel on the other side of the warehouse, flashing red-and-blue lights lit up the surrounding area. Sirens blared loud enough to make her teeth rattle.

Without a backward glance, Cordelia hopped off the barrel and started running for her car. Thick clouds blanketed the moon, extinguishing the light, and shrieks echoed in the near pitch black as a dark figure charged her from between two of the smaller buildings. Cordelia recognized the deputy guarding Honey's cell. She dodged him with ease, her heart pounding faster than green grass through a goose.

The front of her foot slid into a divot in the ground, rolling her already tender ankle, and Cordelia went down hard. Rough dirt bit into her palms. She pushed herself to her knees, but it was too late. The deputy was on her like a duck on a June bug.

"If you fight me, you're only going to make it worse for yourself, Miss Cordelia." The deputy yanked her arms behind her back as she flailed against the useless ground. She couldn't find so much as a loose stick to grab on to. "The sheriff has the others in the back of his car. You're not getting out of this one."

With that, Cordelia gave up the fight. There was no point. She wasn't going to let the chicks be hauled off to jail while she went home and did what? Took a hot bath? Relaxed with a book and a cup of tea? The sheriff already knew they'd broken into the Abernathy compound. His deputy had her on the ground with her hands pinned behind her back. The jig was up.

"I'll come quietly," Cordelia said. "You don't have to pull so hard."

"Sorry about that." The deputy lifted her to her feet and tried to dust off the front of her clothes, then turned red and dropped his hand when he realized just what he was whacking away at. "Corbin Abernathy told us to rough y'all up a bit, but I told the sheriff I don't want nothing to do with that. My momma would tan my hide and sell me at a discount."

"Your momma sounds like good people," Cordelia said absently.

She swiveled her neck as she tried to catch sight of the chicks. They must've been scared out of their minds. Had Belinda Sue taken her heart medication this morning? Was Arline's blood pressure climbing through the roof? She'd get them out of this. Though she wasn't entirely sure how she'd go about doing it, she had a need to protect that ran down her bones.

Maybe this was what it felt like to be a madam.

Chapter Twenty-Two

THE SHERIFF AND HIS DEPUTY LED CORDELIA AND THE CHICKS INTO THE cell next to Honey's. The smug smile on Honey's face as they were ushered in was the least of Cordelia's concerns, though Belinda Sue and Arline had to hold Daisy back from grabbing her hair through the bars. They were in a real mess that went a lot deeper than a simple break-in. Now Corbin knew they were digging into him, and that they'd possibly found something he'd been putting a considerable amount of effort into guarding.

"I knew it was only a matter of time before y'all wound up in here with me." Honey pretended to scratch the side of her mouth with her middle finger. "Y'all know I didn't kill the pastor. The whole time I've been rotting in this cell, I've been waiting for karma to call."

Honey could hardly holler about rotting, considering she had someone bringing her clothes, giving her access to makeup, nicer linens, and a television set. She even had a diffuser sending puffs of lavender-scented mist into the air. To hear her tell it, she'd been chained to a dungeon wall and served nothing but bread and water.

"I've been trying to help you," Cordelia said. "How do you think we ended up in here?"

"I don't much care how you ended up in here, so long as I get out." Honey leaned against the bars, shooting daggers at the four of them. "You don't know what it's been like."

Daisy narrowed her eyes. "You look like you're surviving all right."

"It's still jail." Honey flung her arms out. "Who's feeding my cats? Watering my plants? Unlike some people, I have others depending on me."

"I imagine whoever is helping you decorate your cell is taking care of the other stuff," Belinda Sue said. "Of course, if they were a real friend, they'd post bail. But maybe they're just happy to get a break from your constant jawing."

"And who's bailing you out?" Honey lifted her chin as she stared them down, a cruel smile touching her frosted pink lips when they didn't respond. "That's what I thought."

Cordelia hated Honey Stevens, of all people, getting one over on them, but she couldn't deny the blow had hit its mark. The Chickadee might've been everyone's favorite cathouse, but when it came down to it, who could they lean on when they needed help? The chicks spent so much of their time and effort giving to the town, showing them their hearts, but they were still sex workers in a world that held its judgments as close as its religion.

If they up and disappeared, would anyone look for them? Or would they just think it was an inevitable part of the job? That any hardship that befell the chicks was of their own making? Not so long as Cordelia had breath in her body. That way of thinking was how people like the Abernathys got away with walking all over anyone they perceived to be less than them.

Arline took a seat on the bed and laced her fingers together behind her head. "Might as well get comfortable. We're probably going to be here awhile."

Cordelia had no intention of relaxing. Arline might've been

as comfortable as a cat in a tuna factory behind bars, but the enclosed space was making Cordelia twitchy. She'd never had so much as a parking ticket. She wasn't built for this life.

The door opened, and they all turned toward the sound of footfalls clipping the laminate floor. The sheriff strolled in, sans his deputy. "You ladies are in a world of trouble."

An understatement, to say the least. They would've been in a world of trouble if they'd been caught breaking into the H-E-B or the drugstore, but that wouldn't have been personal. Breaking into the Abernathy compound had been like trying to trap a spider under a glass, only to fall into a pit of snakes. No way would the sheriff let this go with a warning.

Daisy tentatively raised her hand. "Is there any chance of us getting out of here before two tomorrow? I've got an appointment with Clemet Tohen."

The sheriff smoothed his beard with his index finger and thumb. "I'm afraid you're going to have to cancel with Clemet. You can make it your one phone call if you'd like."

"No, that's okay," Daisy muttered. "He'll probably figure it out once word goes around."

Chances were high that word had gone around already. The deputy was like one of those yappy, ankle-biting dogs, the eager kind that was just as likely to lick your face as it was to piss on you. He was too young and too used to seeing next-to-no action. There was no way he wasn't down at the Orb giving half the town a play-by-play by now.

The sheriff pursed his lips. "We're short on cell space for the first time in years. We'll work on getting some cots in here for y'all. In the meantime, try not to fight with the other inmate. She's got her own problems."

He didn't even look at Honey. As if giving her an ounce of his time was beneath him. It would be different if they were in a big city and Honey was a stranger, but she'd probably babysat him a time or two. The disrespect put Cordelia in a horn-tossing mood, and she didn't even like Honey. It just so happened she liked the sheriff a whole lot less.

"I'm standing right here, sheriff." Honey flipped her hair over her shoulder. "And don't think I've forgotten you were the little pervert boy who got suspended from high school his freshmen year for peeping in on me and the other cheerleaders in the changing rooms."

The sheriff's face hardened. "That's enough, Honey."

"Sometimes when we get together, we still laugh at what a creepy little bean pole you were. You might think that badge fills you out, but we all remember where you came from."

If they weren't in a situation of dire consequence at the moment, Cordelia might've laughed. Honey Stevens might've been a walking train wreck, but she had gumption in spades. As a lifelong lover of words, Cordelia couldn't help but appreciate the way insults just rolled off her tongue, as if she'd been born with a sour spoon in her mouth.

The sheriff, turning the shade of Campbell's tomato soup under his beard, spun around and stomped out of the cell room, leaving the five of them alone.

"Girl, I don't know if you're too smart for your own good, or too stupid to look out for yourself." Belinda Sue couldn't keep the admiration out of her voice. "Was it necessary to provoke him when he's holding the keys to your cell?"

Honey flopped down on her bed, arm thrown dramatically across her forehead. "Why should I care about pissing off a small man in his small pond? I'm already going down for a murder I didn't commit. They can't take much more from me."

They could take a lot more from her, like the comfortable conditions she'd been staying in since she'd gotten locked up, but it wasn't Cordelia's place to correct her. Honey was a grown woman who was long past the time of knowing better.

"Don't worry. You're innocent. I'm sure you'll be back to terrorizing the married men of this town in no time," Daisy said.

"That don't mean they'll let me go." Honey rubbed her fists against her eyes. "Not that the four of you care, since y'all seem to know who *did* kill him but don't feel like sharing with the class. Just tell me this: Does it have anything to do with Corbin and Edna Abernathy?"

Cordelia hesitated. There was no point in lying to Honey. She'd already figured out plenty and knew why they'd been arrested. Honey was a lot of things, but dumb wasn't one of them. Putting her off only delayed the inevitable. With all the time she had on her hands, she just might be able to put enough pieces together to start crowing.

"They might be involved," Cordelia said. "But we're not sure yet."

Honey sat up. "I'd be careful if I were you. The Abernathys are slicker than owl dung. I can't say for certain, rumors being what they are, but word is they've gotten themselves tied into a business deal with Sean O'Leary."

The name registered at the back of Cordelia's mind. She'd heard it before, but couldn't quite place where. She looked to the chicks to verify his identity, but the three of them just looked at one another and shrugged. Though by the way Honey had said his name, it probably should've triggered some sort of fear response. Sometimes it wasn't so bad living in the brush country, away from most of the town's doings.

Honey gave them an incredulous look. "Seriously? You've never heard of Sean O'Leary? He owns a couple of restaurants, but people say that's just a front for all kinds of dirty business. Money laundering, tax evasion, racketeering. He's an oilman."

Cordelia stood at attention. If he had a business stake in oil, that could explain the machinery they'd seen at the Abernathy compound. She wondered if Sean O'Leary was the shady gentleman she'd seen Edna with outside the library. The one who was bankrolling their current operation. And he was a restaurant owner to boot . . .

"Which restaurants does he own?" Cordelia asked.

"The only ones I know of are the Flamingo Lounge and Benedict's," Honey said. "He owns about a dozen across Texas, but those two are more local."

"Benedict's was on the list of restaurants that serve Dew Valley," Cordelia whispered to Belinda Sue. "It stood out to me because they only serve breakfast and brunch."

"What's a Dew Valley?" Honey asked. "Is that the wine you were asking after?"

Belinda Sue kicked Cordelia's shin and shot her a look. "Don't worry about it. Why are you telling us this? It doesn't serve you."

Arline held a finger up, startling Cordelia. She'd been sure Arline had fallen asleep. "That's a good question. What's in this for you?"

"What's in this for me?" Honey gestured around her cell as if the answer should be obvious. "The four of you are the best chance I've got of getting out of here."

"You don't trust us though," Daisy pointed out.

"Fine. Don't use the information." Honey laid on her bed, pulled her goose-down comforter up to her neck, and showed them her back. "But if suspicion ends up landing right back on you, having an established record won't do you any favors."

The door opened again, and the sheriff came back in, looking just as annoyed as when he left the last time. "Looks like we won't need to dig up beds for the rest of you after all. Your bail has just been posted."

"By who?" Cordelia asked.

"By me." Archer walked in looking like a ranch girl's wet dream: cowboy hat, cocky grin, twinkle in his tawny eyes, pants so tight Cordelia could see his religion.

Cordelia could feel Daisy starting to swoon beside her, and she elbowed her in the side to keep her from making a fuss. "That was nice of you. What do you want?"

Archer laughed. "Always thinking the world is out to get you, Delia. They got a word for that. It's paranoia."

"Or self-preservation."

The sheriff let out a whistle. "In all my years of serving this town, I ain't never once seen someone trying to argue with the person bailing them out."

"If they don't want it, I'll take it," Honey said.

"Enough of this nonsense." Belinda Sue stood, nudging Cordelia in the back as she filed toward the waiting open door. "Ignore the madam. We're very grateful to you, Archer."

"Speak for yourself," Cordelia said, low enough for only Belinda Sue to hear, which earned her another elbow in the back.

"Thank you, Archer." Daisy fluttered her lashes. "If you hadn't come to our rescue, Arline might've had to get on her knees—"

"Can we not?" Cordelia steepled her fingers against the bridge of her nose.

But Daisy just gave her a look and continued, "—to get at the money she keeps under her mattress for bail."

Archer's mustache twitched, but Cordelia couldn't tell if he was amused or questioning all his life choices. It might've been both.

Once their possessions had been returned to them and they made it out to the parking lot, Archer tipped his hat and walked backward toward his truck. "I'm going to head out now, lest you think I'm hovering because I want something."

All three of the chicks shot Cordelia an admonishing look. But honestly, she had her right to her suspicions. What reason could he possibly have for bailing them out? He wasn't family, he wasn't dating Cordelia anymore, if they'd ever started, and he strongly suspected Cordelia was keeping information about his father's death from him. When presented with the facts, it would've been odd if Cordelia hadn't questioned his reasoning.

"You come over for happy hour tomorrow, so we can thank you properly," Daisy said.

"We'll see." Archer removed his hat and ran a hand through his thick dark hair. "Also, I had a chat with Edna tonight. She said she's not pressing charges, so long as the four of you don't try to send her and Corbin on another wild-goose chase."

After dropping that bombshell, he hopped in his truck and drove off.

Belinda Sue turned on Cordelia, hands on her hips. "Nice job, madam. You done drove him off before we could find out what he said to Edna."

Cordelia rolled her eyes. "It's not like you'll never see him again."

"Why do you suppose she's not pressing charges?" Daisy asked.

"Who knows and who cares," Arline said. "She probably just doesn't want to answer uncomfortable questions about why we were breaking in. And speaking of which, what did y'all find in your buildings?"

While Cordelia had been snapping pictures in the warehouse, Daisy had picked the locks on the three smaller office buildings and they'd each taken one to save time. Arline's was Corbin's sleeping quarters, and she didn't discover anything other than his taste in toothpaste and movies. Belinda Sue had taken an administrative assistant's office, and none of the paperwork contained anything of interest. Daisy had found some documents related to Corbin's father in a second office, but it appeared most of the good stuff had been stored in the warehouse.

"I took this out of his filing cabinet." Cordelia pulled out the papers that were full of notes on how he planned to use her momma to drive her away from the Chickadee. "I wish I could've gotten a look at what was in those locked drawers."

"He had files on all the working girls from the Chickadee?" Daisy asked. "Not just us?"

Cordelia nodded. "As far as I could tell, his files went back to the mid-eighties."

"Ooh, the eighties." Daisy held her squeezed fists to her lips. "What a time to be a chick. We used to have so much fun back then. Remember?"

Belinda Sue and Arline agreed, both wearing dreamy expressions that took them back forty years. The Chickadee was mostly a subdued place of business now that the last of the remaining chicks mainly catered to the married men of Sarsaparilla Falls, but in its heyday, it seemed, the Chickadee had been a nonstop party. A place where the singles in town could let loose and have a good time, according to their particular preferences.

"Why is Corbin keeping all that information?" Belinda Sue asked. "Especially about girls who no longer work at the Chickadee? What purpose does that serve?"

"I'm not sure, but I took pictures of everything." Cordelia pulled out her newly recovered phone, which had been confiscated during the arrest. "We should be able to sort through all these and hopefully get a better picture of what he's got planned."

She unlocked her phone, but instead of the dozens of photos she'd taken in the warehouse, the last picture on her camera roll was of Arline, tipped sideways on her beach chair, drooling into the pool. Every picture she'd taken inside the warehouse had been deleted.

Chapter Twenty-Three

WHATEVER BUSINESS EDNA AND CORBIN WERE INTO, THE SHERIFF WAS in on it. He had to be. How else had Cordelia's photos been deleted? She double-checked her recently deleted folder and the cloud, but they were all gone. While Cordelia didn't particularly like the sheriff, she thought he was like any other bumbling local lawman.

But this went to a level much higher than any of them had been anticipating. It was one thing to piss off the Abernathys—practically everyone in town had done so at one point or another. If the sheriff was stepping into the muck though? There had to be greater forces at play.

And all signs were pointing to Sean O'Leary.

As much as Cordelia hated to give Honey the benefit of the doubt on anything, she'd been pretty adamant about the Abernathys' connection to the shady businessman. That wasn't the kind of accusation people threw around lightly.

As Cordelia drove them home from the police station after getting her car out of impound, they'd all agreed that a trip to Benedict's was in order. Cordelia had a hankering for pancakes and trouble that could not be ignored. Maybe she'd even get a glass of Dew Valley to celebrate their near escape from serious consequences of breaking the law.

After they slept off the dregs of their action-packed evening, they woke up early to get a jump on the morning traffic. Despite being questionably owned, Benedict's was an extremely popular breakfast restaurant. Pickup trucks lined the lot, with overflow parking along the side streets. Cordelia hadn't seen bumper-to-bumper traffic like that since the last county fair.

She hoped the food was just that good, but it more than likely had to do with the fact that a person could get good and drunk at ten in the morning at an otherwise dry time of day. If growing up with her momma had taught Cordelia nothing else, it was that the best cure for a hangover appeared to be a lot more alcohol.

"I don't see why I had to go fancy for this." Daisy pulled the leopard-print caftan away from her skin like the sheer amount of fabric offended her. "It ain't church."

"Because it's a classy joint and we're damn well going to look like we fit in," Belinda Sue said. She wore a floral caftan, another item borrowed from Arline.

One of these days Cordelia would have to take them shopping for proper dresses. Walking around in what amounted to colorful nightgowns didn't exactly scream classy either, but it beat the hot pants and leather. Cordelia opted for a plum pantsuit, which went well with her coloring, but in hindsight probably looked like she was just missing her feathered fedora and chinchilla stole, so who was she to speak on class?

On the way to Benedict's, Daisy leaned forward and stuck her head between the driver's side and front passenger seats. "Here's what I don't get, and I turned this over in my mind all night. Why didn't Edna press charges?"

No one had a clear answer for that, though it weighed heavily on Cordelia's mind as well. Arline said it was because she didn't want to be pressured about why they broke into their compound in the first place, but that didn't ring true. Especially now that they knew the sheriff was in on their dealings. It couldn't have been to save face either, since the Abernathys had been warring with half the town for as far back as their name graced the oldest tombs in the cemetery, so what was Edna up to? She didn't make moves like that without cause.

They found a spot just after seven. To their dismay, it hadn't been in the packed parking lot, so they had to do some walking, to which Arline made several pointed complaints. Daisy's hair began to wilt as the high morning sun burned the dew off the scrub grass, and she patted the styled bouffant with nervous hands.

She didn't need to worry though. Benedict's was three towns over, and Sarsaparilla Falls had the Eagle Cafe for locals, so it was unlikely anyone they knew would be present, but it still felt as if a spotlight was on them. Of course, they tended to draw attention no matter where they went, but Cordelia couldn't help but remain on high alert as they crossed into enemy territory.

Daisy smoothed down the front of her caftan. "This feels worse than when we walked into church. At least then we knew everyone was going to be staring at us."

So it wasn't just Cordelia's so-called paranoia at play. Daisy was feeling an abnormal number of eyes on them, too, and she had an impeccable sense of perception, which made Cordelia feel infinitely better. Archer's comment had wormed its way into her head, and she didn't care to feel as if he'd one-upped her in any way.

Cordelia took Daisy's hands to stop her fidgeting. "You look fine. And we belong here, same as anyone else who wants a shot of whiskey with their eggs."

Normally, they wouldn't have much cared if anyone thought they belonged or not. The chicks had always been their own women who did as they pleased. But their reason for coming to this place had a little more meaning than snubbing their noses at the traditionalists. It would be better for all involved if they didn't stick out so much.

"What's the plan here?" Belinda Sue asked. "Like, theoretically, I know why we're here, but what is it we're hoping to get done today?"

"For now, we're just observing," Cordelia said. "Take note of the staff. See if they defer to anyone in particular. See if there are any men in expensive suits who look like they're commanding the room."

Cordelia thought it would be best to start with just getting a face to go with the name Sean O'Leary, so they would be aware if he approached any of them. If she had to put money on it, she'd bet Sean was the man she'd seen Edna talking to outside the library. But she didn't want to leave something that important to a gut instinct, and Google had been most unhelpful. He appeared to keep a low profile. He wasn't even listed as the owner of the restaurants Honey had mentioned. Both of them were owned by different companies, which were also owned by other companies, screaming red flags in Cordelia's mind.

Inside, they put their name in with the hostess and took a seat in the overflowing waiting area after Arline shamed a group of younger women into giving up their bench. Cordelia took a moment to make note of the décor, gaudy in a new money sort of way. Gold trim around everything, indoor waterfall, abstract art on the brick walls. Not enough exits.

Nearly an hour later, the waitress sat them at a circular red-velvet booth surrounded by curved shiplap walls. Despite the early hour, low lighting offered a certain ambiance to the place. All the windows were covered with thick velvet curtains, blocking out any sunlight that would've killed the serious mood.

Or allowed anyone passing by to see what was going on inside.

"Is it just me, or is this place better suited for romantic

dinners than breakfast?" Daisy asked. "Who wants bacon and eggs by candlelight?"

Apparently, a lot of people. Cordelia took in what little of the surroundings she could see with privacy walls blocking each individual dining table, but most of the patrons appeared to be normal customers. If Benedict's was truly a front for illegal activities, would they try so hard to be legit? Or had their popularity been purely by accident? Texans did love their kitsch.

"I'm going to the bathroom, see if I can get a better look around." Cordelia scooched out of the booth. "Order me an orange juice and a glass of the Dew Valley."

She didn't have any intention of getting tipsy, but she wanted to taste the wine. Get a feel for what made it so special. She figured the more information they were armed with, the better chance they'd have of solving this murder before someone pinned it on Daisy.

As Cordelia made her way to the back of the restaurant, no one paying her much mind, she spotted Stella and Gladys sharing a private moment in a booth. Stella turned her head and Cordelia dove behind a potted plant. The last thing she wanted was to be spotted by a local and have to answer questions about what she was doing there.

Cordelia spread the thick, waxy leaves apart and peered between them. Stella and Gladys sat on the same side of the booth, shoulders touching, sharing an intimate laugh together. It struck Cordelia with the force of a brick to the face. How had she not seen it before? Stella and Gladys weren't gal pals. They were lovers.

No wonder Stella hadn't minded if the pastor spent time with Daisy. Cordelia didn't condone cheating, but was it really cheating if both parties consented? Stella certainly didn't look worse off for it. In fact, she had a glow of happiness around her that had been noticeably absent in Cordelia's youth. She should've known the first time she ran into her in the library. Women could smell joy on each other like bees could smell fear.

Not wanting to interrupt, Cordelia eased her way around the plant and hurried to the bathroom. There was no sense in letting Stella know she'd seen her. There was a reason why they'd come all the way out here for breakfast, and Cordelia had no interest in putting Stella in an awkward position. She had more respect for her elders than that.

As she passed by the kitchen, the door swung open and a man came storming out. He bumped Cordelia's shoulder roughly, sending her careening backward.

"Pardon me." The man had a thick Irish accent. He grabbed both her arms to steady her, and getting a good look at his face, Cordelia felt her blood drain down to her toes.

It was the man with the ill-fitting tan suit, though he wore a closely fitted navy today. The man Edna had been talking to outside the library. His eyes narrowed as recognition dawned on his features. Cordelia didn't need a formal introduction to know she was staring straight into the flat eyes of Sean O'Leary.

His hair was thinner on top than on the sides, with that glaring bald patch she remembered. His thin nose was dotted with the remnants of bologna-colored freckles that had faded to blend in with his ruddy complexion. An old scar marked his chin, cutting a line across the cleft.

His eyes were his most disconcerting feature, so light they were nearly translucent, with the whites threaded with broken blood vessels. But it wasn't the coloring so much as the absolute chill emanating from them. The kind of cold usually reserved for the deepest parts of the ocean.

"I'm s-sorry." Cordelia stumbled over her words, grasping for a smooth exit.

Sean kept his hands on her, his fingers flexing against the

material of her jacket. He eyed her like a teacher assessing his pupil, as if debating how many whacks with a ruler he should dole out. The last thing she wanted was to get on this man's radar, but it didn't seem as though she could avoid it, given his interest in the Chickadee.

"I'm just . . ." Cordelia pointed toward the bathroom. "If you'll excuse me."

"Of course." Sean dropped his hands like she had burned him, but his eyes tracked her pale features and quivering upper lip. Being openly terrified out of her mind was not the best way to go about being inconspicuous.

Cordelia began to hustle away, but a finger snap drew her attention back to Sean.

"I hope you're here simply to enjoy a fine breakfast, Miss West, and not for any other reason. I'd hate to think you were checking up on me." Sean dipped his chin and gave her a knowing smile that didn't reach his near-lifeless eyes.

Cordelia's pulse rang in her ears as all thoughts emptied from her head. "I'm sorry, have we met?"

"Not cordially, no. But your sheriff is an old acquaintance of mine, and I like to keep an eye on my business interests."

"Respectfully, we don't, nor will we ever, have business in common. If you'll excuse me." She turned around and prided herself on keeping her cool until she reached the bathroom. Shutting the door, she leaned against it and held a hand over her racing heart.

How much attention had he been paying to the Chickadee? Had he recognized her that day outside the library? And just how deep did his association with Sarsaparilla Falls go? Once again, Cordelia cursed the sheriff for deleting the warehouse pictures off her phone. If only she'd taken a little more time to read the documents as she sifted through them.

Cordelia splashed cool water over her face and peeked her head out the door. The private dining alcoves made it impossible to get a full view of the restaurant. Tiptoeing her way back into the dining room, she took the long way around to avoid Stella and Gladys. Sean wasn't anywhere to be seen. She should've been relieved, but the unknown engendered fear.

At the table, Daisy slid over to make room for Cordelia and held up her menu. "What do you think sounds better, an omelet or French toast?"

"Either is fine." Cordelia peered around the alcove wall, but the aisles between tables were clear save for a single waitress bringing coffee around. "But I think we should go."

"Go?" Daisy dropped her menu. "What on earth for?"

"I'm not going anywhere until I get my steak and eggs," Arline said.

"It's not safe." Cordelia couldn't be certain of Sean's intentions, but she wasn't willing to stick around and risk a poisoning.

"Of course it is." Daisy gave her a pitying smile. "Look how busy it is. No one's going to hurt us out here in the open." Daisy pulled out a penny. "Heads omelet, tails French toast." She flipped the coin and squealed with delight when it landed on tails.

Belinda Sue leaned forward and cupped the side of her mouth. "Don't look now, but I think I've spotted our suspect."

"Have you met him before?" Cordelia's temper flared. It was one thing to issue thinly veiled threats to her, but he better not dare mess with her chicks. "Has he hassled you?"

"No, momma bear. Settle down." Daisy patted her hand and nudged Belinda Sue with her elbow. "But it's not hard to pick him out of this crowd, considering he's the one staring daggers into the back of your head."

Chapter Twenty-Four

THEY LEFT THE RESTAURANT IN A HURRY, DROPPING A CRUMPLED twenty on the table for their drinks. The chicks mostly stayed quiet on the ride back, letting Cordelia do her thinking without interruption, until they crossed the Sarsaparilla Falls town line.

"At least we know what he looks like now," Belinda Sue said. "He won't be able to sneak around town without us nailing him to the wall."

"Exactly." Cordelia smacked the steering wheel. "It's always good to know your enemies."

Truth be told, Cordelia didn't want to know Sean in any capacity. She doubted very much recognizing him would keep him away from Sarsaparilla Falls if he wanted to be here. And seeing as he had business with the Abernathys and the sheriff in his pocket, he had nothing to fear from three aging sex workers and their untested madam.

"I still want my steak and eggs," Arline said.

"Fine." Cordelia pulled into the Eagle Cafe. "Everyone out. We're getting breakfast and we're going to keep our wits about us. This is just another day."

"Yes, Miss Cordelia," the three of them said in unison.

They were giving her sass, but she didn't mind, so long as they did as she asked. The last thing she wanted was for the chicks to visibly freak out. Investigating a murder took a certain amount of stealth, and they weren't exactly made to blend in.

She should've known walking into Benedict's would be seen as an act of war. She just hoped they could brace for the fallout.

A hostess with a crunchy perm and a missing incisor showed them to a booth with peeling red vinyl. A dollar-store portrait of a howling coyote hung below a set of steer horns and rusted farm equipment tacked to the wall—what passed for ambiance in the town's only diner.

Once they were seated, Daisy leaned in, careful to keep her voice low. "Do you think Sean killed the pastor?"

"Yes." Cordelia didn't hesitate. She'd seen death in his eyes. "I think he has a deal with the Abernathys to tap into the alleged oil on Chickadee land, and I think he'd stop at nothing to get at it."

Belinda Sue shook her head. "All this over a rumor. There's never been proof of oil on Chickadee land any more than there's been a hint of buried treasure."

"Why don't y'all just invite them onto the land and let them drill," Arline said. "When they see there's nothing, they'll leave us alone."

Cordelia tapped her chin. "That's actually not a bad idea."

Belinda Sue gaped at her. "You can't be serious. Don't you know that if you offer to swim a scorpion across the river, you're asking to get stung?"

"It was just an idea." Cordelia absently spun the glass of water the waitress dropped off.

They ordered their food. And while they waited, Cordelia planned. She wanted the person responsible for killing the pastor brought to justice, and the deeper they got into their wayward investigation, the more things pointed toward Sean O'Leary and the Abernathys. But if it was oil under the Chickadee land they were after, calling them on it might reveal more of their hand.

Belinda Sue might've thought it was a bad idea, but Cordelia's back was against the wall. Sean O'Leary wouldn't bother digging into her for fun. He had intentions. It was now on her to shake his equilibrium and throw off his expectations.

She dropped the chicks off at the motel, then made an excuse about needing to pick up a few things from the H-E-B. As she drove through town, she waved to a few people she recognized from her regular trips to the library. The more time she lived in Sarsaparilla Falls, the more it began to feel like home in a way Dallas never had. She always thought she preferred the anonymity of a big city, but maybe that's just what she told herself so she wouldn't have to admit that loneliness hadn't really been a choice.

The Abernathys lived on a quiet cul-de-sac with only two other neighbors. It wasn't hard to pinpoint their house. She just had to look for the red wood shutters and tacky marble fountain at the center of their circular drive. Money could buy a lot, but it couldn't account for taste.

Showing up to the Abernathys' was risky, but Cordelia didn't come empty-handed. If she could keep Edna from straight-up slamming the door in her face, she might be able to find the foot in she'd been searching for all along.

Cordelia rang the doorbell and stood on the stoop, tapping her foot. She knew Edna was home. Her car was in the drive, and Cordelia could hear the notes of a daytime courtroom drama on the other side of the heavy wooden door.

She rang the bell again and was just about to leave a note when Edna finally answered. She had a lazy hold to her stance, like she'd taken her sweet time on purpose. It was a power move that had no effect on Cordelia. She didn't play those types of games.

"Hello, jailbird." Edna's smile dripped with condescension.

"Have I really earned that title if I didn't even sleep over? Feels like appropriation."

Edna wrinkled her nose. "What do you want?"

"I'd like to strike up a deal with you."

"Too bad you don't have anything I want." Edna started to shut the door, but Cordelia stuck her foot out. She'd come too far to let it end here.

"I saw the drill equipment in your warehouse. I know you're looking for oil," Cordelia said, hoping to pique Edna's interest.

She did not.

"And? Is that supposed to be a threat?" Edna sneered. "We're allowed to drill on our own land. You didn't stumble on anything our supplier doesn't already know."

"Is that why you want the Chickadee?"

"Who said we want the Chickadee?" Edna made a big show of examining her nails. "We don't care what you do with your silly little chicken ranch."

She was clearly bluffing. If they didn't care, then Corbin wouldn't have a full drawer in his filing cabinet dedicated to former chicks, and he wouldn't be tracking Cordelia's moves. They might've owned a few squares of nearby land, but the Chickadee's acreage spread as far as the Dewitt County line. Ignoring that kind of reach was just bad business sense.

"If you say so." Cordelia stepped back as if she was giving up the fight. "I was going to make a deal, but if you don't care about our silly little ranch, I'll just quit wasting your time."

"Now hold on a second." Edna stepped onto her front porch, and Cordelia had to suppress her triumphant grin. "What kind of deal are you talking?"

"If you call off your friend Sean O'Leary, we'll let you drill on Chickadee land. Just to set your mind at ease about those oil rumors." Cordelia was taking a risk with the offer. If they did strike oil, they might be looking at an even bigger fight than the one they currently had with just a rumor, but she had to try.

Edna gave her a long, measured look. One that Cordelia couldn't quite read. "I'll think about it and get back to you."

With that, Edna stepped back into her house and slammed the door in Cordelia's face.

Moonlight bathed the Chickadee parking lot in a silvery glow as Cordelia sat on her front porch, twirling the stem of her wineglass. She hadn't taken a drink yet. Sometimes, she liked to pour a glass and hold it just to prove it didn't have any power over her. An old habit from her college days.

Ever since she'd left Edna's house, she wondered if she was going about this entire investigation wrong. So far, nothing had been turning out like those old shows her momma liked to watch. Someone should've slipped up and revealed themselves by now, but even with every sign under the sun pointing to the Abernathys wanting unfettered access to Chickadee land, there wasn't anything that definitively pointed to them killing the pastor.

What would they really gain from a move like that? Sending Daisy to jail wouldn't shut down the whole operation. At the very least, they'd have to get rid of Cordelia and her momma. A thought that didn't sit well with her, but it didn't scream a frame job on Daisy either.

Was it possible James Reed-Smythe had been poisoned by accident?

The pastor told Daisy he'd gotten the wine as a gift from someone, but the poison could've just as easily been meant for someone else. How often had Cordelia pulled a last-minute housewarming item or Secret Santa gift from her own cupboards?

It was almost too ridiculous to consider, but the more she

thought about it, the more framing Daisy just didn't add up. There was no reason to target her.

A noise from the dark cover of the brush country caught her attention. A stilted grinding of rocks against dirt, heavier than the footprints left behind by animals. Like boots crunching on gravel. Cordelia set her wine aside and got to her feet. Of all the low-handed, rotten . . . She'd offered Edna and Corbin a deal. How dare they go sneaking around behind her back?

The crunching stopped on the other side of the motel, close to the wall. If it were Corbin or Edna, wouldn't they have poked around the land? They had no use for the actual motel.

Burglars were always a possibility, though it made little sense for them to come all the way out here when there were plenty of unattended homes in town. Either way, she couldn't sit around all night waiting for an attack. Flight was typically her first response, but she had nowhere to go. She had to act first.

Since her apartment was on the short end of the L, Cordelia grabbed a terra-cotta pot filled with marigolds and snuck around the corner.

A tall figure loomed in the darkness. He had his back to her. Without giving herself time to second-guess, she charged the man and slammed the pot over his head. A loud thwack, like a mallet striking a lobster shell, split the air. He grunted. The pot cracked, and the man went down in a heap of skin and bones.

The pads of Cordelia's slippers dragged along the dirt as she crept up on the person lying face down in the dirt. He didn't stir. Bending down, she reached her hand out, pulled it back, then grabbed the shoulder of his shirt, flipping him over.

"Oh, no. No, no, no." Archer lay on the ground before her, completely knocked out.

Cordelia raised a fist to her lips, biting down hard as she paced. This couldn't be happening. She couldn't be involved with two Reed-Smythe bodies on her property. How had this become her life? She was a librarian with a serious aversion to germs, for crying out loud.

She glanced over her shoulder. The chicks were all busy with clients; there was no way she could interrupt them for this. It would only draw more attention to them. She couldn't leave Archer outside either. Too many critters would be all too happy to make a meal out of him.

Cursing under her breath, she ran back to her apartment and whipped the sheet off her bed. Once outside, she laid it on the ground and rolled Archer onto it, then picked the corners and began dragging him around the corner.

His head knocked against the side of the motel, and she cringed. "Sorry."

Inch by torturous inch, she dragged him back to her apartment. Light spilled onto the sidewalk from her open door. The homey scent of clean cotton and rose oil potpourri wafted on the air, but there was no comfort in the familiar.

"Please don't be dead. Please don't be dead," Cordelia muttered over and over again as she finally pulled him across the threshold and shut the door.

She didn't have the strength to pull him up to the couch, so she grabbed a glass of water and flicked droplets on his face, hoping that would bring him to life. When he didn't move, she got more aggressive and poured the full glass over his head. His eyes flew open. Cordelia screamed and stumbled backward as he sat up, choking and gagging.

Cordelia dropped to her knees and flung her arms around his neck. "Thank God."

Archer held her loosely with one arm as he continued to beat on his chest to clear his airway. "What happened? I went around back to check on your property, and the next thing I know, everything went black."

"If you wanted to check on us, why didn't you just knock on my door?"

"I didn't think you'd want to see me." Archer pressed a hand to the back of his head, his shoulders hunching as he grimaced. A sizable knot had already begun to form. "I got a tip tonight that something might be going down at the Chickadee."

Cordelia's heart sped up. "Like what?"

"Just some bad business with some very bad people."

The screech of slamming a foot on the brakes echoed in Cordelia's mind. That was where she'd heard Sean O'Leary's name before. From Archer. On the way to their disastrous date, he'd mentioned he'd been investigating Sean for some underhanded dealings with oil. How had that not clicked with Cordelia sooner?

Did Archer know about his association with the Abernathys? He must've if he'd been sneaking around the Chickadee, trying to catch him in the act.

"Are we safe out here?" Cordelia asked. The thought of anything happening to Daisy, Belinda Sue, and Arline made her chest tighter than a wet boot.

She buried her face in his neck, well past the time when she should've let him go, but there was a comfort in his pine-scented aftershave. Like everything would be fine if she stayed here, just like this. Possibly forever.

"I don't know, Delia. The God's honest truth is that I'd feel a lot better if you moved into town for a bit, closer to where I could keep an eye on you."

Reluctantly, she released him. His forearm flexed, as if he weren't quite ready to let her go yet. She'd been just on the brink of letting herself need someone, and, true to form, pulled back right when it got a little too real. She stood and took a careful step back as she smoothed down her skirt, closing herself off from whatever had begun to spark between them again.

"That's not really possible." Once Cordelia broke her lease in Dallas, she could kiss her meager savings goodbye, and the chicks would have to be dragged from the Chickadee by their wigs. No way would they leave willingly, no matter the danger.

"That's what I figured." Archer got to his feet, back cracking, and glanced around like he had misplaced his keys. "How did I get inside?"

"I hit you with a pot." When his mouth dropped open, she rushed forward. "In my defense, I thought you were a burglar."

Or someone worse.

"Do me a favor?" He pulled a paper out of his back pocket and unfolded it. "If you see this man in town, call me right away. Don't worry about the time."

Cordelia's fingers shook as she held the print of Sean O'Leary's face. She swallowed hard as she peered up at Archer. "Are you going to tell me why?"

"Hell." Archer ran a hand through his hair, scrutinizing her face. "Don't tell me you already know him."

"I don't already know him." She handed the paper back.

"Delia."

She bit her lip, averting her gaze.

"Damn it all." Archer put the picture away. "How do you know Sean O'Leary?"

"I said I don't." And she wasn't lying . . . exactly. She knew *of* him, but they'd never been formally introduced. A point she was certain Archer wouldn't appreciate.

"Fine." Archer marched toward the door, flinging it open with enough force to rattle the hinges. "That's just great. I don't know why I even bother."

Cordelia followed him outside but stopped at the gate of her small front porch, where she watched him get in his truck and drive away. She didn't attempt to call him back or explain herself. What could she say anyway? So she just stood there, and didn't go back inside until she could no longer see his headlights.

In the distance, a coyote howled. A stark and empty sound that reminded her of just how isolated they were out in the brush country. Before turning out the lights and climbing into bed, she double-checked that all the windows were locked tight.

Chapter Twenty-Five

"WE'RE GOING TO THIS." CORDELIA SET DOWN THE FLYER ON THE POOL-side table.

Belinda Sue had made strawberry daiquiris with red pop, chopped-up ice, and rum. She took one look at the flyer and wrinkled her nose. "No, thanks."

Daisy picked up the corner of the flyer with her thumb and index finger as she pushed her straw around her glass with her tongue. "You said we don't have to go to church no more."

"This is different," Cordelia said. "The whole town will be there."

The church was hosting a celebration to welcome Hollis Thorne, the new pastor, down at the town square. There would be a big potluck, lots of gossip, and plenty to observe. Cordelia also knew that Edna would be present, and since she hadn't heard from her since she offered that deal, she had plans to corner her at the event when she couldn't slam a door in her face.

"Y'all don't have to come with me, but I'm going." Cordelia picked up the flyer and folded it into a neat square, tucking it away in her purse.

"I'd rather skinny-dip with piranhas," Arline said.

Cordelia pinched her lips together. "A simple no would've been fine."

Daisy hesitated. "Do I have to wear another caftan?"

"No, this is a more casual affair." Cordelia gestured to her own ensemble, a tweed skirt and button-down top tucked neatly into the waistband, to illustrate her point.

"Right." Daisy glanced between Arline and Belinda Sue, who both averted their eyes. "I suppose I could come with you. If I get to dress how I want."

Cordelia laid her hand over her heart. "I swear, I won't make one comment."

An hour later, Cordelia and Daisy were headed into town. Daisy had chosen to wear a red tube top with little sheep stitched into the fabric, and hot pants, but Cordelia just got in the car. She suspected Daisy had picked that outfit on purpose to test her. The chicks seemed to forget she'd already raised one overgrown teenager and knew how to play the game far better than they ever would.

They parked a few blocks over from the town center. Bumper-to-bumper cars lined the walkways of every side street. Everyone had come out to greet the new pastor.

Cordelia carried the apple pie she'd bought earlier, nodding at people as they passed. The Newman brothers, reeking of sweat and sour milk; Brian Kobi, who'd played the trumpet in the high school marching band twenty years before and still made it a core part of his personality; Danielle Alvarez-Calderon, who was still known for having a spider crawl in her ear and die at a sixth-grade sleepover; Biscuit McCreedy, who'd rescued a cat from a transmission tower. People who had histories and memories built into the very fabric of Sarsaparilla Falls.

Daisy stopped to chat with a few clients and people she knew from town. Girls with thick brown hair threaded with pink ribbons zigzagged through the crowd with melting snow cones in their fists. A band of middle-aged, balding men wearing matching bowling league shirts played '90s hits from the park's gazebo. The center of town had a bounce house and ring toss set up for the kids and a beer tent for adults. It didn't feel like a church affair so much as a festival.

People stood in clusters, fanning themselves against the oppressive heat. Not even the cooling misters set up around the perimeter of the park could touch the temperature. The air was dry enough for the birds to build their nests out of barbed wire.

Cordelia set her pie on the dessert end of a long table that held the food offerings. Flies buzzed around the fruit dishes, and ice melted in trays set up to keep the salads cold. Sarsaparilla Falls had hosted several town potlucks when she was a kid, but she'd never gone to one. Her momma said they weren't nothing but gossip mills for snooty folks who thought the sun shined out of their cracks. Her way of saying they wouldn't have been welcome anyway.

Times certainly had changed. Daisy was twice the sinner Sherilynn was, but she'd been welcomed with open arms. Of course, her momma hadn't done anything to contribute to the well-being of the town either. All she'd ever done was take and blame.

Cordelia grabbed a spare flyer and furiously fanned herself. Sometimes those old resentments could sneak up on her out of nowhere. Her momma had come a long way since those days, but every now and again Cordelia would be right back there in the past as if she'd never left. It probably wouldn't hurt to make an appointment with her therapist.

"Whew, it's hotter than a honeymoon hotel out here." Daisy pressed a bottle of water to her neck and handed one to Cordelia. "Have you seen Edna yet?"

"Not yet, but—" Cordelia gripped Daisy's arm. "Oh, my. Look who's fresh out of jail."

Honey Stevens parted the crowd. She swished her hips as she gave homecoming queen waves to her gawkers like they were paparazzi trailing her every move. She had a lot of nerve, Cordelia had to hand that much to her. For every dirty look she caught, she blew a kiss in return.

"Damn, I'd like her sass if she wasn't so awful," Daisy said. "How do you suppose she got out? Surely no one posted her bail? It was set at a hundred grand. Ain't no one around here but the Abernathys got that kind of money."

"We could ask her, seeing as she's headed this way," Cordelia said out of the corner of her mouth. "Hello, Honey. Good to see you out and about."

"Don't lie." She flipped her overly processed hair over her shoulder. "You're mad as hell that I got out before you could find a way to clear Daisy."

"That's not true." Mostly not true. Cordelia lifted her chin, choosing to ignore the jab. "How did you end up breaking free?"

"Juan Morales was admitted to the hospital after complaining of abdominal pain and vomiting. The next day, Bart Hewitt comes in for the same thing. Both of them over eighty and both of them residents of the pastor's neighborhood."

"Oh, no. I know Juan from way back. I hope he's okay," Daisy said.

"He's fine," Honey said. "But they tested the well water and it turns out they've been slowly getting poisoned over the last few months. The well got contaminated with arsenic, the kind found in soil. They let me go immediately. The problem for you is that the pastor wasn't old enough to die from the well water, it was only a small amount, so they're going to start looking into what did kill him. I'd be careful if I were you."

Daisy balled her hands into fists, looking about as threatening as a mouse in a catfight. "You know what? I almost felt sorry for you when you were locked up, but then you open your mouth and I remember why no one can stand you."

"I'm just saying." Honey shrugged like she hadn't accused Daisy of murder in broad daylight. "Now that I'm out, people are going to start talking. They might even start listening to Edna Abernathy again, since she was the only one who said I was innocent."

"Maybe he really did die of a heart attack," Cordelia said. "Ever think of that?"

Though that didn't make Cordelia feel any better. If the pastor's death was ruled to be by natural causes, his murderer would still be walking around out there. Still free to kill again.

"They could say it was a heart attack. Except we both know that's not true." Honey gave them a simpering smile. "Good luck out there, ladies."

As Daisy fumed, Cordelia squeezed her shoulder. "She's just trying to rile you up and get people talking about you instead of her. We've got better things to do."

Cordelia threaded her arm through Daisy's, and they walked around, picking up snippets of gossip. Vinner Mendez had gotten a new boat, and some people were saying he'd sold a couple of his toes on eBay to pay for it. He'd been walking funny for a few weeks, so that tracked. Lee Vargas had gotten fired from the Mallory farm for trying to have inappropriate relations with a duck. Someone accused Tilly Gomez-Esteban of selling marked-up Shein, so she blew up her order forms and taped them to the window to dispel the rumors.

Nothing of interest stuck out, at least not anything they could use to figure out who killed the pastor. And honestly, now that Honey was out of jail and the wine bottle was long gone, Cordelia didn't find the matter as pressing as the Abernathys' connection to Sean O'Leary. Protecting the chicks was always her first priority.

"Ooh, look. There's the new pastor." Daisy pointed to a man who stood at the head of a small crowd. Hollis Thorne had shiny blond hair that glinted in the sun like a halo. His teeth were whiter than sun-bleached cotton, and there was something about the way he held himself when he talked to people. Like he was looking down at them from a perch. "He's a handsome one."

"He certainly thinks he is." Cordelia had enough experience with men too pretty for their own good to recognize a fragile ego when she saw one. "I'd like to buy him for what he's worth and sell him for what he thinks he'll bring."

"Oh, stop." Daisy swatted her arm. "You're always so cynical. I think he looks nice."

Cordelia didn't trust nice as far as she could throw it. Her daddy had been nice. The guy who'd asked for help with trigonometry in college, then tried to lock her in his apartment, had been nice. Her ex-roommate, who talked bad about Cordelia behind her back, had been nice. She'd had enough of nice to know she preferred someone honest.

"Let's go get some of that potato salad before the flies get worse," Cordelia said. She'd only come to this event to track down Edna, and since that turned out to be a bust, she planned to take her free meal and leave.

Cordelia turned to Daisy, but she'd already lost her to the allure of the new pastor. She narrowed her eyes, taking in the way Hollis Thorne tilted his head and his blank expression as Georgia Wilson flapped her hands while she spoke. The only reason he gave Daisy a second glance was on account of her outfit, and he dismissed her just as quick, not even bothering with so much as a nod when she interjected. As soon as a man approached him, he promptly dropped the act of half-heartedly pretending to listen to Georgia to engage in what he probably considered a real conversation. The way her face fell for a split second before she brightened and turned to someone else as if nothing had happened infuriated Cordelia.

"Scouting out your next victim?" Edna had slithered up like a snake, taking Cordelia by surprise. "Is it men of God you hate, or just people in positions of power?"

"Bless your heart, Edna." Cordelia gave her the full effect of the Texas charm embedded into her DNA. "It's not even half past five yet and you're already drunk. You ought to know the first step is admitting you've got a problem."

"You're the one who's going to have a problem if another pastor turns up dead after you've been burning a hole into the side of his brain all afternoon." Edna shook her head as if she pitied Cordelia. "The man just got here, how could he have possibly offended you already?"

"I know his type, that's all." Cordelia crossed her arms. "Have you given any more thought to my offer?"

Two nights ago, Cordelia had woken up to the sound of scratching on her walls. At first she thought it might've been a possum in her attic, but then she remembered she didn't have an attic. By the time she got out of bed and peered out her back windows, the noise was gone. The following night, she could've sworn she heard gravel crunching out back. She called Archer to see if he was snooping around her property again, but as soon as his sleepy voice came on the line, she hung up. It could've been animals or clients taking the long way around, but Cordelia would sleep better knowing for sure the threat had been eliminated.

"I have, and I'm not taking it," Edna said.

"Why on earth not?" Cordelia couldn't hide her shock. She thought for sure Edna would use this opportunity to poke around

Chickadee land, if for no other reason than the fact that she was a nosy busybody.

"Why would we use our equipment to drill oil for you on your land?" Edna sneered. "You must think I carry my brains in my back pocket. I'm not trying to make you rich."

"I don't care about getting rich." Cordelia tried to temper the rising shrill in her voice. Remaining calm and cool was her most formidable asset. "I just want Sean O'Leary gone."

"I don't have the kind of pull with Sean O'Leary you seem to think I have." Edna glanced around. Concern etched her brow as she lowered her voice. "Look, it's probably best if we aren't seen talking right now."

"You're the one who approached me." Edna moved to walk away, but Cordelia grabbed her arm. "Hang on. Why shouldn't we be seen talking? What's going on?"

"Nothing that concerns you." Glancing over Cordelia's shoulder, Edna paled as she shook her off. "Just leave it be. I have to go."

Edna's odd behavior unnerved Cordelia, but she didn't want to risk another public altercation, so she let her go. Daisy clearly hadn't let the pastor's brush-off get her down. She stood by one of the picnic tables, licking watermelon juice off the end of her fingers while a girl of about five sat at her feet braiding a daisy chain around her ankle. Porter Sheldon was telling her a story and looking at her like she hung the moon. He held a stack of his reward posters under his arm, the ones offering cash for anyone who had information on his break-in. The sheriff must've been so preoccupied doing Sean's bidding that he didn't have much time left for his actual job.

Martina waved to Cordelia and rushed over. "I was hoping to see you here today. My boyfriend, Stewart, had a fallout with the old pastor, but he's hoping this one will be a little more open-minded. How did your date go?"

Cordelia winced. “Not great.”

“Oh. That’s too bad.” Martina’s face fell. “I hope you at least got a nice meal out of it. I haven’t been to the family restaurant in years, but my tía just told me they did a big renovation on it recently, put in a fancy saltwater tank and everything.”

That would explain why Martina hadn’t mentioned the tank when Cordelia was looking into it. “It was beautiful. You should make a night of it there.”

“We’ll see if I have time after this next election.” Her face brightened as her gaze landed on Stewart, whom Cordelia recognized from his picture. “I’ll catch up with you later.”

Daisy had moved on from the picnic table. Cordelia glanced around, and her attention snagged on the new pastor, who appeared to be in a heated conversation with Sean O’Leary. He must’ve been the reason Edna had been skittish, but why would she be afraid of her business partner? Sean had his back to her, but she’d recognize that bald spot and ill-fitting suit anywhere. Who wore a suit to an outdoor potluck? Cordelia glanced down at her own attire and grimaced.

The pastor caught her staring, and she quickly spun around before Sean could be alerted to her presence. By the time she’d gathered her wits again, Sean was gone, the pastor had his hands full with Daisy, and Edna was pacing the edge of the festival with her phone at her ear. As soon as she spotted Sean, she hung up and bolted.

Cordelia might’ve hated confrontation, but something was going down. The dread gathering in the pit of her stomach had nothing to do with Cindy Baker’s fruit salad.

Daisy caught her eye, and Cordelia motioned for her. Extracting herself from the pastor with some reluctance, she hustled over. “I was just getting to my pitch.”

"Never mind that." Cordelia took her hand, dragging her along as she tried to keep track of Edna. "There's a storm brewing."

"I know. I saw Sean O'Leary." Daisy tried to dig in her high heels at first, but they were really thin, so she eventually gave up and let herself be dragged along. "Can't we just avoid him?"

"No. And Edna's acting strange." Cordelia paused. "Stranger than normal."

They continued to weave around people until they reached the edge of the park. Edna glanced behind her just as Cordelia pulled Daisy behind a stone statue of John Wayne, who had never been to Sarsaparilla Falls, but apparently really liked root beer. By the time Cordelia peeked her head out again, Edna had disappeared into the alley between Parson's Drugstore and the Calico Cat consignment shop.

"Come on, we can still catch up." Cordelia ran across the street toward the alley, with no one at the potluck paying them any mind.

"This might be a bad idea." Daisy's ice-pick heels clicked against the pavement.

Cordelia was certain this was a bad idea, but she was in too deep now. And she needed to know what Edna was up to. She wouldn't get a moment's peace until the business between them was settled for good and Sean O'Leary had set his sights elsewhere.

Digging her keys out of her purse, she thrust them at Daisy. "Go get the car and pull it up to the alley. If she leaves, we need to follow."

"Okay." Daisy bit her lip as she glanced between Cordelia and the alley. "I don't usually drive. I mean, I can, but I haven't driven in a while." She took a few steps back, as if debating whether she wanted to stay or go, before a look of determination crept over her features. "I'll be fine." She broke into a full run toward the street where they'd parked.

Creeping into the alley, Cordelia kept her back against the brick wall of Parson's, sliding along the shadows. The tip of her toe hit an empty soup can and the rattle of metal across concrete made her cringe, but no sounds followed. Cordelia blew out her breath and continued until she reached the back of the buildings.

The low murmur of voices had her ducking behind a dumpster. There was no mistaking the stern Irish lilt in Sean's voice or the nasal whine of Edna's. She sounded like she was pleading with him, and whatever they were discussing wasn't going in her favor.

"I told you, if we make a move on the Chickadee, that FBI agent will be all over us. He's already questioned me once," Edna bit out.

Cordelia strained to hear Sean's response, but she was at the wrong angle and his words carried in the opposite direction.

"He has no idea. I never mentioned you," Edna said. "Cordelia West saw our equipment. She knows we're after oil, but I don't think she knows it's on her property."

Cordelia's brows pinched. How could Edna be so sure of herself? No one would know for certain if there was oil on Chickadee land until they drilled, which Edna had already made clear she didn't want to do. Seemed like they were all going to a lot of trouble for a rumor.

Before Cordelia could contemplate it further, Edna let out an earsplitting scream. Heart racing, Cordelia jumped out from behind the dumpster just in time to see Sean forcing her into the trunk of his car and speeding away.

Chapter Twenty-Six

CORDELIA BURST OUT OF THE ALLEY JUST AS DAISY SCREECHED AROUND the corner with her car and skidded to a stop in front of the drugstore. Flinging open the passenger door, Cordelia jumped into the seat. "Go. Around back. We can still catch them."

Daisy opened her mouth to ask something, when a black sedan peeled out from behind the row of businesses, tires smoking, as it careened around a sharp turn and barreled down the road that would lead them out of town. Gripping the steering wheel, Daisy slammed her foot on the gas and sped after them. Cordelia's head smacked the back of the seat. She grappled with the seat belt, securing it just as Daisy took a corner at a finger-numbing speed.

"Hold on," Daisy said. "We're about to go faster than a sneeze through a screen door."

Cordelia clung to the door, grateful she wasn't the one driving. She didn't have the stomach for greater than five miles over the speed limit. "I saw them talking, Edna and Sean, and then he threw her into the trunk and took off."

"What were they arguing about?" Daisy's jaw was set as she kept her eyes laser focused on the sedan in front of them.

"I couldn't hear him, but she was worried about messing with us because of Archer, and she confirmed they're after whatever oil they think is on Chickadee land."

"These rumors are going to be the death of someone someday," Daisy said.

"Let's hope it's not ours." Cordelia crossed her fingers. "Sean O'Leary has it in his head that Edna's keeping information from him. He didn't like that much."

"I'll just bet he didn't." Daisy's tone was grim.

They reached a stoplight, and she slowed, but the sedan only hit the gas harder, zipping between two cars that had to veer onto the sidewalk to avoid a collision. Thankfully, most of the town was at the park and the area was clear of pedestrians. Instead of following the sedan once the light turned green, Daisy went right.

"Where are you going?" Cordelia asked.

"I don't think they're staying in town," Daisy said. "But they're weaving around different streets like they know we're following them. So I'm going to head out to the highway and wait for them to pass."

"Good thinking," Cordelia said.

Daisy parked in front of the WELCOME TO SARSAPARILLA FALLS sign, hiding the car from anyone leaving town. They sat for a good thirty minutes, just waiting. Cordelia fidgeted in her seat. She normally had the patience of a saint, but the unknown of their situation made her antsy. For all she knew, Sean could've already driven through here and they'd missed him altogether. She was just about to suggest they turn around when a familiar Mercedes turned onto the highway, the crisp white exterior glinting in the early evening sun.

Daisy's jaw dropped. "Isn't that . . . ?"

"That's Edna's car, all right," Cordelia said. "Let's move."

Daisy allowed two cars to pass, then turned onto the highway, keeping a good distance behind Edna's car, not wanting to tip off Sean. Rolling down the window, Daisy turned the radio up and let her arm surf the wind as she kept a breakneck pace on the road. A driver going ninety in the left lane honked when she cut him off, but she wove in between the traffic with ease, ridiculously comfortable behind the wheel for someone who didn't even own a car.

"Where'd you learn to drive like this?" Cordelia asked.

"I lost my virginity in high school to this guy who did amateur racing on a dirt track outside Marne." Daisy pulled her visor down to block the sun. "I learned how to race to impress him, but he didn't want a girlfriend who could compete. He wanted someone cheering for him on the side."

"Did you like racing?" Cordelia asked.

"Yeah," Daisy said quietly, a shadow from a passing cloud darkening her smile. "I did."

Cordelia went as soft as cotton candy in the rain. Here Daisy was, all these years later, a caretaker and cheerleader. A role she'd been put in long before she ever had a chance to stretch her own wings. The only place where she'd felt wanted. How many lives had been shaped by the flippant comments of careless men?

"I think you're amazing, Daisy." Cordelia squeezed her right hand, which rested between them on the console. "In case I don't say it enough."

"You say it plenty." Daisy put her sunglasses on, but not before Cordelia caught the shimmer of tears in her eyes. "Let's see where Sean's taking us."

Daisy hit the gas, catching up to the Mercedes and staying two cars behind it, until it made a sharp turn off an exit advertising a rest stop and not much else. Staying stealthy became much harder when they were the only two cars in the middle of nowhere. Daisy pulled in to the rest stop and parked as Edna's car continued to fly down a dirt road that looked as though it headed to nowhere.

"We're not going to lose them, are we?" Cordelia stretched her neck to get a better view, but all that remained of the Mercedes was a fading cloud of dust.

"There's only one way that road goes, and I don't think it has an exit." Daisy zoomed out on the GPS attached to the dashboard to show that the road indeed dead-ended in about three miles. If Sean wanted back on the highway, he'd have to pass them again. "I figured if we wait fifteen minutes, we'd have a better chance of sneaking up on him."

Cordelia couldn't deny it was a solid plan. It's not like they could pull up right behind Sean and wave at him like they were old friends. That was a good way to end their evening dodging bullets instead of rescuing Edna. If she even needed rescuing.

While they waited, Daisy hummed along to a Dolly Parton song on the radio. A Mack truck pulled up beside them, despite there being several open spots in the parking lot. Daisy took that as her cue to leave. Before the beefy, bearded man could exit his rig, they were speeding down the dirt road where Edna's car had disappeared.

"What if Edna staged this whole thing to lure us out here and finish us off?" Cordelia asked. "I wouldn't put it past her."

"Nah." Daisy swerved, just missing a possum, whose glowing eyes lit with ire at the intrusion. "No way would she have expected us to come for her."

"Why are we doing this?"

It hadn't occurred to Cordelia to question this earlier; adrenaline had thrown her into action mode. But why were they trying to help Edna? If the roles were reversed, she wouldn't have lifted a finger to help them. In fact, she was likely in cahoots with a dangerous criminal to wipe them off the map entirely. And the only reason she'd wound up in Sean's trunk was because she'd made the choice to do business with him in the first place.

"We're doing this because we're good people," Daisy said. "We do for others, even if they probably wouldn't do the same for us."

"Speak for yourself." Cordelia wasn't feeling nearly as generous now that the thrill of the chase had worn off. But that was why Daisy had twice the generosity of those who sat in pews on Sunday mornings and called it good enough.

And while Cordelia wasn't feeling much love toward Edna, they were too far into this now to turn back. About halfway down the road, they spotted the Mercedes parked alongside the gravel road beside a structure that looked more like an oversize oil drum than a building. Daisy shut off the headlights and rolled the car to a stop beside a thicket of dry brush on the other side of the road. It didn't do much to conceal the car, but the sun had set, offering them a little more cover.

Daisy opened the car door, swearing as the overhead light came on, and quickly got out, adjusting her tube top. "I knew I should've worn the three-inch heels today."

She still moved fast enough to catch up to yesterday in her six-inchers, but they made a distinct picking sound against the hard-packed gravel as they snuck up on the rounded building. Clouds gathered in a thick, hazy blanket, blocking out the moon and most of the stars overheard, throwing them into near pitch black.

Once Cordelia's eyes adjusted to the lack of light, she spotted a rusty ladder that clung to the side of the structure, one strong storm away from collapsing. A dim light bulb hanging from a crooked metal hood illuminated the single door at the back. There were no windows, but echoes reverberated against the metal and drifted out of the space between the roof and the wall.

Cordelia pressed her ear against the door. Sean's thick accent mixed with a lower-pitched Texas drawl, one she didn't recognize. She could've sworn she heard Edna weeping, but that might've been the creak of the building settling. They'd never actually seen her in the car.

"There are at least two men in there," Cordelia whispered.

"Should we bust in there, guns blazing, like they do in the movies?" Daisy asked.

"That's a terrible idea, seeing as we don't have any guns." And they'd likely shoot themselves before they'd hit anything they were aiming at. Cordelia pointed to an outbuilding thirty feet away. "I have an idea."

She motioned for Daisy to follow her, creeping toward the metal structure that looked small enough to be a garden shed. One window crusted over with spiderwebs and about a century of dust revealed that the inside held a bunch of old farming tools. Cordelia shuddered at the sight of the rusting hooks attached to the wall. The stuff of horror movies.

"There's a door back here." Daisy pulled on the latch, and it screeched like a tank hitting a guardrail. The voices in the other building fell silent. Daisy glanced at Cordelia with wide-eyed panic. "What do we do now?"

Cordelia yanked open the door the rest of the way and grabbed two hooks off the wall. She didn't have time to freak out about tetanus, but the amount of rust coating those old tools hadn't escaped her notice. She'd bathe in hand sanitizer later.

Raising her arm high over her head, Cordelia tossed the hooks into the scrub. Daisy followed her lead, grabbing more hooks and flinging them into the night. They hit the dirt with a soft thud. If one didn't know where the sound originated, they almost sounded like footfalls.

The door from the opposite structure burst open, and Sean's Irish lilt split the air. "I told you someone was following us. Find them."

Daisy and Cordelia both let loose another series of hooks, and Sean pulled a gun from his waistband and began firing into the night. Daisy squeaked, the noise muffled by the sound of a bullet ricochetting off a rock. A tall man with a stooped build and a wide-brimmed Stetson followed close behind him. Cordelia flung another hook farther than the previous one.

"They're getting away." The man dashed ahead of Sean, who followed on his heels, gun still drawn. "I can't see a damn thing out here."

"Let's go," Cordelia whispered.

They had a five-minute window, if that, to get in and get Edna out. Sean and his partner had left the door of the larger building wide open. Just inside the entrance, Edna was tied to a wooden chair, a dirty cloth stuffed into her mouth. She'd already freed one hand from the rope that bound her and was quickly working on the other. Her forehead crinkled at the sight of Cordelia and Daisy, and she began violently jerking her head from side to side.

Cordelia crouched beside her and began untying her left hand. "We're going to get you out of here, but if I take that cloth off and you start screaming, you're on your own."

Edna nodded, her eyes wide with shock.

Cordelia pulled the cloth free as Daisy went to work on the rope that bound her ankles to the chair. "Who is that man with Sean?"

"Jameson." Edna spit the taste of dirt and oil from her mouth. "He owns a pawnshop in Three Oaks and fences a lot of stolen property for Sean."

"We can get to know everyone later," Cordelia said. "We don't have much time as is."

At the sound of the two men approaching, they all froze. They were too late.

"What now?" Daisy whispered.

They had all but one of Edna's legs untied from the chair and no time to make a run for it. The only thing they could do was fight their way out. In the dark, in an unfamiliar territory, against two grown men with guns. How could this possibly go wrong?

Cordelia instructed Daisy to loop Edna's arm around her shoulders and half drag her away from the entrance. Cordelia grabbed a rusted rake with an ancient wooden handle that was propped up against the wall and waited in the shadows.

As soon as Sean's large frame filled the door, Cordelia swung the rake, cracking him across the temple. He went down like a sack of potatoes, his head lolling to the side. A trickle of blood cut a path across the dirt floor, moving slower than snail slime.

"What the hell?" Jameson stopped short at the sight of Sean and didn't see the rake coming. Cordelia swung wide, and his teeth rattled together like a BB in a boxcar. He went down in a heap of dust next to Sean.

"Oh my God, Miss Cordelia. You never told me you played baseball," Daisy said.

"I don't." Cordelia tossed the rake to the side, a little frightened of what she'd done. She'd never so much as swatted a fly in her life. Her hands shook as fear and fire coursed through her veins. "Let's go before they wake up."

They dug through Sean's pockets until they found Edna's keys and tossed them to her. Just in case, Cordelia relieved both men of their guns, holding them by her thumbs and index fingers, like they might go off if she wrapped her palms around them. Once they stepped outside, she tossed them into a nearby bush. They'd be impossible to find in the dark.

"Should we call the police?" Daisy asked.

"No," Cordelia and Edna said at the same time.

They stopped and looked at each other, unsure of why the other said no. Cordelia didn't want to involve the sheriff because she was certain he'd been the one to delete the pictures off her phone. But what did Edna have to gain by keeping the police out of this? She'd been the one who'd been thrown in a trunk, after all. She had to know Sean would come for her again, and maybe she wouldn't be so lucky next time.

"Why did Sean take you from the festival?" Cordelia asked. "And don't bother lying, I saw the two of you in that alley. That's how we ended up out here."

"You were spying on me?" Edna's eye bulged with indignation.

Daisy's nose scrunched. "And you're welcome for it, you ungrateful bi—"

Cordelia put a hand on Daisy's arm to still her. "Why is he so convinced the Chickadee land is holding oil? You owe us that much."

Edna released a deep sigh as she glanced between them and the building where her abductors had been knocked out. "Let's get out of here first. If you follow me back to my house, I'll explain everything. I swear."

Chapter Twenty-Seven

"I HAVE TO SAY, YOU OUGHT TO SUE YOUR INTERIOR DESIGNER," DAISY said.

Cordelia sat next to Daisy on a gold-trimmed settee and found she couldn't disagree. Edna's parlor, as she called it, had maroon wallpaper stamped with gold fern leaves, a gold mantel over a black granite fireplace, and marble busts of both her and Corbin. It was tackier than a swimsuit competition in a child's beauty pageant.

Edna sneered. "Sorry, I'm not interested in taking the opinions of a . . . someone like you seriously," she said, pulling back the insult at the last second.

Saving her life must've counted for something, but not enough as far as Cordelia was concerned. "One more word, and I'll throw you in my trunk and hand deliver you to Sean." She could put up with a lot of sass, but she wouldn't stand for anyone disrespecting Daisy. "We don't like each other, so just get on with what you have to tell us so we can get out of your hair."

"Fine." Edna shot Daisy another dirty look. "Sean O'Leary has proof that the miner's legend is real. He came across a journal with a map in it."

"Did he happen to come across this journal in Porter Sheldon's safe in his locked house while he was out of town?" Daisy asked.

"I don't know about all that." Heat bloomed over Edna's cheeks. If Cordelia didn't know how heartless she was, she might've said Edna was ashamed. "Sean knows Corbin and I were trying to buy up the land for our own development purposes, so he made a deal with Corbin, and now we can't make good on it. The last person he partnered with who couldn't make good on a deal ended up in a shallow grave a mile from Benedict's."

Cordelia shivered. She didn't doubt that Sean was capable of murder, but having it so bluntly confirmed chilled her to the bone. "What's this miner's legend about?"

"Sarsaparilla Falls used to be a mining town back in the 1800s," Edna said. "Rumor has it a man named Glenn Overbeck went digging for gold but came up with oil instead. Oil was new back then, but he was an educated man and wrote it down in his journal along with a map. Then he headed back to town with plans of getting in touch with George Bissell himself, but he got robbed that night and didn't survive."

"That sounds like a lot of nonsense," Cordelia said. There were rumors like that spread all over Texas. If it were true, it would've been discovered years ago, long before the journal fell into Porter Sheldon's hands. "What kind of deal did Corbin make with Sean?"

Edna shook her head like she couldn't believe the idiocy of her husband. "He told Sean if he helped us acquire the Chickadee, he could have the spot of land that allegedly held oil."

If Corbin's brains were leather, he wouldn't have enough to saddle a June bug. He had no way of getting his hands on the Chickadee, and he should've known that from the get-go. Penelope's trust was as airtight as a submarine. Not even Cordelia could get out of it.

"Is that why y'all tried to frame Daisy?" Cordelia asked.

Edna drew her neck back far enough to crack the bones. "What are you going on about?"

"Nothing." Edna had only just quit accusing Daisy of murder, and Cordelia didn't need to fan those flames again, despite their tentative ceasefire. "So Corbin made a stupid deal he couldn't possibly honor, and you're paying the price for it. Is that right?"

"In a nutshell." Edna's shoulders slumped, exhaustion deepening the circles under her eyes.

"How does the sheriff factor into this?" Cordelia asked.

"Sean has something on him." Edna held up her hands. "I don't know what, so don't bother asking, but the sheriff has been making things easier for us because of our association."

"What are you going to do now? Because Sean won't go away. He might try to burn down your house next." Daisy glanced around. "Although he might be doing you a favor there."

"That's for me and Corbin to worry about." Edna stood. "You've got your answer, so you might as well leave, but don't go thinking you're better off than me. He wants the land the Chickadee is sitting on, and he'll go around us if he has to."

"Thanks for the warning." Cordelia followed Edna to the front door and faced her on the stoop. "And since we saved your life tonight, I hope you'll remember that before starting any more rumors about Daisy and the pastor."

Edna shrugged. "I can't do nothing about that. We already gave our statement to the sheriff, and now that Honey's out, he's going to come calling again. Corbin saw the pastor in the gas station parking lot, where the pastor stopped to fill up before heading out to the Chickadee. Corbin gave him a bottle of wine and told him to split it with Daisy. The pastor didn't even try to deny where he was headed. It's all on camera, so it's not on me to retract the statement."

Daisy clutched Cordelia's wrist. "Corbin gave him the wine?"

"Yeah." Edna gave Daisy a funny look. "Someone had given

it to him, but he doesn't drink red wine, so he gave it to the pastor, mainly just to goad him about stepping out on his wife. That's how we know he was at the Chickadee that night."

"Who gave Corbin the wine?" Cordelia asked, heart racing.

"I don't know, and I don't much care." Edna stared at her nails, making it clear she considered their questions a waste of time.

Both Cordelia and Daisy were at a loss for words. This was the closest they'd come to finding out who killed the pastor, and it was still so far out of reach. When they just stood there, slack-jawed, Edna rolled her eyes and shut the door in their faces.

So much for their tentative truce.

Daisy began to stutter, but Cordelia jerked her chin to the neighbors, who quickly fled from their front window, their curtains still waving. The last thing they needed was to get the town's tongues wagging. They could try to get some answers out of Corbin later, but Cordelia's more pressing priority was getting them all out from under Sean's thumb. And to do that, she was going to need help from someone other than the sheriff's office. It wasn't safe.

"I'm going to take you home." Cordelia kept her voice low as she unlocked her car. "I need you, Arline, and Belinda Sue to cancel all your appointments tonight and hole up together in someone's room, don't care whose, until I get back."

"Where are you going?" Daisy asked.

"To do something I probably should've done a while ago." Cordelia had trust issues, there was no denying it, but she should've been up front with Archer from the start about the palytoxin. Now that all the pieces were falling into place, she could see she'd made a serious error in not giving him all the information when he asked.

They drove home in silence, with Daisy gnawing the color off her bottom lip and shooting worried glances at Cordelia. At the Chickadee, Daisy didn't move from the car. "I think you ought to let us come with you. Safety in numbers."

"I'm not putting myself in danger," Cordelia said. "Just do like I asked. I should be home within a few hours. If I'm not, then feel free to come looking for me."

"I'll hold you to it." Daisy finally opened the passenger door and stepped out. "And in case I don't tell you enough, you're filling Miss Penelope's shoes just fine."

A small smile touched Cordelia's lips. "Thanks for that."

She didn't think she'd ever live up to her Great-Aunt Penelope, but it touched her that Daisy cared enough to say so anyway. Once Daisy had stepped inside Belinda Sue's room and closed the door behind her, Cordelia headed to Archer's office, where she was sure she'd find him working late. This time without the gimmicks or costumes, but for a real honest conversation. Something different for the two of them.

Cordelia parked her car in front of his office window, and just as she predicted, a light remained on. The only one in the building. Blowing out her breath, she approached his door and knocked. When his thick, gruff voice invited her in, her knees wobbled a bit. This would change things between them. He might be angry she hadn't come to him sooner, but with Sean probably coming to on a lonely patch of deserted road in the brush country, she didn't have time to continue playing games or acting like she had everything under control.

As soon as Archer saw her, he jumped to his feet, but he didn't approach her. He just kept his distance and eyed her warily. God, she'd forgotten how much he appealed to her, against her better judgment. How could a preacher's son have been so clearly born for sin?

"Hey," Cordelia said, then cringed. She'd never addressed anyone as "Hey" in her life. "Do you have a minute to talk?"

"I suppose." Archer ran a hand through his hair, sending the dark curls cascading across his deeply tanned forehead. He pulled out the chair across from his desk. "Have a seat."

As soon as her rear hit the cushion and she sank into the soft leather, she realized that placed her eye level with his chest. The spot was meant to be a clear disadvantage to anyone opposing him, but it put her at a disadvantage for another reason. The way his muscles stretched the fabric of his button-down shirt should've been considered an illegal distraction. She tried, and failed, to keep her gaze above his neck.

His knowing look was the only thing that managed to get her back on track. She cleared her throat. "I haven't been completely honest with you."

"Really?" He sat back in his chair. "What a surprise. That you're actually admitting it."

Ignoring him, she moved past the barb, not letting her temper with him get the better of her. For once. "What do you know about palytoxin?"

"I failed chemistry class."

"That's funny. I would've thought you did just fine with chemistry."

His eyes darkened as his gaze dropped to her lips. "Maybe I missed my calling."

"I . . . um." Cordelia's cheeks flushed. They'd gotten off track. Damn those inconvenient pheromones. "It's a toxic substance."

"A what now?" His forehead furrowed as the spell he'd been under seemed to lift. "What does a toxic substance have to do with anything?"

"That's what killed your daddy." Cordelia took a deep breath. Here went nothing. "Someone slipped palytoxin into a bottle of wine, hoping Corbin Abernathy would drink it, but he gifted it to the pastor instead. I'm sorry."

"Hold on." Archer stood, holding his palm out as he pinched his brow. "How do you know any of this?"

"Your daddy didn't die in the church." Cordelia pinched her lips together, knowing what she said next could ruin everything between them. "He died in Daisy's room after drinking poisoned wine. We moved his body because we thought he had had a heart attack and should be found someplace more respectable. For your momma's sake."

"Son of a—" He began pacing. "And you're just telling me this now?"

"We thought you'd pin it on Daisy." Just saying it out loud made Cordelia realize how wrong she'd been about not telling him from the get-go. "We tampered with a body and evidence and all that."

"Hell, Delia. What am I supposed to say to that?" He buried his hands in his hair. "I knew y'all were lying to me, but I thought he'd gotten sick at Daisy's and she kicked him out and felt guilty about it or something. Not this."

"I know." Cordelia could feel the panic rising in her chest, her breath getting shorter. "I screwed up, and I'm so sorry, but I'm trying to be a hundred percent honest with you because we've got a bigger problem on our hands now. Sean O'Leary kidnapped Edna Abernathy tonight. Don't worry, she's fine, but now I'm certain he plans to take us all out."

"For crying out loud." Archer collapsed in his chair. "What exactly have y'all gotten yourselves into? Sean O'Leary is not someone you want to mess with."

"It started when you told us your daddy had been poisoned."

Cordelia went on to explain the steps they'd taken to find the real killer. From the trip to Bramble Park, Val's winery and the stolen guest book and their sudden appearance at church, why she'd been so distracted on their date, the whole fiasco at Benedict's, why they'd broken into the Abernathys' warehouse, how they'd gotten mixed up with Sean O'Leary, what he suspected about the Chickadee's history, what she suspected about the sheriff, and how they ended up rescuing Edna out in the brush country. She spared no details. By the time it was all said and done, he knew it all.

And he was not pleased with her.

"You know how much trouble this would've saved if you'd come to me immediately?" Archer swore under his breath. "Do I even need to ask if you destroyed the wine bottle?"

"It went out with the trash that week."

"That's just great. I'm going to guess you've also got a perfectly reasonable explanation for why Daisy didn't end up poisoned as well?"

"She doesn't drink on the job. It's in her code of ethics."

"Of course it is." He got on the phone with someone and sent them out to round up Sean and Jameson, then hung up. "Chances are, he's long gone by now. I don't want any of you ladies staying at the Chickadee tonight. A B&B just opened up in town. I'll get you a guard."

"You don't have to do that," Cordelia muttered.

"Unfortunately, I do." Archer flung his phone on the desk. "Tell me more about this palytoxin. Knowing you, I assume you've researched all the ins and outs of it."

"It grows on coral, so it can only be found in saltwater tanks. It can be deadly to humans and causes cardiac arrest, which is why Daisy thought your daddy had a heart attack." Cordelia knotted her fingers together. "It was how we initially tried to track down the killer. Saltwater tanks are hard to maintain and not a lot of people have them."

"You said this toxin is only found in saltwater tanks?" The color drained from his face. "Are you sure about that?"

"I mean, I suppose it could grow on coral in the Gulf, but that seemed less likely."

"Damn it." Without warning, he jumped to his feet and stormed out the door.

Chapter Twenty-Eight

CORDELIA DIDN'T KNOW WHERE ARCHER WAS GOING OR WHY, ONLY THAT something inside her drove her to follow. He didn't even get in his truck, just took off down the street. Wherever he was headed had to be in town. She thought about calling out to him, to ask him where he was going, but she hesitated. She didn't know if he'd even want her company, so in the end, she stayed silent as she trailed him. He was so focused, she doubted he would've heard her anyway.

At the end of the street, he turned the corner, and the chain-link fences and squat single-story homes gave way to older, more established architecture. Cordelia's stomach twisted as her old neighborhood came into view. She hadn't taken the time to drive by here since she'd returned to Sarsaparilla Falls, unsure of what memories would be waiting to ambush her.

The Arts and Crafts–style homes with their wide cement porches and thick columns were largely unchanged, as if the neighborhood had a duty to preserve the historical integrity of the properties. Cordelia's daddy had inherited his place from his parents and left it behind when he fled. It was the only reason why her momma had been able to make a fresh start in Dallas. The sale of the premier home in a hard-to-enter area of town had set them up good in their new life.

Cordelia wondered if they'd grown up in another part of town, maybe someplace less fancy, if her momma would've felt as ostracized. Lord knew, she hadn't been perfect, or even acceptable, but being surrounded by people who made it their purpose to act as though they had it all together had to have weighed even more heavily on her. She couldn't keep up with the Hatfields and Conroys in the poorer neighborhoods, let alone the Joneses.

Despite Cordelia's belief in the contrary, stepping back in time and seeing her life from a fresh angle didn't bring old hurts roaring back. Instead, it allowed her to view her childhood through a different lens. Her momma hadn't done right by her, but she'd done the best she could. Maybe that was all any of them could do.

Distracted by her reminiscing, Cordelia didn't even notice Archer stopping until she was a mere twenty feet away. If he noticed her presence, he didn't acknowledge it. He was so lost in his own thoughts, he wouldn't have noticed a tornado barreling down the street. He stood in front of his momma's house with his hands on his hips, just staring up at the place. Worry lines creased his brows. Cordelia found herself wanting to reach out and smooth that crease with her thumb. An absurd lapse in reason.

She waited for him to do something, knock on the door or go sit on the old swing that still hung from his momma's porch. Something. But he just stood there, eyes narrowed, brow furrowed, like he couldn't make sense of whatever he was seeing.

Creeping out from behind the trimmed hedge, Cordelia cautiously approached him, not even giving her old home a second glance. Other than noting that the new owners had decorated their steps with bright-yellow chrysanthemums, she felt nothing, and didn't know if she should be relieved or concerned by that.

"Archer?" Cordelia laid a hand on his arm when he jumped, his muscles tight and tense beneath his shirt. "Are you okay?"

"I'm not sure." His voice sounded faraway, like he was responding from somewhere else entirely and wasn't sure how he'd gotten here.

"Are you going to go in and say hi to your momma?"

Archer shook his head. "I don't think that's such a good idea."

"What's going on?" Cordelia didn't want to press him. It certainly wasn't her place, but that lost look in his eyes bothered her. Archer was always so sure of himself, so confident. This new side of him rattled her.

"Nothing." He blinked a few times, as if clearing his mind. "I can't be here right now. The bed-and-breakfast is up the next street. I'll call Daisy and have her pack your bags."

Without another word, he walked away, but this time Cordelia didn't follow him. She just stood outside his momma's front walk wondering what had spooked him bad enough to make a man like Archer look so haunted. Letting instinct guide her, not that her instincts had been doing a bang-up job until then, she walked up the front steps and knocked.

It took a few moments, but eventually Stella answered the door. She wore a fifties-style polka-dot-print dress with a tight waist and flowing skirt. The top two buttons were undone, and her expression was mildly flustered, but other than that, she was put together. With her salt-and-pepper hair pinned up in a neat twist and a few loose strands framing her face, she looked ready to serve meatloaf to a family of two-point-five kids and a husband named Jim Dear. Or maybe that was just Cordelia's old perception of her coming through.

"Cordelia." She smiled, but it didn't reach her eyes. "What brings you by this late?"

"I was in the neighborhood . . ." Cordelia trailed off when her eyes drifted over Stella's shoulder to find Gladys with her hair mussed and her lipstick smeared. Cordelia's cheeks pinkened.

She'd clearly interrupted an intimate moment. "I'm so sorry to drop in like this."

"Nonsense." Stella opened the door wider. "You're always welcome here."

As soon as Stella opened the door all the way, Cordelia understood what had pained Archer so much and why he'd stood in front of his momma's house like a ghost. There, in the foyer of her home, was a fifty-gallon saltwater tank, brimming with glowing green coral.

Cordelia stood in the open doorway in shock as all the clues they'd chased down knitted together, exposing the full picture. The Dew Valley wine, a single bottle purchased by the pastor, would've been in this home. And now the palytoxin. Everything came together. Why hadn't they focused more on Stella? Cordelia pressed a hand to her stomach as the contents of her lunch threatened to make an abrupt reappearance.

"Cordelia?" Stella reached a hand out to steady her. "Are you sick, dear?"

"It was you, wasn't it?" Cordelia's lips trembled.

"What are you talking about?" Stella glanced over her shoulder, but Gladys had left, possibly to give them some privacy. Did she know? Had she been in on it?

"The wine. The Dew Valley you gave to Corbin." Stella flinched, all but confirming what Cordelia already knew. She could barely form words. Her tongue felt thick and sluggish in her mouth and the insides of her ears buzzed with white noise. "He gave it to the pastor. He drank it and died and you're the one who killed him."

"Keep your voice down." Stella stepped outside and shut the door. "I don't know what you're going on about, but my husband wouldn't drink while writing sermons."

Gone was the soft woman she'd remembered from her youth,

the sweet pastor's wife who had a kind word for everyone. The woman who had been thrilled Cordelia was dating her son. In her place stood a cold and formidable woman.

Cordelia drew herself up to her full height. She wouldn't be intimidated into submission. She wasn't ten anymore. "The pastor didn't die at church. He died in Daisy's room after consuming a bottle of Dew Valley wine laced with palytoxin."

"No." Stella paled and drew her knuckles to her mouth. For a woman who had felt larger than life, she certainly appeared small now.

"You know what that is, don't you?" Cordelia pressed forward. "You can deny it if you want, but I saw the saltwater tank, and I know you had a bottle of Dew Valley in your house."

"The sheriff said it was arsenic." Stella balled her fists under her chin. "I gave that wine to Corbin Abernathy. How did James end up with it?" She seemed so shocked, so suddenly lost, that Cordelia couldn't help but believe her. Her heart now ached for Stella. She might not have loved her husband, but it was clear she still cared for him. The small cry she released was soaked in grief and terror. She hadn't meant to kill her husband, but she did all the same, and she'd have to live with that guilt. Stella could be dismissive of sinners and haughty when questioned, but she wasn't a bad woman. Just flawed.

Cordelia wrapped an arm around her and led her to the porch swing, seating them both on the plush cream cushion. "I think you need to explain what happened."

"I put palytoxin in a bottle of Dew Valley, but I didn't give it to my husband. I never would've hurt James." Stella's eyes filled with tears. If she was faking, she was a phenomenal actress. "I left it on the hood of Corbin's truck with a note, hoping he'd split it with Edna."

"Why would you try to kill Edna and Corbin?"

"I didn't." Stella looked taken aback, like Cordelia had just accused her of harvesting puppies for a fur coat. "I only wanted to scare them out of doing business with Sean O'Leary. The note I left made it look like it was a gift from Sean, so when they got sick, I was hoping they'd see it as a threat. I knew the three of them were planning something with the Chickadee."

"Corbin thought the wine was from Sean?" Cordelia rubbed her brow as she tried to sort out her thoughts.

"I've always had a saltwater tank with coral, and I've been handling palytoxin for years. I know how much a person can come in contact with. It was supposed to be Corbin and maybe Edna drinking it. But James had a bad case of pneumonia a few months back. It weakened his lungs significantly. If it hadn't been for that, he would've only gotten sick too."

"That's awful." Cordelia reeled from the confession. How unfortunate that the one person who wouldn't have been able to stand up to the palytoxin's respiratory triggers was the one person who accidentally ended up with the wine.

"James was so proud when he came home with that bottle of Dew Valley. He thought he got one over on the wine dealer." Stella gave a watery smile as she stared at her lap. "I thought Corbin would buy my fake note, since Dew Valley is only served in a few select restaurants, two of which belonged to Sean O'Leary."

"How did you know the Abernathys were doing business with Sean?" Cordelia had only uncovered their connection because of Honey, but Stella didn't strike her as someone who would give the likes of Honey Stevens the time of day.

"My . . . ah . . . friend Gladys and I are regulars at Benedict's." Stella blushed a pale pink under the soft glow of the porch light. "We were at a booth next to theirs, which are all private and closed off—easier to do disreputable business, I suppose. They struck up a deal to take down the Chickadee. I figured since I was the only one who knew about it, I had a duty to act."

"But why?" Cordelia asked. "What did it matter to you if the Chickadee went the way of the wind? Your husband was a client of Daisy's."

"With my blessing." Stella took Cordelia's hands. "I know you're young, and you might not understand, but my husband and I were much better off as friends. We didn't want to divorce and cause a scandal, but we both had needs we saw to elsewhere."

Cordelia glanced at the front door, to where Gladys was likely waiting on the other side to finish the night with Stella that looked like it had only just begun. Cordelia understood perfectly well what needs Stella had and didn't fault her for keeping them quiet.

The world may have moved forward, but small towns in Texas clung furiously to the past. Her husband's former congregation wouldn't make life easy for Stella. They were downright miserable to Martina just for ordering books about fictional gay couples for the library. And seeing as how the congregation still had say over whether Stella could keep her house, she was just trying to protect herself by flying under the radar.

Taking in Stella's miserable expression and the guilt eating her bones down to the marrow, Cordelia made a decision that might haunt her in the future but felt right in this moment. "I'm not going to say anything about what you told me. Archer might suspect you, I'm hoping he won't for much longer, but I'll never say a word."

"You won't?" The shock made Stella's delicate features paler. "But aren't you afraid Daisy is going to take the fall for the poisoning if you don't turn me in?"

"Not if someone else takes the fall for her."

Stella's eyes widened at her implication.

The old Cordelia was a big believer in black-or-white thinking.

There was right and wrong and she never saw a need to deal with the mess of in-between. But she couldn't deny the last few months had changed things. She no longer held such a singular and narrow view. The Chickadee had opened her world to the rainbow hues of mostly good people trying their best.

As far as Cordelia was concerned, Stella was going to pay for what she'd done to the pastor for the rest of her life. In jail or out, it didn't matter, she'd be paying either way.

But Sean O'Leary would never pay for his crimes. Archer would try to pin him with Edna's kidnapping, but he'd dispose of Edna before she could testify, and take down Cordelia and the chicks without anyone ever speaking out against him. He had too much power, and leveraged fear the way the pastor had leveraged religion.

No, he'd never pay. Not unless someone made him.

"You made a mistake." Cordelia winced. "Mistake" felt like too mild a word to describe the situation, but it was a mistake, nonetheless. "Don't confess. I believe there's another way for this to work itself out."

"How so?" Stella asked.

"If you can get me a vial of palytoxin, I can save six lives." Cordelia weighed her hands up and down in a scale motion. "That will sort of help make up for the one lost, right?"

From the look Stella gave Cordelia, it did not, in fact, make up for her husband's death. But she released a deep sigh and stood. "If you wait here a moment, I'll be right back."

Cordelia once again had to weigh the pros and cons of what she was about to attempt, the right and wrong of it. She was diving deep into the gray—a messy, complicated space to be in—but found it didn't scare her as much as it used to. Sometimes, bad people deserved to pay for their crimes.

And sometimes, they deserved to pay for the crimes of others.

Chapter Twenty-Nine

IT WASN'T WRONG TO FRAME SOMEONE FOR MURDER IF THEY WERE ACTUally a murderer. Hadn't Belinda Sue said they were in the business of community service? And wasn't removing a dangerous man from the chokehold he had on real estate, development, and not to mention the sheriff the best kind of service? Cordelia thought so, and this was the justification she repeated to herself as she drove back to the Chickadee with a vial of palytoxin tucked into the pocket of her sensible skirt.

As soon as she pulled up to the pretty pink motel in the middle of the wide plains, the chicks barreled out of Belinda Sue's room, speaking over one another as Cordelia attempted to exit her car. All of them were asking variations of where she'd been and what they should do next. Cordelia extracted herself from Daisy's tight grip and held up the vial of palytoxin.

"I have a mission for us tonight," Cordelia said. "I can't do this alone."

"Whatever you need." Belinda Sue stood at attention, a general among soldiers, ready to brave the trenches without fear. "We're with you a hundred percent."

Daisy and Arline nodded vigorously beside her, and Cordelia's heart swelled at the sight of the most incredible women she'd ever known putting their full faith in her. They trusted her to keep them safe and put their interests first, and that's exactly what she intended to do.

"I found out who killed the pastor tonight," Cordelia said.

Daisy gasped, drawing her hands to her mouth. "Who did it?"

Cordelia started walking toward the pool and motioned for them to follow. "We should probably sit down for this. It's a long, complicated affair."

Once they were comfortably seated around the table with the pink umbrella for an impromptu happy hour minus the alcohol, Cordelia went on to explain everything she'd learned. How Stella had discovered the connection between Sean O'Leary and the Abernathys, what she'd overheard about their intentions, and how she'd planned to scare Edna and Corbin out of doing business with Sean. What ended up transpiring had been a tragedy that Stella would carry with her for the rest of her life.

The only thing Cordelia didn't reveal was Stella's relationship with Gladys. She didn't think the chicks would be anything other than happy for Stella, but Cordelia felt strongly about letting people keep their personal business personal.

"Poor Stella." Daisy tucked her fists under her chin. "I know doing a murder is wrong, but I don't see her as a killer. She was trying to look out for us and the pastor paid the price. But make no mistake, none of that would've happened if Sean O'Leary had left us be."

"That's why we need to deal with him before he gets back to town," Cordelia said. "We don't have time to let Archer finish building his case, and the sheriff's office is compromised. If Sean makes it to town, he will retaliate."

"How are we supposed to go against him?" Daisy bounced her foot in a nervous rhythm. "He's got powerful connections and eyes everywhere."

"We need to start by calling a truce with Edna." When the

chicks began to groan, Cordelia held up a hand to silence them. "Without her cooperation, this plan will never work."

Belinda Sue's green eyes stared her down, near reptilian in the moonlight. "What kind of plan are you proposing? And how much of a chance do we have of pulling it off?"

Cordelia laid out what she hoped to accomplish and the urgency with which they had to act. If Archer was planning to head back to his momma's house, Stella might not be able to hold up against his questioning. And seeing as how Archer was a do-right through and through, he'd have no choice but to turn in his momma. It would destroy them both. Planting the palytoxin in Sean's home and framing him for the pastor's murder was the only way to save everyone involved from unearned hardship.

Arline lifted her head from where she'd been doing her dozing-while-awake routine. "I ought to come with you. After we went to Benedict's, I took it upon myself to learn the exact layout of Sean's home, as well as his security codes."

Belinda Sue raised an eyebrow. "And how did you manage to do that?"

But Arline just sealed her lips and went back to staring out at the plains. She had more secrets than the CIA had on the murder of JFK, but Cordelia didn't press. Anyone who made an enemy of Arline was a damned fool.

The four of them piled into Cordelia's car. She handed the keys to Daisy, but Daisy just shook her head and climbed in the back. She'd had enough driving for one night. Maybe the memory was too painful for her, or maybe she was sitting with how much she missed it, but Cordelia hoped Daisy would drive again one day, for her own pleasure.

On the way into town, the chicks were tense and silent. None of them relished the prospect of making nice with Edna. It went against their very natures to work with her in any capacity, but they needed her statement to pull off the frame job. The sheriff could dismiss a bunch of sex workers and their madam, but he couldn't dismiss someone he believed to be in just as deep as he was when it came to dirty dealings with Sean O'Leary.

Cordelia parked in front of Edna's, where a single light shone through the front parlor window, and turned to face the chicks. "We're going to play nice tonight. We're not going to insult Edna or talk about her ugly décor."

"It's real ugly though," Daisy said.

Cordelia nodded. "That's God's honest truth, but she doesn't need to hear it from us. Tomorrow, we can go back to hating her as much as we like, but tonight, she's our ally."

The four of them crept up the walk, cognizant of how nosy the neighbors could be and not wanting to draw any unnecessary attention. When Cordelia knocked on the door, Edna opened it right away and ushered them inside. A far cry from how things had gone the last time Cordelia had shown up uninvited.

"Hurry and get in here." Edna motioned for them to pick up the pace as she kept her eyes locked on her neighbors' windows. "I don't need anyone seeing me consorting with the likes of you four. I'd never hear the end of it at bridge club."

"We're not staying long." Cordelia plastered a polite smile on her face and elbowed Arline in the ribs as she eyed Edna's home with an open look of disgust. "We just need you to tell the sheriff that Sean kidnapped you because you overheard him saying he killed the pastor with palytoxin."

Edna's frown cut deep grooves into the corners of her thin mouth. "Why on earth would I do a thing like that? Do you think I have a death wish?"

"You have one if you continue to let him walk around free,"

Cordelia snapped. "You think he's going to stop coming after you just because you got away? That's not how that works."

"I'm going to talk with Corbin when he gets home." Edna's thin lips all but disappeared. "I told you we'd handle this, we don't need you making a bigger mess of things."

"He won't negotiate with you," Cordelia said. "You know he won't."

"He might've before we got the best of him out in the brush country," Daisy said. "But I know men better than just about anyone in three counties, and his ego won't allow you to walk away. The only thing you can do is put him behind bars. You won't be safe until you do."

Edna rubbed her arms as she considered, the closest she'd come to allowing the help she desperately needed. All she had to do was tell a small little lie that would remove Sean from her life and take any heat off her that she got from her association with him. She knew Daisy spoke nothing but facts. Now it was up to her to act appropriately.

"All right." Edna sucked in a deep breath. "Tell me again what I need to do."

They went over what she would say three times before they felt confident Edna would play her part when the sheriff and Archer came calling. She wasn't exactly happy about aligning herself with the Chickadee, and they certainly didn't want to work with her, but a temporary truce was the only way to eliminate the threat to all their lives.

As they drove away, Cordelia kept checking the rearview mirror just to be sure a black sedan didn't suddenly make its way down Edna's street. She exhaled when all remained quiet. Pulling onto the highway, she drove the long stretch out to Sean O'Leary's home.

He lived a good forty minutes away in the town of Catterwood, a small community not unlike Sarsaparilla Falls. The mark of his influence could be felt in the worn-down building fronts, pawnshops, and liquor stores. In the distance, large oil derricks dotted the horizon. Catterwood's charm had been eaten away by the vast wealth and power of one man.

There was so much he deserved to be put away for.

They parked down the street from Sean's home, a grand palace with white pillars and a gray stone facade with prize-winning hydrangeas bordering his walkway. Arline knew the layout and the codes, and Daisy knew how to pick locks, so they decided the two of them would accompany Cordelia into his lair. Belinda Sue would stay behind to keep watch and be their getaway vehicle if needed.

Both Arline and Cordelia wore all black, but they went in the back just to be safe, though Sean didn't have many neighbors—the perk of breaking into the home of someone who valued his privacy. Not so much as a single curtain ruffled as they slipped into his backyard.

The glow coming off the pool cast an eerie light over their surroundings. Mixed with the faint light from the moon, they could see just enough to move about without standing out themselves. The porch lights hadn't been turned on, and Cordelia hoped that was a sign that he hadn't yet made it back from the brush country. Or maybe Archer's man had picked him up, and he was still being held for questioning.

Arline punched in the security code to disable the alarm and Daisy went to work on the lock, making much faster progress than she had at the Abernathy compound. Her hands didn't shake this time around either. She came prepared to end this.

Once they were inside, Cordelia grabbed Arline by the elbow.

"I'm begging you to ignore your instinct to steal just this once. We need to keep it clean this time."

"I know that," Arline snapped. "I already snagged the codes to this house, I can come back anytime I want."

While that didn't necessarily set Cordelia's mind at ease, at least she knew Arline wouldn't take anything now. They couldn't give Sean an excuse to claim a break-in or a frame job. It would ruin everything if he had even the smallest crack to slither through.

Not bothering to take in the fine furnishings or the ornate details that made up his home's impressive interior, the three of them followed Arline directly to his office. A large safe that looked straight from the 1800s stood against one wall. His desk was easily three times the size of the pastor's, with a shiny black surface that seemed to reflect tiny specks of light.

The top drawer closest to the high-back leather chair was open and Cordelia slipped the vial of palytoxin inside. She was just about to shut the drawer when a dusty book with an ancient cracked cover caught her eye. Peeling open the lid with careful fingers, afraid the whole thing might crumble to dust, she scanned the first few pages. There was a map leading to what appeared to be a cave about twenty miles outside of town. A series of *X*'s marked with barely legible symbols dotted the yellowing paper, along with daily excerpts. Cordelia only caught a few sentences before closing the book again, but she'd been right about the cave. The entries were clearly written by a miner who had settled in Sarsaparilla Falls when it was brand-new.

This must've been the journal Sean O'Leary had stolen from Porter Sheldon.

Cordelia slipped the book into the pocket she'd sewn into her skirt, feeling like a downright hypocrite for stealing after the lecture she'd given Arline, but she figured the journal was an exception. Sean could hardly report it stolen seeing as he had stolen it himself. And perhaps Cordelia could finally get a look at what made Chickadee land so valuable there were people willing to kill to get their hands on it.

The slamming of a car door out front caught their attention. A dog started barking, followed by a series of commands to heel, as well as rushed apologies. The commotion allowed the three of them to rush out the back, past the side gate, and into the neighbor's yard without being detected. They hid behind a rosebush and watched the lights come on in Sean O'Leary's home.

If they'd been even another ten minutes, he would've caught them. Cordelia still didn't believe in divine intervention, but she couldn't chalk everything up to coincidence either.

Quiet as a church mouse, Belinda Sue rolled the car up to the neighbors', and Cordelia, Daisy, and Arline hopped in. She then drove to the end of the street and parked behind a large clump of bushes. Cordelia called the anonymous tip in to the local sheriff's office, as well as the FBI. Then they sat there in silence as the flashing lights barreled down the street.

And just like that, the fear and uncertainty that had been plaguing them was over. Several officers from the state police had arrived and argued with the local police. His notoriety ended up being his downfall, and it seemed everyone wanted a piece.

An hour later, Cordelia's heart thumped hard against her chest as she watched Archer pull up to Sean's home. As he led Sean out in handcuffs, she could've sworn his eyes squinted in the direction of their car and a slow grin ate up half his face. This probably wouldn't fully repair what had broken between them, but she had a feeling this would be one time where he'd let a little dishonesty from her slide.

Daisy pulled out a pack of gummy worms. "You should go talk to him."

"Talk to who?" Cordelia pulled a pair of binoculars out of the glove compartment. A handy leftover from her brief bird-watching days.

A man in a brown uniform stopped to intervene in Archer's arrest. Cordelia adjusted the lenses to get a closer look at the man. He had a holster and a badge. He might've been the sheriff of Catterwood, and he didn't look too pleased. Archer's firm stance, his refusal to back down, and the way he owned the scene sent a pleasant flutter through her stomach. Maybe things weren't completely over yet.

Daisy nudged Cordelia's shoulder. "You know who. He was lookin' over here."

"You think now is a good time for that?"

"Maybe not." Daisy bit the head off her gummy worm. "He sure knows how to take command though, am I right?"

Cordelia didn't respond, but a small smile played across her lips.

She went back to observing with her binoculars just as the argument with the sheriff appeared to be over. A few more members of the FBI showed up and started hauling boxes out the front door. Hopefully they contained enough evidence to put him away for a good long while. By that point, the sheriff couldn't do much more than stay on their heels, yapping like an overzealous dog while the feds went over his head.

"What do you suppose he has on that sheriff?" Belinda Sue asked.

"Who knows," Cordelia said. As far as she was concerned, if he wasn't a threat to the Chickadee, he didn't much matter. Catterwood could deal with him.

"Give me a week," Arline said.

"No." Cordelia whipped her head around to face her. "No more funny business. I mean it. We just got ourselves out of the frying pan, I'm not looking to jump into the fire anytime soon."

Arline crossed her arms and grumbled, but appeared to acquiesce. For now.

Belinda Sue took a few pictures of Sean in the back of the police cruiser for her scrapbook, then they headed back to town.

Within two hours, the entire thing was over. Sean O'Leary had been taken to jail, and the threat to the Abernathys, Stella, and the Chickadee had been eliminated in one fell (or foul, depending on the viewpoint) swoop. It wasn't legal, or altogether right, but it was the only option she had to ensure the chicks' safety. When Cordelia's back was against the wall, she found she didn't mind getting a little messy to protect the people who meant the world to her.

She was the madam of the Chickadee, after all.

Chapter Thirty

EARLY SUNDAY MORNING, CORDELIA GOT THE CALL FROM EDNA THAT she'd given her statement to Archer and that the pastor's murder had now been taken out of local hands and turned over to the feds in connection with his other crimes. A judge who couldn't be bought refused to set bail, considering Sean a flight risk, despite a fierce fight from Sean's lawyers.

The kidnapping of Edna and the murder of a beloved small-town pastor were enough to end his reign of terror. As Cordelia's momma would say, good riddance to bad rubbish.

Until the dust fully settled, though, Cordelia wanted to keep her ear to the ground. She still had that book she'd stolen from Sean, though she hadn't opened it yet, and there was still the matter of the sheriff and whatever other associates Sean O'Leary had in town. She and the chicks weren't out of the woods yet, just clear of the most immediate danger.

This was how Cordelia ended up banging on the Chickadee's doors at the crack of dawn. "Up and at 'em. We're going to church today."

Daisy stepped out of her room and yawned, her short gray natural hair sticking up in a dozen odd angles. "I just went to bed an hour ago. I don't got it in me for church today."

"That's too bad, because we're going. All of us. End of story." Cordelia marched back to her room, confident she wouldn't need to say another word. They might grumble, but when it came down to it, they respected her authority and followed her lead.

An hour later, the chicks piled into her car in a kaleidoscope of colorful caftans. After church, they decided they would stop at Tilly's so Cordelia could set them up with at least one proper dress for these types of occasions. The mood was significantly lighter than it had been in weeks, and Cordelia relaxed into the comfort of Daisy's fussing and Belinda Sue's complaining and Arline's silence. They were part of her family now, and she wouldn't trade them for anything.

She parked in a spot near the back, and the four of them spilled out of the car, Cordelia in her neat A-line black skirt and white button-down with the argyle sweater vest, and the chicks in their rainbow-hued floral caftans. Everyone stopped what they were doing to stare, but the chicks liked the attention. They just waved and blew kisses like they were walking the red carpet.

Cordelia spotted Stella standing apart from the two crowds that made up the church's patrons, who Daisy referred to as the fun ones and the boring ones. Stella nodded at Cordelia, a slight dip of her chin, before turning back to Gladys. There were dark circles under her puffy eyes. It was clear she hadn't slept well, but at least she wouldn't be dealing with her guilt behind bars.

As the crowd began to shuffle inside, Cordelia and the chicks stayed back, keeping an eye out for signs of trouble, but everything appeared normal. There had been a few more whispers about the old pastor's murderer being caught on the way in, but since Sean O'Leary wasn't from Sarsaparilla Falls—despite a good number of people knowing of him—the gossip wasn't as juicy. It quickly fell off in favor of Clara Hendricks getting caught stealing packages from her neighbors' front stoops.

One of the final groups to head inside, Cordelia and the chicks took the last pew. The inside of the church was lit up with powerful lights that raised the temperature indoors by about twenty degrees. Several ladies had their fans out. The windows had all been covered with thick black velvet curtains, a mark of respect for the former pastor now that his murderer had been brought to justice.

Cordelia was so focused on trying to listen in on town chatter that she didn't see Archer until he put his hand on her shoulder to draw her attention. She glanced up at him in surprise. "What are you doing here? I thought you didn't go to church?"

"I don't normally, but I thought this would be a special occasion." He grinned and her toes curled in her flats. "Funny seeing you here."

"We thought it would be a good idea to stay on top of the news in town, and what better place to do that?" Cordelia lowered her voice. "I heard you caught Sean O'Leary."

"Yeah. Isn't that something?" He gave her a piercing look. "The night you tell me about the palytoxin, we just happened to get an anonymous tip that Sean had the toxic substance on hand at his house."

"The world is full of odd coincidences," Cordelia said. "But I heard you got Edna Abernathy to corroborate the story, so it sounds like it's all tied up."

"Edna's statement is in. I have no need to question her further." He dipped his head, and, tucking a strand of hair behind her ear, he brought his lips in close. "I know what you did. I don't know why you did it, but I'm going to let that rest for now, so long as it doesn't happen again."

She pressed a hand to his chest, feeling his heart pound firmly against her palm. "I think we understand each other just fine."

"Glad to hear it." Archer straightened and cleared his throat. "I hope you ladies are staying out of trouble."

Daisy giggled and swatted Archer's arm. "You know us, honey. Can't stay out of trouble *too* much. What fun would that be?"

Cordelia just shook her head. Archer headed up to the front and took a seat beside his momma, who immediately threw her arms around him, overjoyed to see him in church. This was why Cordelia had done what she did. Their relationship was too precious to be broken, while men like Sean walked around causing destruction for no reason other than to line their pockets and hold power over innocent people.

Hollis Thorne had just taken the altar, looking as smarmy as he had at the festival, when the back doors burst open. Every head in the congregation turned as Sherilynn West paraded into church wearing a bright-pink tunic just thin enough to showcase her neon-green bra and oversize sunglasses that swallowed up half her face. She pushed them up over her mile-high teased hair and slung her beaded bag over her shoulder, the series of gold bangles on her wrist clinking together and echoing in the open chamber. Her first appearance over that threshold in more than twenty-five years.

Tilly Gomez-Esteban audibly groaned, while Vinner Mendez looked like Christmas had just come early. Porter Sheldon jumped up to move down two pews, keeping his hand over his backside like Sherilynn might fish his wallet right out from under him. Cordelia glanced at Archer, whose eyes twinkled with amusement, like he was pleased to have something to entertain him this fine Sunday morning, when he'd rather be sleeping in. And that was all well and good for him, but all Cordelia was asking for was one solitary day without drama.

It seemed like God was busy answering other people's prayers.

"So sorry I'm late. Traffic on the 281 was hell. Oops." Sherilynn slapped a hand over her mouth. "Probably shouldn't say 'hell' in church. Forgive me, it's been a while."

The entire congregation stared back in silence, most of their mouths hanging open wide enough to invite a whole colony of birds to move in.

"What are y'all looking at?" Sherilynn flapped her hands. "Go on back to your business. I'll just take a seat and mind my own."

"Momma," Cordelia whisper-hissed. "What are you doing here?"

"You have been sending me to voicemail for over ten days now." Sherilynn put her hands on her hips. "Do you have any idea how worried I've been? I got Suzy minding the shop for me so I could drive on down and make sure you were okay. And what do I find? You're sitting in church. I thought I raised you better than that."

Cordelia groaned internally. With everything that had been going on, of course she had forgotten to call her momma, who just let those days slide on by until she had an excuse to come down here. This wouldn't end well.

"Never mind all that." Cordelia tugged on her wrist. "Will you just sit down, please?"

Sherilynn scooched into the pew, introducing herself to the chicks like she didn't just blow in here like a tornado. Only twice as destructive. Daisy threw her arm around her like they were old friends, such was her way, while Belinda Sue gave a polite but firm handshake. Arline just narrowed her eyes. No doubt she'd have Sherilynn's social security number and complete medical history in her back pocket by the end of the day.

The town still gaped at her, unable to process that the notorious Sherilynn West had returned to Sarsaparilla Falls.

The new pastor cleared his throat. "If we could get on with the service now."

Sherilynn waved him off, raising her voice far above what was necessary. "Go on now, do what you gotta do."

"Right." The pastor moved to the podium and shuffled some papers.

Cordelia continued to shoot nervous glances at her. She didn't like the idea of this town getting its hooks into Sherilynn again. And while she had found a home in Sarsaparilla Falls, she still felt very strongly that it was a bad place for her momma, and she wanted to get her out of town as soon as possible.

The pastor droned on. Sherilynn watched him with a near numb smile on her lips and a glaze to her eyes that let Cordelia know she was here in body only. Her mind had wandered elsewhere. Cordelia thought about pulling her right out of the church and sending her back to Dallas, but seeing as how they'd already caused one scene, it was best just to wait.

"And one last bit of business I'd like to address." The pastor folded his hands in front of him. "It's come to my attention that Sarsaparilla Falls is home to a house of ill repute."

The congregation swung their heads around to the last pew. Cordelia sunk lower on her seat as every eye in the room landed on her and the chicks. This was too much attention for one morning. It was already hot in the church thanks to those oppressive lights, but the temperature raised another ten degrees.

Only a small handful, Edna and her ilk, looked smug about the callout. The rest of the women in the congregation shot each other worried glances. They'd gotten real comfortable with their alone time and weren't looking to give that up anytime soon. Maureen Claremont shot the pastor a dirty look. The only reason she got to catch up on *Real Housewives* was because Daisy kept her husband occupied and out of her hair.

"I plan on making it my duty to shut this sinful business down," the pastor said. "This is God's country, and there is no place for prostitution within the borders of this town."

Sherilynn snorted. "Good luck with that, buddy."

The congregation broke out in murmurs, and none of them seemed to be favoring the pastor. Least of all because they didn't consider the subject matter Sunday-morning appropriate. Ashlynn Vick covered her toddler's ears while her five-year-old pressed her face into her side. Her husband was a little too young to pay a visit to the Chickadee, but her kids benefited from the books Daisy donated and she appreciated them all the same.

"If you'll excuse me." Arline stood, her bright-purple caftan splashed with irises swishing at her ankles. "I've got to use the bathroom. Tell me if I miss anything good."

Cordelia opened her mouth, then closed it again. It wasn't worth the effort.

Daisy crossed her arms. "And to think I was going to offer him a discount as a welcome to town. He can forget about it now."

"The old pastor, rest his soul, might've been okay with the goings-on in this town, but I'm not the same." The pastor paused and looked out on the congregation to gauge their reaction. A few of the men hung their heads—the spineless ones who didn't deal well with a direct shaming of their proclivities—while most of the women looked ready to stage a walkout. "I won't stand for heathens making a mockery of you any longer. We're going to take our county back and make this a Christian land once more."

Only four people broke out in applause, which quickly died out once they realized they stood alone. Cordelia was pleased to see that Archer and Stella weren't among them. But it worried her that there was any support from people at all. Now that they'd been fully cleared of any wrongdoing in Pastor Reed-Smythe's death, she figured things would go back to normal.

The lights flickered overhead. The pastor raised a finger. "And one more thing."

The lights suddenly went out, plunging the church into total darkness thanks to those light-blocking curtains. Panicked whispers rose above the din as people stepped over one another to figure out what had gone wrong. They weren't expecting a storm. What had taken out the lights? And why hadn't the generator kicked on?

A loud thud echoing from the pastor's microphone brought everyone to a standstill. The lights flickered again, and a few screams broke out in the front. The lights flickered one more time before coming back on.

And at the front of the church, slumped over the podium, was the new pastor. Still and unmoving. With a knife in his back.

The room erupted in pandemonium. Archer tried to herd people away from the body to preserve evidence as several deputies in their Sunday best ushered people toward the exit. In the flurry of activity, a flash of movement caught Cordelia's eye, and she shifted her gaze just in time to see a scrap of purple fabric covered in irises disappear through the side door near the front of the church. Arline still hadn't returned from the bathroom.

Sherilynn began crying, and Cordelia had to help her to her feet and get her moving toward the exit, with Daisy and Belinda Sue bringing up the rear.

Looking back, Cordelia caught Archer's gaze. His expression was set in a grim line. Had he seen anything? Or anyone?

"Excuse me." Cordelia passed her hysterical momma off to Daisy, who planted Sherilynn firmly against her bosom and tried to usher her forward.

"Where you going?" Sherilynn clung to Cordelia's arm, her chipped pink nails digging into the skin. "The exit is the other way."

"I'm just . . ." Cordelia glanced back at Archer. She couldn't just leave with everyone else, not knowing what was happening or what any of this meant.

"We'll talk later," he mouthed across the room. "Tonight."

Cordelia nodded. He wouldn't leave her in the dark. With no other options, Cordelia joined the people who poured out of the church like ants running from a flood hill.

Daisy kept her voice low as she ran a soothing hand down Sherilynn's back, her brown eyes wide and worried. "How did this happen?"

"I don't know," Cordelia said, her frantic gaze still searching the crowd. "But I think it's going to be on us to figure it out."

"I don't like the sound of that," Belinda Sue said grimly. "Where's Arline?"

That was the question of the hour. And while it would've been nice to have a break from being implicated in another murder of another pastor, it looked like their luck could only go so far. Cordelia pressed her fingers to her temples, knowing she had no choice but to step up.

Just another day for a madam.

Acknowledgments

First, thank you, readers, for going on this journey with me. These characters have lived in my heart and mind for years, and now they belong to you.

Thank you to my agent, Becca Podos, who has been this book's fiercest cheerleader since I first brought them the idea of a group of senior sex workers and their reluctant madam solving a murder. It was probably my most ambitious project to date and would never have seen the light of day without their unwavering support.

Huge thank you to my editor extraordinaire, Sophia Kaufman, who loves these characters as much as I do and completely understood the exact story I wanted to tell. Your notes were all spot-on and working with you was an absolute pleasure.

I'd also like to thank production editor Suzette Lam and copy editor Jane Cavolina and the entire team at Harper Perennial for making this story shine and bringing it to shelves. I've been a mystery lover since I was old enough to read, and because of you, my dream of writing in this genre is coming true. I've had such an amazing publishing experience and I'm incredibly grateful to work with such a skilled and dedicated team.

To my coven, thank you for encouraging me when I was doubting myself, especially my Canadian crew, Annette Christie, Kelsey Rodkey, and Auriane Desombre, who talked this out with me over dinner and drinks on the most magical and soul-nourishing trip of my life. You not only believed in my, admittedly, bonkers premise, you talked me through my imposter syndrome and reminded me why I do this.

Brian Kobi, I'm sorry your character's namesake didn't get as big of a role as Vinner's. He asked first, but I'll make it up to you in the next book. Until then, I will continue to provide you with plenty of pickles and will yell at Vinner if he tries to eat yours.

Shelly Waalkes, thank you for providing me with the name Arline, I can't picture her as any other name now. And Bree Smith, I have to give you a shout-out because I know you'll pout if I don't.

To Mr. Sonia and my girls, you are the reason I can. Love you always.

About the Author

Lyla Lane is a pen name for Sonia Hartl, the author of the rom-coms *Rent to Be* and *Heartbreak for Hire*, which has been optioned for television, as well as the YA novels *Not Your #Lovestory*, *Have a Little Faith in Me*, and *The Lost Girls*. She lives in Grand Rapids with her husband and two daughters. She was born in Michigan and has spent significant time in Michigan; Baton Rouge, Louisiana; and Phoenix, Arizona.